TOO BIG A STORM

MARSHA QUALEY

DIAL BOOKS

NEW YORK

Published by Dial Books
A member of Penguin Group (USA) Inc.
345 Hudson Street
New York, New York 10014

Designed by Lily Malcom
Text set in Garramond 3
Printed in the U.S.A. on acid-free paper
10 9 8 7 6 5 4 3 2 1

Library of Congress Cataloging-in-Publication Data
Qualey, Marsha.
Too big a storm / by Marsha Qualey.
p. cm.
Summary: When serious worrier Brady Callahan meets vivacious
Sally Cooper, daughter of a wealthy Minnesota family, they develop
a close friendship that helps them both grow and survive during
the turbulent Vietnam War era.
ISBN 0-8037-2839-5
[1. Friendship—Fiction. 2. Vietnamese Conflict, 1961–1975—Protest
movements—Fiction. 3. Family life—Minnesota—Fiction. 4. Minnesota—
Fiction.] I. Title.
PZ7.Q17To 2004
[Fic]—dc22
2003016399

ACKNOWLEDGMENTS

Thanks first and foremost to my editor, Lauri Hornik. We've worked together on eight books over thirteen years, a fact I cherish.

Thanks also to: Tracey Adams, my patient and supportive agent; Regina Castillo, a skilled and thoughtful copyeditor; Lisa Westberg Peters, who shared her memories of working on the *Minnesota Daily* and will, I hope, forgive me for changing some things so they'd work in the story; Dave, Laura, Ellen, Jane, and Ben Qualey, who provide the structure, spirit, and soundtrack in my life.

Special thanks to Ann Catherwood, Sarah Hanna, Margaret Peck, and Kathy Seestadt, who weathered the storm with me. As Shawn Colvin sings, "We were raising each other in a strange land." We may not have made sense of it all yet, but we sure have found things to laugh about.

At one level, this novel is a story about two girls and their brothers. So I figured, why not dedicate it to mine?

For Scott, John, and Al

TOO BIG A STORM BLEW OUT OF THE SKY.

—Margaret Wise Brown, *The Sailor Dog*

PART ONE

1

Brady Callahan pretended not to see the two guys who were watching her from behind a nearby tree. Instead, she faked interest in the conversation her mother was having with the couple that stood near them in the slow-moving buffet line.

The couple had the cottage next to the one Brady shared with her mother and two younger brothers. The Callahans had arrived at the resort that afternoon too early for check-in, and were told to wait on the lodge patio and enjoy the complimentary beverages. While her mother went looking for a restroom, Brady went to the patio and was immediately accosted by the jovial man and woman.

"For pig's sake, call us Myrt and Jack, just Myrt and Jack," the woman had gushed.

When Jack let his eyes roam over Brady and said for the third time, "*Quite a young lady*," she'd excused herself.

"I need to find my brothers," she explained. "They disappeared the moment we got here. Our cottage will be ready soon, and we'll want to unload the car."

She found them in the boathouse. Thirteen-year-old Cullen was sitting on a tall stool, watching two older boys fiddle with an outboard motor. Eight-year-old Sam was caressing the smooth wood of a water ski. "Guys," she said, "I need you."

Sam spun around, knocking down the entire row of skis. The boys with Cullen looked up and growled.

"Way to go, Sammy," Cullen said, assuming the irked attitude of the boathouse boys.

Sam bit his lip and colored, a familiar prelude to tears. "I'll help you put them back," Brady said softly. "I shouldn't have surprised you."

She carefully replaced the skis as Sam handed them to her. "Can we water-ski while we're here, Brady?" he whispered. "They take people out skiing, that's what they told Cullen."

"We'll see," she said.

As soon as she and Sam had hung the last ski, Brady said, "Let's go. We need to unpack the car." Cullen swore, but obediently hopped off the stool and ran ahead, giving Sam a light slap on the back as he passed him. Brady ignored the boathouse boys on her way out, but as she hurried along the boardwalk that followed the shoreline, she could feel them watching.

They watched again now, and again she pretended not to notice. When she reached the end of the buffet line, she looked up as she turned away from the table. Her eyes inadvertently met theirs and she had to nod. The tallest one motioned.

Her mother and brothers had followed Myrt and Jack to a cluster of picnic tables. Jack was making introductions. His hand rested on Brady's mother's shoulder as he recited names. Cullen and Sam walked past the adults and sat on a flat boulder by a flower bed.

Brady weighed options for a brief moment, then she smiled at the boys and went over.

The taller one said, "Thought you'd never see us."

"Why didn't you just come get me?"

"Drake and I are off duty. It's against the rules to socialize with guests on our private time. Old Jack the Lecher, the one you were in line with? He's been coming here long enough to think he runs things. He'd report us on the spot."

The other guy, Drake, cleared his throat and said, "Besides, he likes to keep the girls for himself."

"You're here to warn me about a dirty old man?"

"We're here to tell you that there's a party later. A moonwalk party at someone's cabin. A few of us have the night off and we're going. If you want to come, be at the boathouse at nine."

4

"There's supposed to be a party here," Brady said. "They're setting up televisions in the lounge and the game room."

Drake tugged on his friend's sleeve. "Steve, there's Howard. Let's go before he sees us."

Brady turned and saw the resort's friendly program director moving among the tables. When she faced the boys again, they were backing up and inching toward a getaway. "Nine," Steve said. "Don't tell."

Mary Callahan made room for her daughter at the table by sliding closer to Jack the Lecher, who didn't move.

"I can stand," Brady said. "I'll need to go track down the boys soon anyway. They've run off again."

"Quit worrying," her mother said. "What could happen to them?" She turned to the others at the table. "My daughter carries the weight of the world on her shoulders. But, the world being what it is, only her brothers can be managed."

Barely managed, Brady thought as she spotted them among a cluster of children just as a young girl in the group backed away from the others, her eyes opened wide in terror. Brady excused herself from the adults and hurried toward her brothers. As she approached, she heard the little girl whine, "Don't kill it!"

"What are you doing?" Brady asked Cullen, who seemed to be at the center of it all.

The girl said, "It's a hurt bird. He said he was going to put it in the barbecue pit."

Cullen's eyes met his sister's. "Not until it was dead, which it will be any second now."

"That's kind of sick, Cullen," Brady said.

His eyebrows shot up. "Yeah? Then why'd we do it to Dad? That's all I was going to do—cremate the bird."

Sam tugged on Brady's shirt. "Don't let him."

She pulled him in for a hug. "He's only trying to freak out the others," she whispered. "I'll get someone from the resort."

Brady spoke to one of the buffet attendants. Within moments there was a flurry of activity. Minutes later the bird was gone, the spot on the walk where it had lain was scrubbed, the children had scattered.

Cullen and Sam took off with a few boys, destination unknown. Brady checked: Yes, their still-full plates were on the boulder. Cullen's ketchup-covered hot dog was disappearing bit by bit into a huge gray squirrel. The boys would be starving by bedtime. Well, they'd have to survive on popcorn. No way she was going to let them buy any snacks at the resort store. Too expensive and, besides—

Brady caught her breath and glanced at her mother. Forget it, she thought. If she's not worrying, I won't. If she doesn't care that the boys don't eat, I won't care.

She sighed and checked her watch. In ninety minutes she could be escaping in someone's boat. She knew why she'd been invited to the party, of course. Knew that her appearance at the boathouse that afternoon had sown the seeds. Knew by the way the boys had watched her walk away that she was being evaluated for . . . possibilities. Apparently she had passed some qualifying test of acceptable company. She didn't have a doubt in the world that the test was short and idiotic:

Breasts? Yes. Fat? No.

She'd possibly lost a few points for not being blond and tan, and probably even more for being just a few inches short of six feet; still, she'd passed. So the boys had flouted rules, lurked behind a tree, and invited her to a party. They didn't even know her name.

Why wasn't she outraged? Why was she even considering going?

A sudden "Hoo-hoo, baby!" pierced through the shell of her thoughts.

Two middle-aged men wearing pastel shirts and plaid shorts were demonstrating dance steps on the patio by the barbecue pit. Behind them, a half circle of other middle-aged people shouted approval and clapped a rhythm. Brady found her mother. Mary Callahan's eyes were opened wide in wonder as she watched the dancing men.

Brady went to her mother and hooked a hand on her slender, pale arm. "Let's get some watermelon," she said. Halfway to the buffet she whispered, "I've been invited to a party somewhere on the lake. It's okay if I go, isn't it?"

Not that it wasn't her own decision. Asking was just a courtesy. For as long as she could remember, she'd been making her own decisions about where to go, what to do, what to wear, how much to spend.

"Why?" her mother asked. Brady had to smile. So typical. Not, Where? Not, Who with? Not even, When will you be home?

Why? Forget details—her mother wanted to explore motivation. But really, what else should she have expected from the ex-nun-now-psych-nurse?

And what answer would satisfy?

I'll go nuts if I stay here. (But people are so interesting, Brady.)

I don't want to spend the night chasing after my brothers. (Then don't.)

It's time I lose my virginity, and this seems like a really good opportunity. (You joke about the oddest things, dear.)

"Brady?" her mother prompted.

She focused and smiled. "I just feel like being with people my own age."

They both considered this, though neither stated the obvious: Except for sitting in class at Marshall-U High—the third school in three years—she rarely was with people her own age. They'd moved far too often for Brady to have kept friends.

Mary said, "But you'll miss the moonwalk. You don't want to miss that."

"They said it was a moonwalk party, so there must be a television. And you can't tell anyone because I'm going with a couple of guys who work here. They said they'd get in trouble if they fraternize with the paying guests."

She knew that once again the same thought had hit them both, because her mother's eyebrows rose and a slight smile appeared. They weren't paying guests. No way in the world could they afford to be paying guests at a place like Potter's Family Resort, not on her mother's salary, not even if they added in her own income from working part-time at the church, not even if Cullen chipped in his paper route money. They'd won the vacation in a fund-raising raffle at Sam's school.

They helped themselves to large slices of watermelon. Mary idly picked at the seeds on hers as they walked back to the table. She said, "Do you suppose Will can somehow watch the moonwalk? Do you suppose they'll stop the bloody war for even a few minutes and let them watch?"

Brady shooed flies away from their fruit. Her older brother, Will, had been in Vietnam for six months. She sighed. Somehow she didn't think army privates trapped in jungle hell would be watching astronauts walk on the moon. But she said, "I hope so."

Mary stared at the blue lake for a moment. When she faced her daughter, her eyes were glistening. She whispered, "Go. Have fun."

2

Parties were bad luck. Brady thought she was probably crazy to imagine that this one would be different.

The first party she could remember was also the first bad one. At Will's seventh birthday party she'd tried desperately to keep up with the pack of boys he'd invited by riding his bike around their new neighborhood. Five-year-old Brady had run with the boys to a park across the street from their house. Her father, exhausted from two weeks of no sleep since Cullen's birth, lagged behind. Brady climbed with the others onto the merry-go-round. Just as her father started shouting and running, Will and another boy spun the merry-go-round.

Brady flew off with the second revolution. She hit the ground, rolled, and landed hard against the steel and concrete footing of a jungle gym.

The party ended immediately. The trip to the emergency room lasted for hours.

The next party to end in disaster was her own tenth birthday party. The family had just moved to Minnesota and she had started at a new school. The guests were mostly strangers to one another and to Brady, who—with her mother's prodding—had invited the girls almost at random. No one at that party was destined to break an arm, a nose, and need seventeen stitches; however, the guests were again all sent home early, most of them whining about not even getting cake. They'd been playing American Bandstand, dancing to records cranked up loud on the hi-fi when the party ended. Intent on her moves, Brady hadn't heard the phone ring and she was the last in the room to see her mother enter and walk toward the record player. Mary Callahan, with always-fussy baby Sam cradled in her arms, stopped the music and told all the girls that they had to go home. A neighbor was waiting out front to drive them.

After everyone was gone, her mother told her that there had been a car accident. "Your father . . ." she said, then stopped. Sam's arms flailed against his mother's chest.

There were no injuries or fatal accidents associated with Will's going-away party last January; nevertheless, it was a sour memory. The party had been Father Tom's idea, and her mother had resisted loudly when Brady conveyed the priest's suggestion.

"Why should I celebrate my son's participation in an immoral and illegal war? Why should I celebrate his conscription and forced participation in an evil, racist war?"

"You shouldn't," Brady had snapped back, "but we should get together with everyone we know to say good-bye."

"Like a funeral?"

"Like a party, Mother."

Mary Callahan refused to attend. "You know how she feels about the war," Brady explained to the younger boys as they got ready. "You know how she felt about Will dropping out of college and letting the army draft him." They knew. For years their mother had been active in the peace movement. She'd often hauled Brady and the younger boys along on marches and demonstrations.

Not since Will enlisted, though. Since the day he'd reported for his induction physical, Mary had quit attending marches and meetings. Sometimes it seemed to Brady that her mother had even quit paying attention to the war. She wondered at times if her mother had given up hope for peace when she'd said good-bye to her son.

"Would she go if it wasn't in a church?" Cullen asked. He had their mother's green eyes and coal black hair; he also had her unflinching stare.

Brady glanced at him. When did you get so old and wise? she thought. "I don't know," she said.

The patriotic flag-waving members of St. Bernard's parish turned out in force for Will Callahan's party, the third Vietnam send-off at the church that winter. Brady and her family didn't belong to St. Bernard's or any church. Brady and her brothers had never been baptized, confirmed, or otherwise religiously ritualized. Brady's parents—her mother only two steps out of the convent—had even been married by a judge at the Cleveland city hall.

But the day Will had reported for his draft physical, while her mother was still in a fuming rage, Brady had bicycled the mile from their house to St. Bernard's and volunteered at its Open Door People's Center. She'd read a newspaper article about the center and its outreach work. It had started as a drop-in spot for vagrants and runaways, but recently the center had been helping veterans. The article said that every day more and more vets came to St. Bernard's. By the time Will was drafted, the war had used up a lot of men.

Father Tom McGann ran the center. After Brady had volunteered there for several weeks, he asked her to join the staff part-time. When he heard that her brother was due to be sent to Vietnam, he suggested the party, even though he'd met Will only once.

"You're part of our community," he said to her. "That means your family is too."

When she mentioned it to Will, home on leave before being shipped overseas, he said, "Why not? Can I bring my own friends?"

Unlike Brady, he had plenty of friends his own age. Two years earlier, right after Will's senior year of high school, Mary Callahan had announced that the family was leaving Minnesota temporarily and moving to Madison, Wisconsin, while she returned to school for another graduate degree. Will refused to move. He stayed behind, found a job, and got an apartment with friends. In the fall, he enrolled at the U. He'd partied more than he'd studied during that first year, and his grades were worse than bad. When the second year started, he dropped out after a few weeks and was soon drafted. After several weeks of basic training, he was home on leave before being sent overseas.

He brought his friends to the farewell party, they brought liquor they drank on frequent visits to their cars, a neighborhood band played, and the church ladies cooked.

At ten, Mary Callahan arrived to take her younger sons home. She stayed long enough to meet and thank the priest. At eleven Father Tom made a speech, and Will said his thanks. At eleven-thirty Brady parked Will's car in their driveway, hands frozen to the wheel as her very drunk brother sobbed hysterically.

" . . . can't go, Brady . . . can't do it . . . get killed . . . don't want to . . . die."

"Then don't go."

"Huh?" He choked down a sob and was silent. He looked at her.

"I'll drive you to Canada. We'll leave right now. We'll get across somehow. You don't have to go to Vietnam."

Will's head twitched, as if he were trying to shake thoughts back into place.

"You don't have to go," Brady said crisply. "Father Tom helps guys get to Canada. He has connections. I'll call him now."

Will sat erect. The muscles of his jaw tightened. "Mom's right," he said. "You spend too much time at that place. What do you do it for, Brady? Saving the world? Or maybe you're just like her: Searching for the perfect wounded animal to love."

She leaned back. She took a moment. Then she said, "What's the point of anything if you don't do something, Will? Father Tom says—"

He made a noise. His body convulsed. He opened the car door and leaned out. When he was done heaving the night's food and drink onto the snow, he lifted his head and glared at his sister. He got out of the car and stumbled toward the house.

When Brady got up early to help her mother with a big going-away breakfast, she found her sitting in the kitchen holding a note. Will was already gone.

3

Nine o'clock.

Three guys and two girls waited at the boathouse. I'm someone's panic date, Brady thought. They did the math and realized they were short a girl, and I was the best they could come up with. Which guy is the lucky one?

Apparently it was Steve, the tall one who'd tracked her down at dinner. The other four stood in pairs as he recited names.

Brady gave hers when he admitted he didn't know it.

One of the girls giggled. "That's a weird name for a girl."

"Weird name for anyone, really," Brady said. "It's a family name from somewhere on my mother's side."

Steve motioned them all out of the boathouse. He pointed toward a huge motorboat tied to the dock. "We're taking the Larson."

Drake and his girl claimed the spots in the back of the boat. The other couple sat in the front. Brady stared at the empty side-by-side seats right behind the wheel and controls.

"No life jackets?" she asked Steve as she stepped in.

He shrugged and slid into the seat behind the wheel. "Won't need them. Nothing will happen."

The roar of the motor deterred conversation. After a couple of minutes Steve said something and pointed. Brady turned to look and saw that Drake and his girl were already making out furiously.

"Beer, please," Steve shouted to Brady.

She got a can from the cooler behind his seat and handed it to him. She glanced toward the front, then again toward the back, and decided that no one else would want to be interrupted for refreshments.

Steve increased the speed and the boat raced. Brady's hair flew in the wind. Why hadn't she thought to tie it or bring a hat? It would take forever to comb through the tangles.

They slammed down hard over a series of waves. Brady squeezed her seat cushion. She'd never been in a boat. She hoped they didn't hit anything, because she couldn't swim. She looked at Steve. He slowly turned his head and returned her stare. After a second he resumed looking ahead.

Not a flicker of interest, not even basic animal interest. Why had they asked her along? Why risk their jobs by bringing her to a party?

Suddenly, Steve cranked the wheel hard. There were thumps and shrieks as the lip-locked couples rolled off their seats and hit the bottom of the boat. Brady and Steve exchanged smiles. He pointed and shouted. "See the bonfire? That's where we're going."

At least a dozen boats were pulled onto the beach or tied to a long L-shaped dock. Steve eased the Larson into a narrow space on the shore. Brady helped him haul the cooler out and then stood with it while he and Drake pulled the boat securely onto the sand.

The party was in high gear. A crowd clustered near the fire, upwind of the smoke and flames. When everyone spotted the new cooler arriving, a loud cheer rose. Someone threw a log onto the fire. Crackling embers shot high into the air.

Brady checked her watch. Almost nine-thirty. Tonight men were walking on the moon for the first time ever, and it looked like she might miss it. She tapped Steve's shoulder. "Television anywhere?"

That earned the second smile of the night. Was he relieved she wasn't interested in staying glued to him? "We'll ask. There's our host."

A portable stereo powered by a long extension cord blasted the Stones. A tall, slender boy danced furiously. His dark chin-length hair whipped around in the air. He seemed to be the center of a circle of dancers. Everyone was in swimsuits. The boy stopped when he saw Steve, then stepped forward when he saw Brady. The others stopped dancing and stood in formation behind him.

He looked Brady over. Then, with his eyes locked on hers, he said, "Good job, Steve. Well done."

Now she understood. Some people bring potato chips to a party. Steve had wanted to please his host by finding a new girl. Brady was his contribution.

The boy said, "Welcome to Chez Cooper. I'm Paul, your host, which means that everyone here is my responsibility." He pressed a finger to her lips and stroked. "Especially strangers." He turned, took a can of beer someone was holding, and held it out to Brady. "Have a cold one. Then let's get acquainted."

She took the can and emptied it over his bare feet. She told him what to do with himself. She dropped the can and blindly walked away, stumbling as she crossed the uneven sand.

She heard her mother: *Why?*

The power cord fueling the dance music snaked across the sand and disappeared in the dark beyond the bonfire. Brady followed it until she reached the steps of a cabin.

Inside, several people sat on the floor in front of a small TV. Brady sat at the edge of the group and was immediately offered a joint. She passed it along without taking a hit.

The image on the television screen jumped, and Walter Cronkite's face melted into lines that rippled like gray and black waves. A loud groan rose from the group. A girl hopped up and adjusted the rabbit ears. When the picture reappeared, applause broke out and she bowed. As she took her hands off the antenna, the picture fell apart.

"Just stand there and hold it, Sally," someone said. "It's almost time and we don't want to miss it."

Brady said, "Tinfoil." People turned and looked at her. "We have an old set at home. It works better if you wrap foil on the antennas. Don't ask me why it works, but it does."

The girl at the front said, "Eddie, run to the cabin and get some. Jenny's up there making popcorn. She'll show you where it is." One of the boys took off.

"This isn't the cabin?" Brady said to a guy sitting next to her. He shook his head as he inhaled on the fat joint that had made its way to that side of the room.

He exhaled slowly. "Boathouse," he said, gasping.

Brady looked around more carefully. It was a one-room building, almost larger than the entire first floor of her house in Minneapolis. And it was for boats?

A massive picture window at one end overlooked the lake. She rose and walked to it. Just as she pressed her forehead against the cool glass, the soft pink of the fading sunset was overtaken by star-specked inky blue.

All around the dark shoreline white and yellow cabin lights twinkled. Out of the corner of her eye, she saw the flames of the bonfire. The music throbbed and people laughed. A girl shrieked. Brady heard a splash, then a series of splashes. Soon she could see swimmers headed toward a square raft that bobbed on the water a few yards beyond the end of the dock. One boy briefly crouched in the shallows before standing and waving his swim trunks above his head. He flung them back to shore. Other swimmers began tossing their suits toward the beach.

The first swimmer reached the raft and climbed the ladder. Soon there were several naked bodies on the raft. A pushing game began and bodies toppled into the water.

A loud cheer reclaimed Brady's attention and she turned back to the group around the television. Eddie had returned with the foil and was wadding it around an antenna.

A clear image filled the screen. Everyone applauded. Eddie said, "Hail to the genius," and bowed to Brady. The others thought that was funny, and without prompting, everyone rose from the floor of the boathouse and bowed. Then all but one of them tumbled back onto the floor in a tumult of arms, legs, pot smoke, and laughter.

Brady stood her ground, watching, then she raised her eyes and caught the gaze of the girl someone had called Sally.

4

Looking like a crude toy, the astronaut hopped from the spaceship. As he cavorted on the moon, the crowd watched quietly. The longer he played, however, the less it claimed people's interest. By the time the announcer returned to pass judgment on the wonder of it all, joints were again circling rapidly and a few people had left to join the dancing. Brady remained to watch and listen to the commentators.

"You look distressed," a girl said. "It's supposed to be wonderful. Don't you think it's wonderful?"

Brady said, "It is." She sighed, chided herself silently, then turned and smiled at the girl, the one called Sally.

"Then why were you shaking your head?"

"A private thought."

"My favorite kind. Tell me."

Brady started twice to speak, but held the words back. She'd only get in trouble, no doubt about that.

Sally said, "Oh come on, are you afraid of hurting my feelings? You don't even know me, so why be polite? And no one else is listening."

True enough. "Did you hear the commentators? 'America at its best,' one of them said. 'The true spirit of this country.'"

"Missed it. Too dizzy with joy, I guess."

"Evidently America at its best is a bunch of white guys. That's the message. Screw the protesters and people trying to stop the war, screw the hippies, screw the blacks, oh yeah, especially the blacks. Give me a bunch of white guys—"

Sally pointed at the television image of the jubilant engineers in mission control. "In short-sleeved shirts."

"Exactly. White guys in short-sleeved shirts and, golly, that's America. I work . . ." Brady shook her head. Shut up, she told herself. Shut up and figure out how to get out of here.

"What's your name?" Sally asked.

"Brady Callahan."

"What about your work, Brady Callahan? And I'm Sally Cooper."

Cooper? That was the name the obnoxious boy had used. Her brother? Yes, same thick dark hair, same deep-set brown eyes, same slender build. Sally was short, though, and apparently sober.

"I work at a community center in Minneapolis," Brady said. "We see a lot of people who need help. We see soldiers just back from the war who are incredibly messed up, and spaced-out runaways whose brains are fried, and girls who are pregnant and have been kicked out of the house by their parents. And old people, lots of lonely old people. So all this—" Brady pointed at the screen and sighed. "Yes, it's amazing, I do think it's wonderful and amazing. I love the puzzle of it, you know? How they solved the puzzle of going to the moon. But it's not America at its best."

"What is it?"

"A distraction."

"From thinking about things that are not so great?"

Brady nodded.

"Brady?"

"Yes?"

"You need to relax more."

"That's what my mother says. I thought I would tonight, coming to this party. I thought it would be fun. I'm staying at Potter's Resort. It's awful. It's full of people dressed in golf clothes."

They both laughed.

Brady said, "I wish . . ."

"Wish what? Tell me, please. I've just decided I want to make all your wishes come true."

Brady stared evenly, her lips set. Finally, she said, "I met your brother outside. He was obnoxious too."

Sally laughed. "I believe it. We can't help ourselves. Now tell me, what do you wish?"

"I wish I could leave. Do you have a car?"

"It's faster by boat. C'mon, I'll take you back."

Only a few people remained by the bonfire. Drake sat alone. When Brady told him she had a ride to the resort, he nodded, lifted a can of beer, and drank deeply.

Brady followed Sally onto the dock. The metal slats clanged under their feet as they walked. "Just a minute," Sally said as she hopped into a boat. After a moment she got out, walked to another, and climbed into that one. She repeated this three times before calling, "Here we go. Get in."

Brady hesitated. Maybe the girl wasn't so sober, not if she couldn't remember where she was parked. "Are you sure you should be driving?"

"I'm not drunk, if that's what you mean."

"I just wondered, because it looks like you can't remember which one is yours."

"Ours is blocked in. We'll take someone else's. I was just looking for one with keys in it."

"You're stealing a boat?"

"No one will notice for hours. Besides, they'll get it back. Hop in."

No one came running after them as Sally eased the boat out of its tight parking spot. She turned toward open water, the boat's motor humming at moderate speed.

"Where did everyone go?" Brady asked. "The beach was almost deserted."

"Up to the cabin, I guess."

"Your parents must not be home."

"They're in Washington watching the moonwalk with a general, a couple of former cabinet members, and some senators. Perhaps a foreign ambassador or two."

"Are you joking?"

"Nope. Mom and Dad fly pretty high."

"Do you live in Washington?"

"No. Near the Twin Cities, on Lake Minnetonka. You?"

"Minneapolis. Is Paul your older brother?"

"He is. My only brother, for that matter. And I'm his only sister. I should have guessed you'd met him when you came into the boathouse. You had such a panicked look on your face, like you were escaping a hall of horrors. He's not so bad when he's sober. He just turned twenty-one, and I think he's already had enough intoxicants to last a lifetime. Look at that." She slowed the boat and pointed.

A new moon hung like a ghostly outline in the sky.

Brady leaned back, stretched out her legs, and dropped her head on the seat. "They'll leave tons of litter."

Sally idled the engine. The boat rocked and drifted on gentle waves. "Do you ever stop worrying?"

"Do you ever worry at all?"

When Sally didn't answer, Brady rolled her head along the seat back and looked at the other girl. Sally was staring at some spot in the dark. She turned and faced Brady, her brow furrowed.

Brady thought, Holy crap. I think I know what's coming.

Sally leaned over and kissed her quickly. She pulled back and stared ahead.

Brady said, "This has been the strangest night. Please don't do that again."

Sally said, "An impulse. I never have before—I mean a girl—and for a second it just seemed like I had to."

"Do you always act on your impulses?"

"I have a history."

"Then you probably should stay away from the edge of high places. Did you like kissing me? Didn't do much for me."

Sally nodded thoughtfully. "Same, I guess. I want something to do that, Brady. I want to feel something and be shaken up."

"Be careful what you wish for."

"It was so peaceful and nice sitting here looking at the world. And I thought, already I feel like I've known you forever, but at the same time I want to know more—everything about you. What could that mean? It has to mean something, to have it all mixed up that way. And then I thought, Well, why not?"

"You don't have to explain."

"I know. But I have to understand." Sally put the boat in gear. "I want to feel something," she said again.

Potter's patio was packed with dancers. Under pale yellow lights, they shimmied and glided to soft piano music.

"Want to come in?" Brady said. "The lights are on in our cottage, which means my mom and brothers are still up. They're probably playing cards."

"What's Dad doing?"

"Dad's dead."

Sally slumped. "I didn't know."

"How could you? We just met tonight."

Sally said, "Did we really? Just tonight? It seems longer."

Brady said, "Are you always melodramatic?"

"Do you hate me?"

Brady stepped onto the dock. "Oddly enough, no. Thanks for the rescue."

Brady watched Sally speed away. Would they meet again? Did she want to? She was just about to turn and walk back to the cottage, when the boat made a sharp turn and raced back.

Sally brought it to a stop inches away from collision with the dock. "Do you water-ski?" she called.

"I don't even swim. But my brothers might like to, if that's not too rude to mention."

Sally waved good-bye and turned the boat back toward open water. Brady watched until its twinkling lights dissolved in the darkness.

5

Brady watched her mother snap down a row of playing cards.

"Two hours of solitaire, Mom? That must be a record, even for you."

"As the boys would say, don't make a federal case out of it. I've lost interest in the books I brought, you're taking your time with that one, and I don't feel like walking to the library in the lodge. With weather like this, there's not much else to do."

True enough, Brady thought, her attention turning again to the gray world outside the window. The downpour that began as they'd returned from the lodge after breakfast had slowed to a persistent, mood-dampening drizzle.

"Thank goodness there are rainy-day activities for kids in the lodge," Mary continued.

Brady readjusted the position of the book on her lap. As long as the boys were busy, it would be nice to have a day inside, if only because it made it less likely that she'd run into Steve or Drake or either of the girls who'd gone to the party last night.

"How was the party?" Mary said.

Brady resisted the urge to turn and stare at her mother. Was she a mind reader? That was too scary to contemplate. How typical, though, that she'd wait hours before asking about the party and then toss off the question oh so casually, either because she didn't want to seem like she was prying and eager, or because her interest truly was casual.

Which was less annoying—a calculating mother or a disinterested one?

"The party was a drunken revel," Brady said. And I was kissed by an interesting girl, she added silently.

Snap, snap, snap. "Do you know," Mary said, "that I've never been to a drunken revel? Did you see the moonwalk?"

Brady dropped her head to hide a smile behind her hair. This was like so many conversations she had with her mother, the professional confidante who tended to talk with a one-two punch. First came the personal, then the impersonal. Brady could choose which thread to pick up. "The moonwalk made me sad, then mad."

Mary looked up from her cards. "How so? I thought it was thrilling."

Before Brady could explain, a poncho-shrouded figure walked in front of the cabin. It turned and looked in. Sally.

Brady leaped out of the chair. Her book slid to the floor.

"Whoa," Mary said when a blast of cool air flooded the cabin as Brady opened the door.

Sally stepped under the eave and pushed back the hood of her poncho. "Are you doing anything?"

Mary called out, "She's hogging the book I want to read."

"My mother," Brady said.

Sally peered in through the screen. "Hello, Brady's mother. Can she come out and play?"

"I warn you, your shoes will get ruined. I brought my brother's old boots along. I thought they might be the right size."

Brady looked at her tennis shoes. There were tiny frayed openings where her big toes rubbed the canvas. "Doesn't matter," she said. "They're old. And I don't want to wear his boots."

Sally's attention shifted from her driving to Brady. "Look at you blush. Your face is practically the color of your hair."

"I blush at anything and everything, okay? Sometimes when I'm scared I blush. Maybe your driving scares me."

Sally grinned, shifted, and the old pickup truck careened around a curve in the narrow gravel road, sending up sheets of muddy spray.

Brady bounced in her seat. "Are you going to tell me where we're going?"

Sally said, "My favorite place in the world."

• • •

"This is a swamp. You brought me to a swamp."

"A bog," Sally said. "More accurately, a floating bog. You'd better coat yourself with bug dope. The mosquitoes are fierce."

Brady said, "I never would have guessed that you were a nature girl."

Sally sprayed repellent on her hands and then smeared her face. "I'm not, exactly, but I do like hiding places. Dad and I come out here sometimes. He likes hiding places too."

Brady pushed back her poncho hood. The drizzle had stopped. The air was sweet and still, protected from the wind by a tall break of trees that rimmed the bog. She breathed deeply, inhaling the silence along with the air.

Sally peeled off her poncho and tossed it into the cab of the truck. She pulled out a plump green knapsack. "Ready? Follow me exactly. If you step off the trail, you might go through into the water underneath. Leeches galore down there."

Brady stopped in her tracks. "You're kidding."

"Just stay right behind me. You'll be fine."

Brady checked the sky. Still dark, but nothing was coming down. She took off her poncho, twisted it into a long rope, and tied it around her waist. As soon as she stepped onto the trail, the ground rolled under her feet. "How weird. Is it really safe for us to be walking on this?"

"It's safe enough for us, if we're careful, but not so great for the bog, so we don't hike out here very often. Dad hired a naturalist to look over the place. She spent days exploring and taking samples. She pretty much mapped out a route across the bog."

"You own all this?"

Sally paused, testing the trail with her foot. She nodded as she prodded a spot, then stepped over it. "Dad was out snowshoeing one winter. He likes getting out and exploring. He was here and fell in love with it. And of course he had to own it, he had to acquire it and make it a possession. Eight thousand acres."

Brady stopped. "That's a lot. How far are we walking?"

"About a mile."

As they walked, Brady realized when and where she'd experienced this sort of discomfort before: every single time she had entered a new school, feeling out of place and knowing the next step was potentially the wrong one. She looked up and spotted three huge crows perched on tree branches. One cawed disapprovingly. Yes, just like a new school, where her every move was watched.

Brady said, "Do you know that I've gone to seven schools in my life, including three high schools?"

Sally said, "How come?"

"My father kept taking different teaching jobs in colleges. And the last two were because my mother moved us out of state when she went back to school for another degree. When she was done, we moved back to the Twin Cities, but to a different neighborhood."

"Another degree?"

"Masters in social work. For some reason she didn't think her graduate nursing and public health degrees were enough. She . . ." Brady bit her lip. There was no way she could explain her mother.

Sally held up her hand. "No more. Not while we're walking. It's too interesting. I'm curious, though: What made you think of it?"

Brady turned and eyed the crows. "Everything."

Sally said, "Don't you love everything?" She waved her arms. "I mean, all of this?"

Brady said, "Not really, but I'm trying to be a good sport. I love that I'm not spending a day trapped in a cabin with my mother. I love the quiet."

"Was that a hint? Okay, I'll shut up."

They reached the other side of the bog. The trail continued onto what looked like solid ground. "See that rise on the east edge?" Sally said.

East? West? Who could tell with a sky this overcast. Brady said, "I guess."

Sally pointed. "Beaver house. It's almost forty feet wide. Can't even imagine how far down it goes. You don't care, do you?"

Brady said, "It is beautiful here, but I feel out of place."

"That's why you thought about all the schools, isn't it? Ha! I'm not so dense."

The narrow trail they followed meandered through woods. Every now and then Sally pointed out a wildflower or bird. Brady always missed the birds.

"You're hopeless," Sally said.

"I've always lived in cities," Brady replied. "And the first science teacher I ever had was horrible, so since then I've tuned out stuff unless it was going to be on a test. Wildlife was never on a test. Blame Mrs. Bronson, evil Mrs. Bronson."

The trail ended abruptly at the edge of a tiny lake. Brady said, "This is beautiful. This I like. Is it yours too?"

Sally said, "I'm pretty sure. I've never asked. He doesn't know I've hiked this far. We only ever go to the bog. For some reason he wants to keep this a secret. By the way, we've walked through lots of poison ivy. We'll wash up when we get there."

"There" was a tiny shack set back a few yards from a small beach. Brady said, "His?"

Sally nodded. "I told you he likes hiding places. I think he built this himself. He must have brought the materials in by sled during winter. Of course, it's even more likely that he hired someone to do it."

"What if it's not his?"

Sally leaned down and pulled a plug of wood out from under the sill of the shack's only window. She probed, then pulled out a key. "I'm pretty sure it is. This is exactly how we hide the key to our cabin, and then one time I came here and there was a fishing pole like his and some books that are the kind of crap he likes to read."

She swung the door open and motioned with her head for Brady to follow. Brady said, "This seems wrong. It feels like an intrusion."

Sally smiled. "I know."

The shack was bare except for a cot and chair and a small table. "It's not much, but it's comfortable," Sally said. She dropped her knapsack on the table and unbuckled it. She pulled out towels and a bar of soap. "Fels-Naptha. Let's go scrub off."

The sun broke through just as they reached the beach. Brady shielded her eyes.

"There's suntan lotion and a hat in the cabin. It's in the small pocket of the knapsack."

By the time Brady returned to the beach, Sally had stripped and was walking naked into the lake. Brady sat on the sand and rolled up her pants. She took off her shoes and socks, and studied her wrinkled pink feet for a long time. She ignored Sally, who was standing waist deep and looking out over the water.

Sally shouted, "Don't be shy, Brady. There's no one around." She dove and started swimming parallel to the shore.

Brady contained her fury with precise motions as she washed her arms and legs.

Sally swam for a long time. When she finally stepped onto the dry sand, Brady balled up a towel and threw it at her. She said sharply, "Why did you bring me here?"

The towel unfolded in Sally's hands, draping her front. Her head jerked back in surprise. "What?"

"You heard me."

Sally wrapped herself, shivering slightly. She frowned as she looked at the sand around her feet. Then she laughed. "God, no. Brady, *no*. This has nothing to do with last night. That was, I don't know, an impulse, like I said." She sat down on the sand. "You are so uptight. I did not bring you here to seduce you." She stretched out her legs and dropped back onto the sand. Brady leaned over and closed Sally's towel where it gaped.

"Very uptight," said Sally.

The sun had disappeared again. Brady decided she preferred the gray. "I am uptight," she said. "Probably because I'm always worrying."

"How old are you? About my age, right?"

"Eighteen."

"Me too. Done with high school?"

Brady nodded. "I'm going to the U this fall."

"I'm going to Connecticut College. It's where my dad's mother and all her sisters went. I'm not thrilled."

"Don't go."

"Not that simple. So you're eighteen and constantly worried. About what?"

Brady thought, How long a list do you want? She said, "My mother. I worry about when she's going to feel settled. I worry about my two younger brothers and how screwed up they're getting with all the moving we do. I worry about the people I see at work. I worry about money, if you must know. But mostly I worry about my older brother. He's in Vietnam."

Sally made a noise. "God, that's awful. That must be the worst. If I were a guy, I'd go to Canada. Jail would be better. I absolutely would not go."

"I feel that way too, but it's easy for us to say, isn't it? We're never going to be drafted. What we believe will never be challenged."

Sally sat up. "So we should shut up about the war just because we'll never have to fight?"

"I wasn't saying that."

Sally shook her head. "Never silence yourself, never. If something is wrong, say so. You have to speak up."

Brady said, "And what then? What do you do after you speak? Lots of people make noise but never take action."

They stared at each other a long moment before Sally said, "Not me. Watch this." She dressed and went back to the shack. She returned after a moment with her knapsack. "Time to feed the hungry. I brought lunch. And even better: dry socks for the hike back."

They built a fire, ate, and watched the clouds gather. They saw two deer come to the water's edge. They watched the breeze make patterns on the dark water.

Brady said, "I think you have seduced me."

"How?"

"With this place. The view. I'd love to be able to sit in such absolute peace every day. But even just to do it for an afternoon—you have no idea how wonderful this feels."

"You should see the view in the morning. I spent the night here once and the sunrise was incredible. We should come back sometime and spend the whole night." Sally lay back on the sand, one arm under her head for a pillow. She closed her eyes and didn't speak.

As the silence settled, Brady felt something lighten and lift.

The weight of worry. The years of loneliness.

6

The next afternoon Brady was coating Sam's back with suntan lotion, when there was a knock on the door. Cullen, still in pajamas, growled and retreated to the cottage's tiny bunk room. Mary looked up from a newspaper. "Is that your friend again?"

Brady shrugged, patted Sam's shoulders to wipe the last of the lotion from her hands, and went to the door.

Sally stood there smiling. "It's a hot one. Anyone want to go skiing?"

Cullen and Sam both did, of course, though Cullen, who had emerged from his room in swim trunks as soon as he heard the question, feigned cool indifference.

"Sure. I guess," he said as he leaned against the wall.

Brady opened the door and waved Sally in. "Did you steal another boat?" she asked.

"Steal a boat?" Mary said. "We're going in a stolen boat?"

"*We're* going?" Brady said.

"In the event Sam and Cullen actually get up on skis, I want to be there to see it. As long as the boat's not stolen."

"More the merrier," Sally said. "And the boat's ours. My brother's waiting down at the dock." She turned to the boys. "Why don't you guys go on down. Paul will fix you up with life jackets. Red boat with a silver stripe. Tell him we're coming." The boys took off like light, the screen door slamming behind them.

"We brought all different sizes of life jackets. Enough for everyone," she said to Brady. "And I've got hats and suntan lotion and stuff to drink. I figured you'd worry about all that."

Mary laughed. "Sally, exactly how long have you known my daughter?"

"Not long, but she's not much of a mystery; everything shows on her face."

Mary said, "I'll get my suit on. Thank you, Sally, this should be fun."

After the bedroom door closed, Brady said, "I'm not so sure this will be fun. I don't think I want to spend the afternoon in a boat with your brother."

"I'm not surprised. He finally sobered up this morning and told me what happened. Well, what he could remember. He told me what you did. Way to go, Brady."

"So why is he here?"

"Because I asked him."

Brady nodded curtly to Paul as she climbed into the boat. His greeting was equally cool. But he was sweet to her brothers and mother, so later when they accidentally made brief eye contact, she managed a slight smile, even though under her breath she was still calling him names.

With Sally in the water coaching, Cullen was successful on his second try. As the boat pulled away, his solid body rose from the water and he stayed up for two full circles around the bay.

Sam couldn't do anything but topple over whenever the boat began moving. Brady watched in terror as he tumbled again and again. He gave up after fifteen minutes. When Paul hauled him into the boat, Sam's stick-thin body was shaking with cold and fatigue. Paul handed him a towel. "Nice try, buddy. Why don't you sit by me and help drive the boat."

Sam's gloom changed to a sun-bright smile. At that moment Brady was ready to forgive Paul for anything.

Sally climbed into the boat, grabbed a towel to wrap around her shoulders, and said, "Who's next?" as she looked straight at Brady.

Brady shook her head.

"I'm a good teacher."

"I'm a bad swimmer." She was saved from making more excuses when her mother stood and said, "My turn."

Mary tightened her life jacket, swung her legs over the side of the boat, and slid into the water. Sally started to follow. "I'm fine," Mary said. "I've done this."

Paul and Sally looked at Brady. "Beats me," she said.

With the first burst of speed Mary rose from the water. Paul circled the bay once, then, nodding at some hand signals Brady's mother was making, passed the resort dock. Mary Callahan dropped a ski, slid one foot behind another, signaled again, and Paul opened throttle.

While the others cheered, Brady shielded her eyes with a hand and watched her mother do tricks on the water. She turned to Sally. "I didn't know. She never told us."

Cullen shouted from the back of the boat, "Hey, Brady, think she learned this in the convent?"

"Convent?" Sally said, then turned to watch the skier, now leaning so sharply into a turn that her shoulders nearly touched the water.

Sally waited with a towel as Mary climbed back into the boat.

"You were in a convent? You were a nun?"

"Three or four lifetimes ago. Oh my, I'm going to be stiff in a few hours. I haven't done that in a very long time."

"At least not in *my* lifetime," Brady said.

"At least. Don't look so surprised, dear."

"It's just that we never knew, Mom."

"I gave it up when I entered the order, of course. This and a great deal else. And then when your father entered the picture, I was so enthralled with him that I completely forgot about things I used to do as a girl." She stared dreamily at the water as she hugged herself with the sun-warmed towel.

"That's what I meant, that's it exactly," Sally whispered to Brady.

"What?"

"That's how I want to feel about something."

Brady again refused to ski; instead, she asked for a ride around the lake. Paul let both boys drive. Cullen confidently let it run at high speed. During his turn Sam gripped the wheel with nervous joy as the boat went about as fast as a floating leaf.

They arrived back at the resort after nearly three hours on the water. In spite of layers of lotion, Brady suspected she'd be painfully red. Already she could feel her skin tightening.

As everyone climbed onto the dock, Mary thanked Sally and Paul. "Won't you join us for dinner?" she asked. "Please be my guests at the lodge."

Cullen and Sam looked at each other, then at Brady. She knew what they were thinking: How expensive would that be, two extra people?

"Good idea," she said, and the boys relaxed.

"We always play cards after dinner," Cullen said. "Killer Hearts. You could stay for that."

Sally and Paul declined with one voice. "Our parents get back tomorrow," said Paul.

"We need to clean our cabin," Sally added. "But maybe tomorrow night or Thursday? You're here all week, right?" All the Callahans nodded. "Then for sure I'll be back." She faced Cullen directly. "But don't think for a moment that you have a chance of beating me at any card game."

"She cheats," Paul said.

"I'm good," Sally said, her eyes still on Cullen.

"That'll be great," Cullen said, and he blushed.

Brady's throat tightened as she watched her brother. She was certain his heart was on fire.

7

True to her word, Sally showed up two nights later with Paul in tow. True to her word, she immediately won the first game—with no sign of cheating, though her brother insisted she was doing it somehow.

"She has ways," he said to the younger boys.

"One more round," Mary said, "then how about a break for the sunset?"

Watching the sunset that week had become her mother's major preoccupation. "Do you think it will go down again tonight?" Brady asked, handing her a glass of lemonade as they set out for the small wooden fishing dock down the shoreline from their cottage. She picked up the bowl of popcorn she'd just popped, and pushed open the screen door with her foot, holding it for the others. "We'd better go watch in case it doesn't."

"Do you tease your mother?" Mary said to Sally. "I bet you don't." She ran ahead to join the boys, who were already on the dock, lying on their stomachs and grabbing at something in the water.

"Did your parents mind that you went off tonight?" Brady asked Sally. "I mean, what with them just back and all."

"They have friends visiting. They didn't mind. We had dinner, they showed us off, they said good-bye. Hey guys, you can't catch fish that way. Don't listen to my idiot brother."

"Your idiot brother," Cullen said, "did catch one with his hands."

Paul rolled over onto his back and smiled up at the girls. "I am truly great."

Sally scooped a handful of popcorn from the bowl Brady was carrying and dropped it on his face. A few kernels rolled into the water. All at once there was a feeding frenzy as a mass of fish converged on the popcorn. Sam and Cullen immediately plunged their arms into the water.

"What is the point of this?" Brady asked.

"None whatsoever," said Paul. "Toss some more popcorn, would you?"

"No, I want to eat it."

"Don't you dare touch it," Sally said as he reached for the bowl.

"If we want to use our share as bait, what's wrong with that?" Cullen said.

"Yeah," said Paul, sitting up and looking tough. "What's wrong with that?"

"Yeah," echoed Sam, looking deliriously happy.

Mary was staring at the sky. Already the sun was touching the narrow band of trees that rimmed the distant western shoreline. "What does it matter?" she said softly.

Brady dropped a handful of popcorn into the water, and the feeding frenzy resumed. Sam scooped up a tiny yellow-breasted fish not much larger than his palm.

"Not too tight, buddy," Paul said. "You don't want to kill it."

"Look, Brady, I caught it with my bare hands!"

She looked, then turned away, repulsed by the pulsing gills and blank eyes of the fish.

"Toss it in, it needs the water," Paul said. Brady heard a soft splash. "Don't you like fish?" he asked.

"She ate enough at supper tonight," Mary said, still watching the sky.

"What I ate didn't have heads or scales." Or soulless black eyes.

"Hey, sis," Cullen said, "look at this."

Stupidly, she looked. He waved a gasping fish right before her eyes.

Reflexively, she pushed him toward the water. Sally caught him by the arm. The fish went flying, landing on the dock, where it flopped and gasped until Mary calmly pushed it into the water with her foot. She said, "Shall we settle down, children, and watch the sunset?"

They lined up like ducks and then sat facing the sunset. Paul stage-whispered to Cullen, "Don't ever be mean to girls."

Cullen shrugged.

Paul said, "They're too good at getting even."

Just as the sun was disappearing, Brady, sitting nearest the shore, heard faint knocking. She glanced back toward the cottages.

A man in a dark suit peered into the front window of the Callahan cottage. He turned and faced the lake.

Brady noted his stiff bearing and short haircut. At first she thought, Cop. What was he doing? What did he want?

Their eyes met. The man ran a hand over his very short hair.

That's not a cop, she thought. He's military.

Her jaw tightened. Air caught in her throat.

He's here to tell us Will is dead.

Will is dead.

Will.

The man approached. She moaned softly. Not here. Brady rose and halted him with her hand. She walked around Sam to her mother, squatted, and whispered, "I need you. Can we go to the cottage?"

Mary turned around, still laughing at a bad joke one of the boys had made.

Her sage green eyes, Brady thought. That wide-as-the-world smile.

Will.

The smile vanished when Mary saw her daughter's face. She looked over Brady's shoulder, saw the visitor, and understood immediately.

"We'll be back," Brady said to the others, though they weren't paying much attention, intent again on catching fish.

"Mrs. Callahan," the man said as they approached.

"Inside," Mary said tersely.

Brady followed them into the cabin. She stood just inside the door. Sally had watched them walk away, but the boys remained focused on the water. Brady caught Sally's gaze and shook her head slightly.

"Is it Will? You're here to tell me he's dead, aren't you?" Mary said. "Go ahead and tell me. A child in Vietnam, every day I expect the worst."

"Ma'am, I'm Special Agent Daniel Blake. FBI." He pulled an ID from a pocket, flashed it, and put it away.

"FBI?" Brady whispered. He looked at her, his head pivoting slowly on a thick neck.

"Why are you here?" Mary said.

"I'm here to inform you that your son William Callahan is absent without leave from military service." He withdrew a white envelope from an inside pocket. "This is your official notification letter."

AWOL. Brady felt a cool rush sweep through her; her breath escaped in a slow, nearly silent whistle of relief. Out of the corner of her eye, she saw activity through the cabin window. Sally and Paul were leading the boys toward the boat dock. Sam broke away in a run, racing toward the red and silver boat.

Mary took the letter and sank into a chair. "What?" she said.

Brady thought, Yes, say it again. Once again tell us anything except that he's dead.

The FBI agent smoothed his tie. "I realize that you're feeling tremendous relief right now."

Panic returned with pinpricks.

"You're probably not familiar with standard operating procedure when a soldier goes AWOL."

Probably not, Brady thought. Her mother said it aloud at the same instant.

"In routine cases the family receives notification by mail as soon as it's been determined there's an AWOL situation. One month after the absence begins, the soldier's status is changed to DFR. Desertion, commonly called." Again he smoothed his tie. "At that point the FBI serves as the civilian liaison with the families."

"He's been gone a month?" Brady said. "Then why didn't we find out sooner?"

Agent Blake shook his head. "Private Callahan's case is not routine. He left his platoon nearly three weeks ago. We've been called in to assist earlier than normal because his is an unusual situation."

"Why?" Mary asked.

"Have you had any contact with or communication from Private Callahan since July 2?"

Mary shook her head. "No letter for almost a month."

Brady said, "Why isn't this routine? If you don't usually get involved for four weeks, why are you here now?"

Agent Blake kept his eyes on Mary Callahan. He pulled another envelope out of his pocket. Both Brady and her mother recognized the handwriting immediately; they both leaned forward.

As her mother took hold of the letter, Brady saw the edges where the envelope had been sliced open. "You've read it."

Mary lifted her eyes to the agent. "You intercepted this." Her voice tightened. "You ignored my daughter's question. I'd like an answer to that question. Why isn't my son's case routine?"

"In ten days," Agent Blake said, "your son's status officially becomes that of a deserter. It would be in his best interest for that not to happen. Any information you might have—"

"What would I know? I told you that I haven't heard from him in nearly a month." Mary held up the envelope. "You held this from me. You read it. And you still haven't told us why this isn't routine."

"Mrs. Callahan, I regret to inform you that your son, along with several others, participated in a mutinous act. Further, the army believes it's possible that he received aid and assistance from the enemy. It does have evidence that he is in hiding and is inciting other soldiers to desert and commit acts of resistance."

Brady's gasp rolled into a sharp laugh, her mother's into a vehement curse.

"That's outrageous," Mary said.

"We have reason—" Agent Blake began.

"What reason?" Mary snapped.

Agent Blake's stony face taunted, I'm not telling!

Mary folded her arms, tucking both letters out of sight. "You track me down and toss your little bombshell. You don't give me your reasons why you think my son is a traitor. And you expect me to cooperate."

"It's in his best interest—"

Mary silenced him by slashing the air. The notification letter went flying from her hand. "Don't tell me what you think is in his best interest. That's an obscene joke coming from the government that sent him to war. Just tell me what you know."

He said, "Two days before your son disappeared, his entire platoon engaged in what's commonly called a combat refusal. They refused to obey orders."

"What were the orders?"

"I don't have that information. Private Callahan, along with the others, was of course reported. Two days after that refusal there was a similar incident that ended abruptly when the unit came under fire. Air support was called in. By the time the situation was under control, Private Callahan and three others were missing."

Brady's brain spun wildly. Lost, she wanted to say, my brother's only been lost.

Mary said, "Taken prisoner, perhaps."

Agent Blake tipped his head slightly. "That was assumed at first. Within days, however, there was evidence that he was in Saigon. Saigon's quite a distance from the district where he was last seen. Far enough that an American soldier on his own would have a hard time getting there in such a short time."

"Has he been seen in Saigon?"

"Mrs. Callahan, any communication you've had from him—"

"Five letters," Mary said softly. "Five letters, that's all I've had in all the months he's been gone."

"If I could see them and take them with me. They'd be returned, of course. To know where he's been, who he's seen, the names of his friends in the platoon—all this would help us clarify the situation."

"Help you fabricate a conspiracy," Brady said.

Mary glanced toward the bunk room. Brady knew the letters were there, in her mother's purse.

Brady said, "You searched our house in Minneapolis, didn't you? You didn't find any letters. You didn't find him. That's why you came here."

"We did not do that, miss."

Mary took a breath. "You can't have them. I won't let go of them."

"That's understandable. If I could just read them, it would help."

"No. My daughter is right. You're patching together a story with my son at the center. You say you have evidence that he's alive but you won't tell me what it is."

Agent Blake rose. Brady realized then that there was more that he knew. More he was choosing not to tell.

"What else is there?" she asked. "What else aren't you telling us?"

Agent Blake reached into his pocket. He removed a business card and set it down on the table. "I'm assigned to the Minneapolis office. Until Private Callahan is apprehended I'll be checking in with you. But if at any time you hear from your son, or should you change your mind about the letters, please get in touch."

He paused at the door. "I'm very sorry, Mrs. Callahan."

Brady was frozen in place. She closed her eyes and saw Will sobbing in the car, frightened to death about going to war. "Why did he come here to tell us that? Why now, after Will's been gone three weeks?"

Mary sat at the table and put her head in her hands.

"What do we tell the boys when they get back?"

"Get back?" Mary looked up. "Where did they go?"

"Sally and Paul took them out in the boat."

Mary looked out the window at the lake. "We can tell them that he's not dead. Just missing, that's what we'll say. AWOL, yes, it's only fair they know that much of the truth. Until we know what really happened."

Brady thought, We'll never know.

8

They waited on the dock. When the boat returned, the boys hopped out, excited about having seen the northern lights. "I counted thirty shooting stars!" Sam shouted.

"Brady will explain," Mary said to Sally and Paul. "Thank you, with all my heart."

Cullen said, "What's up? What's wrong?"

"I need you inside, darling. Please say good night."

Cullen made a face, unhappy about being called "darling" in front of Sally and Paul. But he cheered when the older boy hugged him around the shoulders and said, "See you again, okay? We'll do some more skiing."

Sally kissed Sam and said, "You too, dreamboat."

After her mother and brothers had gone, Brady told her friends what had happened.

Sally erupted. "What a fascist, coming and finding you on your vacation. Especially when they've known for so long. It's so incredibly fascist. You'd be home soon. Why did he have to track you down and interrogate you like that?"

Paul said calmly, "Element of surprise. He might even have waited until you were gone so they could search your house."

"That's what I thought. He said they didn't."

"You don't believe that, do you?" Sally said.

Brady shrugged. "I bet we'll never know anything except what they permit us to know."

Sally said again, "Fascists." She pulled Brady into her arms and said, "I'm so sorry about your brother." Brady felt Paul's hand briefly touch her shoulder.

She turned and faced him, the first time they'd stood eye to eye since she'd dumped the beer on his feet. "Thank you for being so nice to my brothers," she said.

He started to answer, then simply nodded and looked down as he slid his hands into his rear pockets.

Sally took Brady's arm and walked her back to the cottage.

"It's so hard to believe the story he told us," Brady said. "Collaborating with the enemy? That's pure bull. I can half accept him going AWOL. He was so scared, Sally. The night before he left, there was a party. He got loaded and he broke down and admitted he was scared. He didn't want to go. Maybe it all kept building, maybe the fear won, and he just had to run. But working with the enemy? Inciting other soldiers to resist? Not Will. It doesn't make sense. What could they be talking about?"

They reached the cottage lawn. Sally said, "Go in to your mom and the guys. I'll be by tomorrow."

"I don't think we'll stay here. She'll want to go home."

"Well, I'll be home soon too, and I'll call. We'll get together."

Brady stared out over the lake. "Maybe he saw something that made him snap. They said his whole squad resisted orders. They refused to do something. What was it they wouldn't do?"

"Who knows? Don't you suppose there are quite a few things to resist? Brady, I won't leave if you want. I'll stay here all night and we can figure it out. We can guess at the things he wouldn't tell you. But I bet your mother probably wants you with her."

Brady looked toward the cabin. "Yes."

Mary insisted on leaving that night. "I don't want to talk with anyone, I don't want farewells, I don't want questions about our visitor."

They arrived home at 3 A.M. Both boys were sound asleep. After they'd hauled them out of the car and herded them into bed, Brady and her mother sat at the large, round kitchen table. The maple tabletop was chipped and gouged around the edges. Mary fingered one of the blemishes. Her pink oval nail filled it exactly.

They sat without speaking as the blue plastic clock on the pale yellow wall ticked, ticked, ticked. Brady stretched her arms out on the table and laid down her head. Out of the corner of her eye, the last image before sleep, she saw her mother's eyes flare and her mouth burst into a small round O, as if she were suddenly recalling a nightmare.

9

The milk carton wobbled in Sam's hands as he held it over his glass. Brady took it from him and finished pouring.

"What will happen to him?" Sam asked.

"You mean, what will happen to him if he's not already dead," Cullen said, stirring his cold cereal.

Sam said, "He's not dead. Mom told us they didn't find his body and they don't know what happened to him. He might be a prisoner of the other side and he might be hiding because our army thinks he did something wrong. You can't be everybody's enemy, can you?"

Brady and Cullen exchanged looks.

"So what will happen to him?" Sam asked again. "If he's not dead and someone finds him, what will happen to him?"

"I guess he might go to an army prison, Sam." If he's lucky, Brady added to herself.

Sam nodded, happy to get one answer he understood. He stuffed a load of Cheerios into his mouth.

Brady rose and put the milk in the fridge. "I'm going over to the church to pick up my paycheck."

"Where's Mom?" Sam asked.

"Getting the mail from the post office. Then she was going to try to talk to someone, to see if she could find out more about Will."

Cullen made a noise. "I bet we'll never know anything."

Brady thought, We'll never know the truth.

• • •

Ten a.m. and the heat was unbearable. By the time she reached St. Bernard's, Brady was coated with the summer slime unique to the city.

One of Will's letters to Mary had been filled with complaints about the heat and humidity in Vietnam. A short letter, but all complaint. Was that what had cracked his spirit and made him run—the climate?

On a brown patch of grass next to the church's parking lot a dog lay alongside its owner. The human at the end of the worn leather leash was either passed out or asleep. The handle of a syringe was visible under the man's leg. The dog panted and looked at Brady, its head turning slightly to watch as she walked closer.

Brady leaned down to pet the dog. She froze when a gravelly voice said, "He bites." The dog whimpered and put a paw over its head.

She went to the church kitchen. It was empty and quiet before the noon rush. She found an old bowl, filled it with water, and carried it back outside to the dog.

The man was snoring. The dog inched cautiously toward the water after Brady set down the bowl. She debated unhooking the leash and spiriting the dog away from the junkie. She could give it a safe home and thrill the boys at the same time. Her mother had always resisted pets, claiming the family wasn't settled. Well, if they weren't settled now, they never would be. Surely a stray—okay, a stolen—pooch would be just the thing.

Suddenly Will's sneering voice echoed: *Are you searching for the perfect wounded animal to love?*

It was the last conversation they'd had.

Her breath snagged. Last conversation ever?

10

Father Tom was in his office, which was unusual because it was Food Day, and normally all hands were required to help distribute the government surplus canned meat, cheese, and powdered milk to the several hundred people who always began lining up at least two hours beforehand.

He motioned Brady in and closed the door. She looked for a space to sit. On the visitor's side of his desk were three chairs and a sofa—all covered with books, magazines, and shopping bags of donated clothing. The walls were dense with posters, pictures, cartoons, and newspaper clippings.

"Don't get too close to me," he said. "I'm contagious. Summer cold."

"Is that why you're hiding out here?"

He shrugged his shoulders and then rocked his head—maybe, maybe not. He gestured toward the sofa under the window. "Find a spot." Perched on the desk, he stroked his gray beard with a thumb and looked at her, his blue eyes steady but tired.

She was supposed to be gone the whole week, but he didn't seem surprised to see her. "Oh, God," Brady said. "You know."

He nodded. "The FBI was here yesterday. Well, there was one agent. Blake, I think it was."

"He came here before he talked to us?"

"I'm pretty sure he was at your house and at the neighbors before—"

"The neighbors? Does everybody know? Does everyone in the neighborhood know about my brother?"

"Another person's action is no reason for your shame, Brady. Besides, some might say what he did was admirable."

"We don't know what he did, just what the army says he did. And I'm not ashamed. I just don't like it that the whole world knew before we knew. What did he ask you?"

Someone knocked on the office door. Bang, bang, bang. Pause. Then three soft knocks. Brady said, "Dee's secret code?"

Father Tom smiled. "Yes. We're expecting an ambulance." He rose from the desk and moved toward the door.

"What happened?"

"Mr. Tremain broke into the kitchen last night through the basement window. We assumed it was an ordinary break-in until Deanna found him hiding under a pew in the sanctuary about half an hour ago. He was rather cut up from going through the glass. Worse, his night alone in the church seems to have disoriented him a bit further. Please stay, Brady, while I attend to this."

He opened the door and spoke to Deanna, the senior social worker employed at the center. She poked her head around the door while the priest reviewed and signed some papers.

"Hey, Brady. Short vacation."

"Came home early. Family stuff."

Deanna nodded. "I didn't tell the FBI a thing. Not that there was anything to tell, but why let them know that?"

Brady felt the color rise, toes to scalp. Her breathing quickened and her hands tightened into fists. Everyone knew. "I'm surprised he talked to you, Dee. You didn't—" She bit her lip. "You don't even know my brother."

"He wasn't interested only in your brother. He was obviously fishing for information about resistance activity. I wish I did know your brother. I like guys with guts. Anyone who says 'enough' to the war has guts. Oh, Tom, sign here too. I hope they keep Mr. Tremain long enough to get some food in him this time."

Deanna and Father Tom stepped into the hallway to talk privately. Brady slouched on the sofa and stared out the window.

She'd come to get answers but now felt more confused. Resistance activity? It was no secret that the priest counseled young men who had qualms about being drafted. And among the staff, it was no secret that he knew how to assist those who decided to go to Canada. But why tie Will into it? He had wanted no part of that.

Tom shut the door and walked to his chair. He sat down heavily and ran a hand across his head as he sighed.

"Why do you think the FBI agent came here to ask about my brother?"

The priest said, "Let's start from the beginning. What do you know, Brady?"

She shook her head. "What do *you* know?"

"Fair enough. Yesterday an FBI agent came by. It's happened before. We're watched, surely you know that. My fault, mostly. My activities have landed me on some government unpopularity list. I'm never surprised when they stop in for a visit. Much nicer, really, than wondering what van parked on the street might be covering up their watchers and microphones. But this wasn't routine harassment. This agent, this Blake, was asking after your brother. He said that Will is listed as AWOL. The FBI is interested in any communication anyone might have had with him."

"Which is ridiculous. He didn't know anyone here."

He shook his head. "Not ridiculous, Brady. The Birthday Brigade had added Will to its list."

The Birthday Brigade was an informal group of church ladies who met regularly to send cards and letters to church members who were ill or shut in or celebrating some sort of milestone. "I didn't know they included servicemen," she said.

"Since 1942." He picked up a pencil and tapped the desk.

"So he goes AWOL, the army digs through the stuff he left behind, and they find newsy letters from church ladies. That's worth a visit?"

"They also found two letters from me."

Brady sat back. "Why would you write him?"

"Part of my job. It's not just the Birthday Brigade that's been writing to soldiers since 1942."

"He doesn't belong to your church."

"He belongs to my community. My community is my church."

"What did you write about? Did you encourage him to disobey orders? Did you encourage him to go AWOL, Tom?"

He held up a hand. "I wrote about the weather. Baseball. And a bit about you and your activities here and how we value them. What do you mean about encouraging him to disobey orders?"

Brady inhaled slowly. "Will and his platoon had refused to carry out some orders."

He sat back and clasped his hands on his stomach. "A combat refusal. It's happening more and more, I hear."

"They think Will is collaborating with the enemy. That's what they said. It's not just that he's AWOL."

His eyes widened. "Why do they think that?"

"Because he's apparently showed up in Saigon and they say he couldn't have done that without having help."

"That explains a lot."

"Not to me, Tom. None of it makes sense, especially the collaborating part. Not my brother."

"It explains the quick involvement of the FBI. If they were looking for more than just a single soldier . . ." He gazed toward some spot on the wall.

"Looking for what?"

"Looking for some way the refusals were being organized or coordinated."

"Through St. Bernard's draft counseling center, for example. Through letters from a notorious priest, a well-known peace activist. Do you think they're looking for a conspiracy?"

He said, "They couldn't have found any conspiracy in my letters. That must have frustrated them."

Brady said, "My brother's not political. He hated the demonstrators. My mother used to be active in the movement, before she went back to grad school and before Will was drafted. She used to make us go to demonstrations with her. But not Will, he was old enough to say no to her. He gave her so much crap about her politics. Sarcastic crap, all the time."

Father Tom said, "That is also political, Brady."

"He was so mean to her about the war. It was making them hate each other."

"I doubt that."

"I love my brother."

"I'm sure you do. He knows you do."

Does he? she wondered. "They wouldn't have found any letters left behind that were from me. I never wrote. Not once."

"Brady, dear, don't allow—"

She held up a hand to shush him. She whispered, "He got mad at me the night before he left. We didn't even say good-bye."

Deanna wasn't the only one who'd heard about Will. After Brady left Father Tom, she went to the church office to pick up her paycheck. Big mistake. Food Day was always the busiest day of the month at the center, and the rooms and halls were crowded with volunteers. As she made the long walk down the hall to the administrative office, she thought again about what a troubled place St. Bernard's was, its personality split between St. Bernard's Catholic Church and St. Bernard's People's Center. Volunteers came from both sides, though they usually self-segregated around favorite projects. Birthday Brigade, all-church parties, and the annual rummage sale were the pet projects of the politically conservative working-class families that had long been the backbone of the church. The staff and supporters of the center tended to develop and support political activities geared toward issues of racial justice, peace, and poverty.

But volunteers from both factions supported Food Day and turned out full force. Brady knew them all. People wanted to talk.

"I'm so sorry."

"Man, what he did takes guts."

"He'll turn up."

"We didn't tell them anything."

She knew that not everyone was sympathetic. They were the silent ones. She could feel their eyes on her back, she could sense the murmuring that would begin as soon as she was out of sight. She wrote the script in her head:

Have you heard about her brother?

When so many other boys are dying . . .

Criminal, coward, traitor . . .

11

What was normal now? Brady wondered.

Was the way that woman was looking at her normal? Was that the normal expression you pull on when you see the sister of an AWOL traitor?

Was it normal to hear whispering voices as you walked through the produce section of the grocery store?

Was it normal to hesitate each time you reached for the ringing telephone?

Was it normal to turn and walk away when you heard your mother crying?

One night, going to the kitchen for a glass of water after waking from a troubling dream, Brady found Sam asleep on the living room sofa. He was hugging a framed photo of Will. She carefully pulled it from his arms. The frame had been lodged against his cheek and left a triangular red mark. She stroked it with her thumb, then went to get him a blanket.

Brady took the grocery bag from her mother, who dropped onto a kitchen chair. "What did you hear today?" Brady said.

Mary sighed. "I've called every government office with even a remote connection to the military. Nothing. Even our bloody congressman—our bleeding-heart, liberal, war-hating congressman—wouldn't talk to me. Even his aide wouldn't talk."

"Mom, not so loud. Sam—"

49

"They're watching television."

"It's just that he absorbs it. They both do."

Mary slumped. "I did finally talk to some low-level clerk at the Pentagon. He was so tight-lipped. Officially, Will's status is AWOL and that's all he wanted to say. Except for one unbelievable thing. Astounding, really." She picked at the skin around her left thumb, a new tic. Brady could see where it had begun bleeding. "He said, Yes, there was always the possibility Private Callahan was a prisoner of war and not AWOL. He said Vietnam was a confusing place. Can you believe that? Confusing. He said that sort of mix-up— mix-up—could happen. Then he asked me if I knew anything about how prisoners were treated by the Viet Cong." Mary stared at her daughter with lifeless eyes. "He said that it would be better for Will if he were dead. That's what I'll never forgive them for, Brady. Telling a mother to hope her child is dead."

Cullen got in a fight and came home bleeding. Brady was hanging laundry on the clothesline when he sped into the backyard on his bicycle, hopped off, and pushed it forward. It crashed against the garage and toppled over. She turned, clothespins in her mouth, and watched him rush toward the house. She followed and found him in the kitchen—twisting, kicking the air, and trying to get away as their mother restrained him in her arms.

"Let me look," Mary said calmly.

"Let me go," he shouted.

"Brady, wet a cloth," Mary said.

"Let me go," Cullen said again. "They didn't hurt me. It's nothing."

Brady got the cloth and handed it to her mother, who pressed it against Cullen's face as she held him. He stood still for a moment, then kicked a cupboard door.

"I wish he'd just been killed," Cullen said. "Just killed straight out."

Brady, Sam, Cullen, and Mary ate an entire meal in silence.

Brady thought, So, now, I guess this is normal.

PART TWO

1

The end of the supper line finally reached the serving counter in the church dining hall. Brady quickly tallied the hash marks she'd made on paper: 154, capacity once again. Twenty-three more than they'd served at lunch. Not surprising, considering the heat. It was the third day of ninety-plus temperatures, and she suspected that most of the people had come for the air-conditioning and not the sandwiches. A good number of those were still piled on the serving trays. Fine, they could wrap them up—

"Brady!" Father Tom's voice broke into her thoughts. He stood in the far corner of the room. He pointed with one hand and held an imaginary phone to his ear with the other. As he shouted to another staff person, Brady looked to where the priest was pointing.

A girl faced the milk machine that stood between the far end of the serving counter and the kitchen door. She alternately kicked and pounded it. "I want chocolate milk," she screamed. "Chocolate!"

The dining room quieted as everyone watched the girl's battle.

Brady recognized the girl. She knew that she lived in a nearby squat house and that chances were good that the girl was wired on speed. Brady also knew the rules: Don't intervene when someone goes off. Leave that for the social workers. She saw Dee and Jerry racing toward the scene.

The girl's screams grew louder. She picked up a chair and banged it against the machine.

As Brady moved toward the kitchen to call for an ambulance, she heard a loud crash. Out of the corner of her eye she saw a chair skid across the smooth linoleum floor. The next thing she knew she'd been thrown to the floor and the girl was pounding on her back. A sharp point ran up her arm. Brady sucked air as the pain spread.

In an instant the weight was gone. Brady rolled her head around and saw that the girl was locked in the arms of one of the diners, a man wearing jeans and a T-shirt. Brady looked at her left forearm: a scratch stretched the distance from elbow to wrist. Blood oozed out of the red line.

The social workers took the girl from the man. He went back to his place at a table, picked up a book, and started reading.

Brady rose slowly to her feet. "Thank you," she called. He looked up and nodded. Brady saw then that she'd been wrong about his age: He wasn't much older than she was. He returned to his book.

Father Tom motioned everyone back into their seats before he put his arm around Brady's shoulder and gently led her out of the room. "Are you okay?"

"I think so. Did someone call County?"

"Yes. An ambulance is on the way. How's your arm?"

"It's not too bad, but I'd better go clean it up."

"Why don't you pop into the free clinic? One of the nurses can take a look."

Brady checked her watch. "It's a half hour early, but maybe I'll just head home. Do you mind?"

"Good idea. Go home, my dear. And if you don't feel up to being here tomorrow, I'll understand."

"I'll be here. Who was the guy who pulled her off me? Do you know him?"

Dumb question. He knew everyone. "Mark Walker. He's just out of the army, back from Vietnam. He's in the GED study class, but I think he's doing as much tutoring as learning. I told him to stay and have a bite to eat."

"A vet? He's so young."

Father Tom sighed. "So many of them are."

The arm tingled and burned. Brady pressed it with her hand and squeezed back the pain the entire walk home.

Three houses away from her own she stopped. A black car was parked in the driveway. At first she thought, Government guys with more bad news. Then she thought, Government guys don't drive Jaguars.

She pushed open the kitchen door onto merriment.

Sam shouted, "Sally's here and we're making pancakes!"

2

While the boys and Sally made a big show of preparing the simple supper, Brady sat at the kitchen table and let her mother fuss over the cut.

"This doesn't look like a knife wound," Mary said as she swabbed antiseptic on Brady's arm. "A pin, maybe."

Brady shook her head. "Probably a broken fingernail." She grimaced. "Are you this rough with your patients?"

Cullen sat at the table and dug into his pancakes. "She's out of practice," he said as he chewed. "The only thing she puts on a patient anymore is a straitjacket."

Mary closed up the first aid box. She shook her head. "That place . . . " She set her lips.

Sally said, "That place sounds interesting. Are you ready to eat, Nurse Callahan?" Without waiting for an answer, she set a heaping plate on the table. "More, Monsieur Chef!" she shouted. "The diners will soon be wanting more!" Sam, grinning widely, carefully poured batter onto the sizzling griddle.

"St. Bernard's is a wonderful place," Brady said. Her mother made a face.

Cullen said, "Mom, I don't see why you get so cranked about Brady working there. Bums and crazies—that's your line of work too." He turned to Sally, who was sitting down with her own plate of pancakes. "She hates anything church, even if it's not religious."

"That's not true," Mary said.

Brady and her brother exchanged looks. "What about you, Sally?" Cullen asked. "Do your parents make you go to church or do they make you stay away?"

"Neither, I guess. Dad doesn't belong to any church. Mom's Catholic. Technically, so are Paul and I, but once we were confirmed she quit making us go. She's still very faithful about it all. I'll go to mass with her every now and then. Holidays, usually."

Sam said, "Here you go, Brady. Four. Is that enough?"

She smiled at him. "Perfect. You sit down and eat too."

Sally said to Mary, "So why do you feel that strongly? I mean, once you were completely immersed, right?"

Brady watched her mother cut carefully through the stack of pancakes.

"Yes, I certainly was immersed."

"What happened?"

Brady waited for the answer to Sally's question, one she'd never asked. The family's distance from religion was always just a fact of life, just part of the way they lived, nothing more extraordinary than the fact that they always drank 2 percent milk.

Besides, she had always assumed that it had to do with her parents wanting to get married. She said, "She met my dad. People weren't happy about that and she got angry when they tried to keep her from leaving the order and marrying him."

Sally shook her head. "But something had to have been going on before you were . . ." She searched for what she wanted to say. "Before you were open to falling in love. Right? Something undercut your faith, otherwise you'd never be thinking about guys. About passion. About feeling something."

Mary laughed. "Don't be so sure. The sisters were all very human. And as for passion and feeling, Sally, I bet you find more of it in a religious order than anywhere else. After all, passion is the very thing that brings the women there in the first place." She raised a forkful of pancakes to her mouth, then hesitated. "There was no one thing. I just came to believe in other things."

"But you're so pissed," Cullen said.

His mother eyed him sadly as she chewed.

"Really pissed," he said to Sally.

Mary said, "Brady's right. It wasn't a smooth exit when I left. Their father was also estranged from the church. It all added up."

Sam sat down, crowding in between his mother and sister. He said, "She ran off from the convent and got married right away to our dad."

Sally dropped her fork on her plate and leaned forward. "You were really that swept off your feet?"

Mary nodded, smiling as she remembered. "I was doing graduate work in Ohio. Kieran was a visiting lecturer at the same school. He had been on the faculty of the University of Ulster, in Northern Ireland. He'd been dismissed from that position because of his political activity, so he took a job in the States."

"A poet," Brady said. "A visiting Irish poet."

"Holy crap!" Sally said, sitting back. "Cullen, go find me a picture."

He was gone and back in a flash. He handed Sally a small framed photo.

Sally let out a long sigh. "What a heartbreaker. No way you'd say no to this guy. Definitely a First Date Yes."

"Excuse me," Brady said, "but that's our father."

"What's a First Date Yes?" Sam asked.

Mary tapped fingernails on her glass as she stared sternly at Sally.

"It means your dad was really handsome." Sally looked at each of the boys, then again at the picture. "It's not that you two aren't good-looking, because you are—especially with that dribble of syrup on your chin, Cullen—but I think Brady looks the most like him." She smiled at Brady and lifted her eyebrows. "A real heartbreaker."

Sam giggled and Cullen snorted.

"She does look like her father," Mary said. "She has the same fair coloring and wild red hair. He was tall too."

Sally set the photo down. "What about his poetry? Do you have any books with his poems?"

This time Sam made a quick trip to the living room. He returned with four thin books, which he handed to Sally. "My dad's," he said proudly. "He was only forty when he died, otherwise I know there'd be more."

Sally paged through the top volume. Her brow furrowed. She looked up, puzzled.

Brady said, "He only wrote in Irish. None of us know the language."

"Aren't there translations?"

Brady shook her head. "He refused to do that and to let anyone else do it.

You see, English is the language of the oppressors. For an Irish radical, at least. A nice political stance, but it sort of limited his audience."

"Not his listening audience," Mary said. "He often gave readings; they were always crowded." She gazed off. "It was like listening to sweet music to hear him read."

Sally exhaled in satisfaction. She opened a second book, then a third. "Well, I can understand this." She pointed to a word. "*Mary*. This one was dedicated to you."

Mary Callahan nodded. She reached for the book. Her finger stroked the spine.

Brady watched, her breath taken away by the exposure of her mother's sadness and longing.

3

Brady felt a tap on her shoulder. She turned and saw the guy who'd pulled off her attacker.

"Are you okay?" he said.

She set down the tray of coffee cups. "I'm fine. Thank you for being so quick yesterday. I've got one scratch and a couple of bruises, that's all."

"That's good," he said, and turned to leave.

"Wait, please." She caught up with him at the dining room door. They walked together down the hall toward the offices and meeting rooms. His fingers tapped a rhythm on the notebook in his hand.

He paused at an open door, looked in, and waved to someone inside.

"You have class," Brady said.

"Dropout High," he said.

"Father Tom told me that you help the others a lot."

He shrugged.

"Mark." She hesitated; what did she want to say?

He waited. When she remained silent, he said, "Brady." They both laughed, introductions over.

He was a good inch shorter then she was, no more than five eight, but built so solidly, he seemed large. He seemed to fill the door to Dropout High.

She licked her cracked, dry lips. When had she last used lipstick? She focused, meeting his steady ice blue gaze. "When you were over there, did you ever feel like running?"

He scratched his chin and looked away, staring into the middle distance.

"I didn't," he said finally. "But there were times that I sure felt like hiding. Curling up somewhere and hiding. You're the girl whose brother went AWOL, right? The one the FBI was asking about."

"Yes."

Two girls turned the corner from a stairwell and stopped at the door. Brady stepped back to let them through. "Isn't that cute?" one girl said to her friend. "He's about to ask her out."

"Markie," said the second girl, "remember that you promised to help me with some math. The test is tomorrow and I really, really need you." Their laughter hung in the air as they disappeared into the classroom.

Mark said, "Will you be here tomorrow afternoon?"

Brady said, "Until two."

He said, "I have something for you."

Brady fingered the rough edges of a crumpled newsletter. "Where did you get this?"

Mark traced the rim of the mint green coffee cup with an index finger. "A buddy of mine who's still at Ft. Lewis just sent it to me. This one's out of Saigon. They make their way back. Guys bring them."

Brady shook her head slightly, her eyes busy scanning the mimeographed sheet in her hand. *Deserter Times.*

"Not exactly what you'd call a newspaper, of course. It hardly even qualifies as an underground paper. You see a lot of this stuff circulating around army bases, here and overseas. Some are mostly humor, some more political. This one, of course . . ." He shrugged. "Cal sent it because a guy we both knew, Jeff, went AWOL. He's still somewhere in Saigon. There are plenty of places to hide in the city. Every now and then Jeff has something in here. A book review, usually." Mark shook his head in disbelief. "He's probably living in some rat's hole and he's writing book reviews."

Brady picked at the staple in the upper left corner. She tried again to read the lead article, but her eyes couldn't move past the title and byline: *"A Newcomer's Guide to Cong Ly Street," by William Butler Callahan.*

"Cong Ly is a street in Saigon with a lot of bars and flophouses. Places like that. A good place to hide, I guess." Someone dropped a tray of dishes in the kitchen. Brady's eyes widened and her head whipped around. Mark laughed and pressed a hand on top of hers. "Whoa, there. I think I'm the one who's supposed to get jumpy at loud noises."

She blinked, not really seeing him. He pulled his hand away.

She smoothed the paper and focused again on Will's name. "He's alive. And he's not a prisoner."

"Apparently so." He tapped the credit at the bottom of the article. Her eyes followed, reading.

"Former PFC Callahan liberated himself from military slavery in early July. This is his second article for *Deserter Times*."

"I don't have the other one, sorry. And Cal, my friend, is about to get out, so it's not likely he'll be sending any more." He leaned forward. "Father Tom might be able to get a copy. He knows people. You know that, don't you? You know what he does?"

She had finally started reading past Will's name. She nodded absently. "Draft counseling," she murmured.

"More."

"I know. He's helped guys evade the draft and get to Canada."

"More."

She looked up.

Mark said, "It's like the old underground railroad, only this is for deserters, not slaves. Most of them have cut out of army bases stateside, but a few have made it from overseas. He helps them move around, make it to Canada, or go deep underground."

Brady looked again at the paper. This time, she read it all the way through while he talked about the underground network.

"I'm sorry. I shouldn't talk so much. You want to read."

She lifted her eyes from the paper. As she met his gaze, she made a fist, twisting the paper in her hand. "How do you feel about Father Tom helping them? How do you feel about guys running, when you obediently answered the call?"

Right away, she wished it back. She hadn't meant to challenge him. Before she could apologize, he spoke. "I wasn't drafted, though I would've been soon enough. I enlisted when I was seventeen. Either that, the judge said, or a youth facility. My parents had disappeared years earlier and the state had finally run out of foster homes that would take . . ." He looked down at his hands a moment. When he looked up, he wore a false smile. "Very bad boys."

"I like very bad boys!"

Brady looked up. Sally stood there, grinning.

Brady glanced at Mark. He pushed back from the table. His lips were set and his eyes narrowed as he looked at the interruption.

Brady said, "Sally Cooper, Mark Walker. What are you doing here, Sally?"

"I came to see the famous and controversial St. Bernard's. I also came to see if you wanted to go out to our house and go sailing." Her eyes darted between the two at the table. "It looks as if I stumbled into the middle of something."

"We were talking."

"About foster homes and bad boys and the army," she said. "I heard."

"Mark was in Vietnam."

Sally took a seat. "I get it."

Mark raised an eyebrow. "You do?"

"It was a foster home or the army. I've heard about that. Well, mostly I think it's jail or the army, that's what you hear about. That is so outrageous, that they'd do that to you. So outrageous that society has no place for you, so they send you off to kill."

Mark paled. Brady realized she felt like slapping Sally.

He rose. "I need to leave."

Sally said, "Come sailing with us."

"No."

Sally looked at Brady and made a face. "I tried."

Brady stood close to Mark. "Congratulations on being done with the class and the test. I bet you aced it." She kissed him directly on the lips. "And thank you."

He regained some color and smiled. He left without looking at Sally.

"That was not a thank-you kiss," Sally said. "Not by a long shot was that a thank-you kiss. He knew it too. I wouldn't have guessed you'd be so bold. C'mon, let's go. You can tell me about it in the car. And don't say you have to work, because I know you don't. I called your house and Cullen said you got off early today."

"For a reason. I have to register for classes."

"Fine. I'll drive you to campus, you register, we head out to the lake."

Brady rolled up the newsletter and held it behind her. "I can't. I need to go home after I go to campus. My mom expects me at home."

"Bring her. Bring your brothers. Go chase down that angry guy you just kissed and bring him. I bet he'd say yes to you."

Brady whacked the *Deserter Times* against the table. "I said I can't go, Sally. Don't think you can push me." She walked a few steps, stopped, and turned. "And you may as well know, I don't like being a novelty. A pet. I don't like being anyone's source of amusement."

4

Brady watched her mother read the newsletter. The muffled sound of the television and Sam's giggles drifted in from the other room. Tires squealed outside as a car peeled away from the stop sign at the corner.

Her mother looked up and around. Her eyes met her daughter's. "I don't know what to think. I don't know what I'm feeling. I'm relieved, I guess. Oh, God, yes, I am so relieved."

Brady felt an ice-cold hand grip her heart. She watched as her mother scanned the article again. The cold hand squeezed harder. Brady leaned forward. "No."

Mary looked startled.

"He didn't write it, Mom. That's not Will talking."

"Oh, honey. His name, it's there."

"Mom, he did not write that article. I knew the first time I read it through. He is not responsible for the things that are printed there."

"Some of it's harsh and crude, but people change the way they think."

"I know people change, but they don't suddenly become good writers. My brother did not write these words. He did not string together these sentences. I started rewriting his school papers for him when I was in the sixth grade, Mom. I know his writing."

Her mother stroked the paper. "I wish I could read the other one he wrote. It must explain why the army thinks he's complicit."

"He didn't write anything. I'm sure of it."

"There was probably an editor or someone who fixed his writing."

Brady snorted. "Have you read the whole newsletter? No editor fixed the other articles."

"Then he worked with someone. What's the alternative, Brady? What is it you're suggesting?"

She reached to touch her mother's hand, then pulled back when Mary folded her arms. "Will's missing. Remember what the agent told us that night, how it would be hard for anyone to get from Long Binh to Saigon on his own. How did Will do it? How did he do it so quickly and get hooked up with this newsletter?"

Her mother's eyes flickered, as if she were making calculations. "They thought he had enemy assistance. He turned against his platoon, and the Viet Cong helped him, and, oh, God, I don't know, Brady."

"Mom, he's missing. What if someone knows that and is using his name?"

"Missing and dead, you mean. You'd rather believe that, Brady? You'd rather believe he's dead?"

"Of course not, but I also don't want to believe a lie." She jabbed the *Deserter Times*. "This is a lie."

5

Brady stayed away from work for two days. She called the church office and said something had come up. True enough, she told herself. One hell of a mood had come up. She knew she'd miss the money, but she couldn't face the problems, the people, the need.

She took Sam and Cullen shopping for school supplies. She mowed the lawn. She washed windows.

Several times she went into her mother's bedroom and took out Will's letters, which were kept in the drawer of a bedside table. Several times she almost dialed the local FBI office to say, "Come and get them, Agent Drake." She stopped each time, unable to go behind her mother's back, to deceive her and make an end run around the hope that Will was still alive.

When she returned to the center, she spotted the Jaguar in the parking lot. Someone had slashed its tires and broken the windows. A bumper sticker was stuck onto the hood: *Comfort the troubled and trouble the comfortable.*

"Taking a stand," she said aloud. "Some idiot thought he'd smash a rich person's car and make a point."

She went to the office to sign her time sheet for the week. Dorothy, the secretary, welcomed her back cheerfully. "Father Tom's gone to a United for Peace meeting at the U. There's a big march planned for the fall. Jerry called in sick, and so Dee was hoping you could help with Bitch and Gripe." Brady groaned. Twice a week the center had people on hand to help anyone write a letter to a politician. The official name of the program was Speak Up!

"Can't she corral a volunteer? The parking lot was full. There must be someone else."

"Rummage sale," Dorothy said. "Today's the setup day, and all the church ladies are here to help."

"By the way," Brady said nonchalantly, "there's a car in the lot that's had some trouble."

"That would be your friend Sally's father's car. We know. Happened two nights ago. You might have told her that she shouldn't park a car like that in a neighborhood like this. She's lucky it wasn't stolen or stripped clean. When she was here this morning to leave the keys, though, she didn't seem too upset. My guess is she hasn't told her father yet." Dorothy pointed to a set of keys on her desk. "We're waiting for the tow truck."

"*This* morning?"

Dorothy shrugged. "Get the story from her. It's none of my business where she's been spending her nights."

Had Sally really been hanging around since Tuesday? Where had she stayed?

Brady passed the large room where the volunteers were setting up the rummage sale scheduled for the weekend. She spotted Sally in the middle of an army of older women, everyone picking and sorting their way through piles and bags of donated clothing. Brady knew most of the women—they were the church regulars who showed up whenever a call for help went out, the same women who had provided the food and crowd for Will's party.

Mrs. Woitz was talking Sally's ear off. Brady could guess what she was talking about: her painful arthritis, the two sons killed in World War II, a husband disabled by emphysema. She had heard the lament herself, time after time. Just as Mrs. Woitz paused to catch her breath, Sally reached into a donation bag and pulled out a lacy red bra with massive cups. She said something and held it up for all to see. The ladies laughed, and Mrs. Woitz put her hands on her hips and did a stiff little jig.

Brady looked at her friend and was hit by a hard wave of longing. She wanted to feel those solid arms around her shoulders. She wanted to rest her head, weaken, and weep.

Sally looked toward the door, saw Brady, grinned, and started swinging the bra overhead. Just as Brady shook her head, Sally let go. The bra went flying across the length of the room, held aloft by an explosion of laughter.

6

"Do you have any idea what goes on here at night?" Sally took the towel from Brady and picked up a pot from the sink. She dropped both and swore.

"Be careful," Brady said. "I rinse with very hot water."

Sally shot her a look as she turned on the faucet and held her hand underneath cold water.

"I'm sorry. I should have warned you sooner."

"Not your fault."

"I'm almost done for the day," Brady said. "I'll drive you home. I'm sorry about your car. I should have warned you about the neighborhood too."

Sally turned off the water and looked at her hand. "What happened to the car is also not your fault. Okay? Not. Your. Fault."

"I'll finish up here and find someone to cover for me the rest of the afternoon. We can go."

Sally picked up the towel. "We can stay. The car is getting fixed and I can drive myself home. Back to my original question: Do you know what goes on here? Well, I'm sure you do. You must know everything. All I've heard about for two days is Wonderful Brady this and Wonderful Brady that."

"Bernie's After Dark—that's what people call it. Yes, I know all about it. I know the room that used to be the school library turns into a coffeehouse at night and I know that there are yoga classes in the dining hall and other classes in the school rooms. I know there's an alternative book store. I know that when the federal government rammed the highway through the middle of the neighborhood, families moved away and the school died. The church has to use the building for something."

They finished drying the last pots. Sally wiped a counter. Brady took towels to the laundry bin.

Sally said, "The fun stuff that happens here doesn't interest you. The work does. Am I right?"

Brady shrugged. "I always have to get home before night. Speaking of which, have you really not been home in two days?"

"I found other things to do."

"Where did you stay? You could have crashed with us."

"Oh, right. After the way you exited that day?"

"I'm sorry about that. I never—"

Sally held up her hand. "Don't apologize. Don't be sorry for everything. I deserved to be told off, okay?"

"If you needed a place, you could have called or just come over."

"I didn't want or need a place. I was with some people I'd met at the coffeehouse and we weren't done talking when it closed. So when I walked out of the church and saw that the car had been trashed, I figured, Screw it for now. I crashed at their place and ended up staying for a couple of nights."

"Your parents don't mind?"

"They're still at the cabin and don't know. Besides, who needs parents? Not with you for a friend, not the way you worry about me. Are we done here?"

Brady put her hands on Sally's shoulders.

"Whoa—are you going to kiss me?" Sally said.

Brady turned her around and pointed to a pile of carrots on a counter. "We're not done until every person in the long line forming outside this room has been fed. Start peeling."

She peeled three to Sally's one. When Sally held up her first carrot and slowly examined it before tossing it onto the pile, Brady said, "Don't think too much about it."

Sally set down her peeler. "Do you realize that's the exact opposite of what people usually tell me? Usually they're screaming, Didn't you think first!" She picked up another carrot and studied it. "Perhaps I've found the perfect occupation. By the way, the house where I crashed? That guy lives there. Mark."

Brady couldn't help it, she started to say, "Oh?" but she caught herself in time. Instead, she blushed.

"Ha! I knew it."

"There's nothing to know."

"My brother will be so jealous."

Brady finished another carrot and tossed it onto the pile. "You're not being helpful. You're being a pest."

A volunteer walked by with a tray of sandwiches. Sally grabbed one and bit into it. "You're not the only one who's fond of the truth," she said as she chewed. "I cannot tell a lie, except when it suits me, of course. But this is no lie: Paul digs you. He might not know it, but he does."

"You know that, do you?"

Sally finished the sandwich and resumed peeling carrots. "He won't admit it, that's the sad thing. You confuse things for him."

"Because I'm not appropriate? I'm not an acceptable girlfriend for a Yale man?"

Sally slowed her low-gear peeling. "No, it's not that. We're not snobs, Paulie and me. I'll say that for old Mom and Dad. They raised two spoiled brats, but not two spoiled snobs. My brother would never think that you were unacceptable, whatever that means."

"What, then?" Brady pushed a pile of carrots into a colander for rinsing. Across the dining hall someone dropped a tray, and silverware clattered as it hit the floor. Brady picked up a tray of clean silverware. She carried it to the serving counter, set it down, and signaled to the volunteer.

Sally nibbled on the carrot she'd been peeling for at least two minutes. "Unexpected, that's what you are. Meeting an interesting girl he could be serious about before he's ready to be serious isn't a scheduled part of the plan."

Before Brady could ask about the rest of Paul's plan, there was a piercing scream. She spun around. An older volunteer stood in the center of the dining hall, her hands pressed against her chest as she screamed. Crazy Jack, one of the regular diners, screamed back as he took off his clothes.

"Holy cow," Sally said.

Brady walked to the phone.

7

Sally idly tapped her water glass with a fork. "Your daughter works at a wild place."

Mary raised an eyebrow as she put jam on a biscuit.

Sally nodded. "The stuff I've seen. I tell you, it's crazy."

Cullen reached for another piece of chicken. "That's his third leg," Sam whined. "He can't have all the legs."

"We asked for extra drumsticks," Sally said. "There should be plenty."

"She's a psych nurse, you know," Brady said. "Nothing seems wild to her."

Sally sat back in her chair and looked from mother to daughter. Then she said to Mary, "Do you suppose people think *I'm* exactly like *my* mother, even though we look different?"

Mary said, "Odds are, yes."

Sally released a howl, put her head on the table, and pretended to cry.

Sam said, "Yuck, she got her hair in her potatoes."

Sally said, "No one falls in love with me, not ever."

Brady stretched her legs out and prodded an anthill rising from a crack in the front walk. "My brothers have."

"They're little boys. Doesn't count."

"Mom and I have too, for that matter."

Sally hooked her arm through Brady's. They both stared out at the street, where the Jaguar, pristine again after its day in the shop, glistened under a streetlamp.

How much had it cost? Brady wondered. How much clothing, how many meals, how many prescriptions could have been bought with that money? "Do your parents give much to charities?" she blurted. "God, I can't believe I said that. It's none of my business."

Sally said, "It's a beautiful car, isn't it? Scandalous, really, what it cost them. Scandalous what it cost me to get it fixed today. Jag repairs are so expensive. No wonder Dad won't take it to the lake. Driving on those country roads could do a lot of damage."

"You're a mind reader."

"No. You're transparent. That fair skin and your burning conscience are a revealing combination. My parents give away tons of money. Money and art. There are little wall plates with their names all over the art institute: *Gift of Robert and Sylvia Cooper*. Why shouldn't they give lots? It eases their conscience and we have zillions and get zillions more by the hour. Every time someone in the world makes a cake or a batch of cookies, we get richer."

Brady's jaw dropped. "Cooper Flour? You're *that* Cooper?"

"Cooper Flour, Cooper Cakes, Cooper Ag International. Yes, we're *that* Cooper. You didn't know?"

Brady shook her head. "Does your dad run the company?"

"His cousin does. Dad actually quit working for the company about ten years ago and started doing more interesting stuff. Well, interesting to him. It's mostly behind-the-scenes political stuff. He's a lawyer."

"I shouldn't have asked about the money."

"Why the hell not? It's hard to ignore. And as long as we're on the subject of 'none of my business,' are you a virgin?"

Brady slowly swiveled her head to face Sally. Then, slowly, she again faced the street.

Sally said, "I'm not."

That's no surprise, Brady thought.

"You're not surprised," Sally said.

"I am."

"Really? I'm surprised that you're surprised."

Brady shook her head. "Not what I meant."

"Ah, I get it. Well, don't be offended, but *I'm* not surprised."

"Why?"

"The risk."

"What risk?"

"All of them, you'd have thought about all of them: pregnancy, VD, intimacy. Letting down your reserve, maybe that's the riskiest thing of all."

Brady pulled her arm from Sally's, drew up her knees, and hugged them.

"You don't want to talk about this, do you? That's okay. Of course, talking doesn't hurt a thing. But, then, if you're not used to talking, I suppose it's not easy to do. That night when we were making pancakes and talking about your father? I kind of had the feeling that you were all saying things for the first time."

Brady didn't answer.

"But like I said, it's okay. Of course, I'll have to make up your end of the conversation. And sometimes my mouth is uncontrollable, so if I raise a subject that's uncomfortable, it's your fault."

"Ah, something is my fault."

Sally laughed. "Yes, but don't say you're sorry."

Brady said, "Why do I think that what might come out of your mouth will make me sorriest of all?"

Sally nodded. "'Fraid so. That guy Mark—you know what he said to me the other night?"

"What?"

Sally punched her arm. "So that's the secret: I just need to find the right subject, then you look interested. Actually, he didn't say much. You two have that in common."

"Did he say something about my brother Will?"

"No. As I recall, what he said was, 'Everyone shares the peanut butter, but be careful what bread you use.' I ran into him in the kitchen. I was hungry. He gave me some of his bread. Whole wheat from the co-op, in case you're curious. He disappeared into his room after that. Why would he have said something about your brother? Do they know each other?"

Brady shook her head. "Right before I blew up at you that day, before you interrupted us, he'd given me this underground newspaper written by deserters that an army friend sent him. There was a front-page article, supposedly written by Will."

"Supposedly?"

"His name was on it, but it didn't sound like his writing."

"Meaning what?"

"Meaning he gave permission for someone to use his name, or he didn't give permission."

"Why would anyone take his name? And how could they do that?"

"I don't know how it works over there. Mark said there were places where deserters go underground. I'd like to talk to him. He might be able to explain things."

"Of course, it could be that your brother did write it. That's the simplest explanation of all."

"It's the one my mother believes."

"Can you blame her, Brady? That way she can hope he's still alive and that he might get a message to her. She can hope that she'll see him again."

"You don't think I'd like that too? I'd love to believe he's hiding out in Saigon writing anti-American crap for some mimeographed newsletter. I'd love it because, yes, that means he's not a prisoner and he's not dead. But Sally, the guy never had a political thought in his head and he could never, ever, put together a sentence with more than five words. Don't tell me to want something so much that I choose to believe a lie."

Sally said, "It's a purple house next to a pizza parlor on Riverside."

Brady blinked.

"Where Mark lives. If you want to go find him, we could leave now. Well, you don't want me tagging along, but I'd drop you off. I should head home, anyway. I should shower, call the cabin, let them know I'm alive. I'll take you to the house. I bet he'd love it if you dropped by."

Brady shook her head. "I need to stay here, help Mom with the boys. She's so empty and worn out. I hate to think what will happen to her when we do know the truth."

"She seemed fine tonight."

"I can't cheer her up. You do. She obviously loves it when you're around."

Sally said, "That's me, the class clown. Good for a laugh. Good for a good time. Speaking of a good time . . ." She slipped two fingers into her shirt pocket and pulled out a joint.

"Put it away."

Sally stared at the joint a moment, then dropped it back into the pocket.

"I hate smoking alone. It seems so, oh, like a habit, not a pleasure. You don't ever, I bet."

"Alone? No."

"I mean ever. I bet not. There's the risk thing again. You wouldn't risk getting busted because that would be a huge and expensive complication. You wouldn't risk appearing wasted and stoned in front of other people. Too revealing. And, also, it's illegal and requires deceit. Therefore, you don't. And don't look so mad, I'm not making fun of you. Just working through your logic."

"Don't be so sure you know me," Brady snapped.

"Maybe I don't. So tell me. Who are you? What do you think? What do you want? What do you dream about, Brady? Hey, there's no risk to dreaming."

Brady rose and stretched. Her arms touched the branches of an unkempt bush that drooped over the sidewalk. "I don't want to talk to him, Sally, though I need to hear what he knows. I'm afraid I'll fall for him."

Sally's laugh startled a rabbit out of the bushes. "You are so pathetic. Can't you tell you already have?"

Brady whacked her friend on the shoulder, then pulled her up and hugged her for a long time before pushing her toward the Jaguar. "Go away," she said.

Sally hadn't gone two steps before Brady moved. She grabbed her arm, then let her hand slide until she was holding Sally's.

Brady said, "I do have dreams. I dream about the war being over and about my mother not being tired and worried. I dream about Cullen and Sam being happy in school, and I dream about being in your boat again and flying over the lake. I dream about the people at the center getting more than sandwiches or soup for supper. I dream about the bruised, beat-up girls I see finding a safe place to rest. Mostly though, I dream about my brother being home and my father being alive. I dream I can hear him, reading his poems as I fall asleep.

"You couldn't be more wrong, Sally. Dreaming is incredibly risky, maybe the riskiest thing of all. You conjure up thoughts and you allow yourself to want things. That's risky, don't you doubt it, because most of it never comes true."

8

The screen on the porch door of the purple house by the pizza parlor on Riverside Avenue bulged out like a mesh hubcap. Someone had painted a peace sign on it. Brady pushed her palm against the screen, reshaping the bulge into two hills with a narrow valley.

A stereo was cranked up. No one answered her knock. She pulled open the door and stepped onto the porch. Two guys sat on the floor, intent on the flame of a low-burning candle. She walked past them through an open doorway into the house.

Smoke and incense. A Cream song throbbed so loudly, she didn't recognize it until Clapton's guitar soared. Brady closed her eyes, struck by the sudden memory of when she'd first heard the album. Will had brought it home one night and made her stop doing homework to listen. She'd been studying world geography. Capitals of European countries.

On her right the hallway opened to a large room. Two girls danced while a boy drummed the air. One of the girls sashayed over to Brady.

Brady shouted, "Mark Walker?" The girl pointed down the hall with one arm as the other made figure eights above her head. Brady followed the hall to a kitchen, where two guys about Will's age sat at a table. One was reading aloud, the other was eating pudding. Books and papers were piled on the table. As she walked in, a paper fluttered to the floor. The guys ignored it, their eyes pinned on Brady.

She said, "I'm looking for Mark Walker."

The one who'd been reading closed the book and set it down. "I know you. You're Father Tom's chick." He smoothed his long hair, then stroked his bare chest.

"I work at St. Bernard's center. I'm not his chick."

"Marx had it right. Religion's a drug for fools. Pardon my paraphrasing."

"Father Tom's okay," his friend said through a mouthful of pudding. "He fights back."

"Fighting back isn't enough."

"What would be enough?" Brady asked.

He set two fists together, then sprang them open. "Boom!" he said softly. "Destroy it all."

Brady eyed him steadily. Were these guys the people Sally had stayed with? "Violent revolution?"

He said, "What's the alternative? Handing out sandwiches day after day after day? What sort of difference is that going to make? Your bologna politics is worthless, sweetheart."

His pal chuckled. "Brian, I think you made her mad. She's beet red."

For the millionth time in her life, Brady cursed her give-away complexion. While the boys laughed, she said, "I'm looking for Mark Walker."

"So you said. Soldier Boy isn't here."

"Probably out gunning down more innocent villagers."

Brady walked out of the kitchen.

"He went down to the Viking to hear the band," one of them shouted.

Just as she reached the front door, she felt a hand on her shoulder. Brian said, "Wait a sec."

She stared at the open doorway, anxious to get outside. The cigarette and dope smoke was thick in the hall. She didn't doubt the air in the house always hung heavy.

This guy's eyes were clear, though. Sharp and piercing. He said, "It's not that I despise people like you and the priest. But what you do is worse than doing nothing. You're complicit in the oppression. Don't you see that? As long as you keep people fed, you keep them quiet."

"You're saying it's better that they go hungry? Not see a doctor? Not get help finding somewhere safe to live?"

"Change is coming. It will happen, Brady Callahan."

She stepped back, startled that he knew her name.

He was pleased he'd surprised her. "There are other things going on. If you want to be part of something that matters, there are people you can hook up with. It's going to happen, Brady Callahan. Be part of it."

She felt his eyes scrape a mark on her back as she hurried from the house.

A knot of people came up the front walk. "Party's just starting," someone said as she wove through the group. "Don't go now." Brady turned in the other direction—away from home and toward the Viking.

Summer nights in the city meant heat, smells, and sounds. Her shirt clung to her back. She was glad she'd changed out of her jeans to a skirt, even if it was long. The India print fabric hung lightly, cooler than denim. A bus wheezed past, its diesel fumes covering up the sickening sweetness of garbage cans set out for morning pickup. Car horns, disembodied voices, cat-calls, and radios. Brady hurried through it all toward the neon red sign of the street's busiest bar.

Act like you do this all the time, she thought as she approached the open door of the Viking. Fifteen feet out she could hear the music—a rippling guitar, a thumping bass. Just as she walked in, a harmonica took off, spark-ing a roar from the crowd. As she waited for her eyes to adjust to the dark room, her head whirred, calculating the immediate risks: She could get carded and kicked out; she could be hassled by drunks; Mark might not be here; he could be with someone.

The bar was crowded. Most everyone faced one side of the room, watch-ing the musicians. Her hand tapped her thigh as she pushed through. She glanced around, avoiding eye contact.

For the first time in my life, she thought, I'm in a bar. I'm underage, alone, and looking for someone who probably doesn't want to see me. He's come here to listen to music and I want to make him talk about war.

I walked over some line, she thought. I must be crazy.

Mark was leaning against a far wall. His arms were crossed against his chest. He nodded his head and bit down on his lip as he concentrated on the music. His short wavy hair was tousled. When the number ended, he was the first to respond—grinning, standing erect, running his hands through his hair and then clapping them high overhead. There was space on either side of him, and he didn't talk to anyone once his hands came down. Brady pushed her way to him.

He seemed unsurprised. He tipped his head toward the stand and said, "Blue-eyed blues and it's pretty darn good."

"I didn't know you were twenty-one," she said.

He smiled, but kept his eyes on the band. "I didn't know *you* were twenty-one." He shrugged. "I'm not, but I've never been hassled or carded. Which is good, because the food is cheap and the music is the best in town."

The best music in town started up again. Brady settled in, doing her part to hold up the wall.

Two numbers later, she was edgy. Mark was right—the music was good, too good. She wanted to move, to dance. The crowd was listening respectfully, hands on their laps or tucked in pockets. Here and there, heads nodded.

Once or twice Mark turned her way and smiled, but he stayed glued to the wall.

A woman at the nearest table handed her a glass of beer. "My birthday," she said. "Drink up."

Brady sipped twice. She licked the foam off her lip and handed the glass to Mark. He shook his head, then changed his mind. "Drink it all," she said. And he did.

A saxophone entered the musical mix, its sensual blurt rising and falling as it was chased by the guitar. Brady leaned back and closed her eyes, loving the sound. It was like bathing in hot bubbly water.

Then, a voice in her ear: "These idiots. Don't they know they should be dancing?"

Brady opened her eyes and looked at Paul Cooper. His brows bobbed as he emptied a glass. She closed her eyes, counted to three, and then looked again. Paul set his glass down on a table and said, "Dance with me, Brady." He took her by the arms and they swayed and circled to the blues.

When the set was over, Brady introduced the boys. "You've met his sister," she said to Mark.

He thought a moment. "That one."

Paul laughed, "God, exactly: 'That one.' I'm sorry to break in on your date, but I couldn't stand still, not to music like that."

Mark said, "It's not a date."

Brady said, "I thought you were up at the lake."

"Tiller broke on the sailboat. I came down to pick up a new one at the boat works."

"What brings you to this part of town?" Even as she asked, she knew. The neighborhood was near the university; drugs of any type were easy to score.

His eyes held her gaze a moment. "Grocery shopping." He stretched. "And I wanted to hear some music. I head back tomorrow."

Mark edged away. "You two probably want to talk. I'll be going."

Paul put a hand on his shoulder. "Like I said, I didn't mean to cut in. She's all yours."

"I'm nobody's to hand around, okay?" Brady growled. She turned to Mark. "I have nothing to talk about with him."

Paul said, "Why do I think it's funny when you tell me off?" He turned to Mark. "That's the whole basis of our relationship: I make her mad and she tells me off."

Brady said, "It's no relationship."

Mark said, "I should go."

Brady said, "I came here to find you. I'd like to talk."

Mark said, "It's too noisy in here for talking."

Paul said, "I'm hungry. Does anyone else feel like bacon and eggs?"

9

The Cake and Steak parking lot was full. They circled in Paul's station wagon, waiting for a spot to open.

"Lot of hungry people tonight," Brady said.

"Or a lot of people who aren't ready to end the night," Mark said. "This town is dead after midnight. When I first got back, I couldn't get used to it."

"Back?" Paul said.

"From Vietnam."

"When were you there?"

"I left in March of '68. I got back in May."

Brady said, "I thought tours were only for twelve months."

"I extended for two, which cut short my whole enlistment. I got out after less than two years. This is ridiculous, we'll never get a spot."

Paul said, "Anyone have a curfew?"

Mark and Brady looked at each other.

"Good," Paul said. "I know the perfect place, but it's a little ways away."

Mark shrugged.

Brady said, "Let's go."

Paul drove like a starved man headed toward the last food on earth: rocket acceleration, sharp turns, sudden stops. Brady, sitting in the middle of the front seat, gripped her thighs because there was nothing else to hold. She looked from side to side: two nice-looking guys in T-shirts and blue jeans.

Nothing else she dared to hold.

Come on, she chided herself, just enjoy what's happening. Nothing like this had ever happened before. She glanced at Mark. He was staring out the window. His eyes closed tightly as Paul swerved to pass and overtake a car turning slowing onto the highway ramp.

The car veered from lane to lane on the interstate. Paul whistled softly. Brady thought she heard Mark release a small sound, not a whistle. She glanced over. His eyes were still closed.

Paul turned on the radio. He started twisting the dial through stations. The car zigged and zagged as he drove with one hand on the wheel. Brady touched his arm. "I'll do it."

"No Top Forty crap," he said. "Unless by some fluke they're playing the Stones."

She rolled through stations. At one spot there was a snatch of singing and Mark said, "Hold it; that's Carmen McRae, doing Monk, I think."

Brady sat back. The car filled with a rippling rich voice.

"Purrrrfect," Paul crowed. He crouched over the wheel and looked at Mark. "You like jazz too, man? Not just blues?"

Brady stuck out her arm and pushed him back. "Drive, Paul. Don't talk."

The song ended and the announcer said, "That was Carmen McRae—"

Paul hit the wheel. "You knew it, you knew it. Man oh man, we're gonna be friends." He hit the wheel again and the car swerved.

"Jeeesus, Paul!" Brady cried.

Mark said, "Pull over. Now."

"Highway. Can't stop."

"I didn't survive fourteen months in Nam to come home and die in your mother's Buick. Pull over now."

Paul obeyed, bringing the car to a gravel-spraying halt on the shoulder of the highway.

Brady released her breath in a long, slow *S*. She turned and kissed Mark on his shoulder. "Thank you." She let her head rest a moment.

Paul turned off the car. "Maybe this was a good idea."

"You bet it was a good idea," Brady said. "You're too damn drunk."

"Not all that drunk, but you know, I think I have to admit that even four or five beers kind of wires me weird and stupid." He kissed Brady on the cheek. "As you may remember. No, kids, the reason this is a good idea is that I've really gotta pee." He got out and walked around the car and down into the ditch.

Brady set her hands on the dash and rested her head on her arms. How had this happened? She'd gone out to get answers and had ended up on the shoulder of a highway in the middle of the city with two guys she barely knew. One of them was peeing in a ditch and the other had apparently gone mute.

She sat back, looking out the driver's window. Middle of the night and still the cars streamed by. Where were they going? Had anyone else tried to escape and ended up in a surprising place?

"Can you drive?" Mark asked. "I only got my license three weeks ago and I'm not that comfortable on the highway yet."

Brady slid over behind the wheel. Mark hesitated, then moved to the middle position next to her. "How long have you known this guy?"

"A few weeks. I don't really know him. Somehow, though, this adventure doesn't surprise me. The one other time I saw him drunk, he was pretty obnoxious. When he's sober, he's nice and fun. I guess maybe that's the guy I thought we were with."

Do you ever change personalities? she wondered, looking at Mark's profile and studying the way his hair curled over his ears and along the back of his thick, tan neck.

Don't be stupid, she thought. Do not let on, do not let anything out. "Have you been working outside?" she blurted.

The muscles of the thick, tan neck tightened slightly as he turned to face her. A wide grin, then he bit down on a lip as he stared. Three lanes over, headlights streamed past, spurting light into the car. "You're blushing," he said as he leaned over and kissed her.

After a moment Brady pulled away. "He's coming back."

Paul returned to the car, zipping his pants as he walked up the incline. He stumbled slightly and landed heavily against the car. He grinned, then pressed his face against the window.

"My little brothers really like him," Brady said, laughing in spite of herself.

"I feel a lot better," Paul said as he got in.

"So do I," Mark said, "now that you're not driving."

"Sorry to scare you, man. Are we still eating or have the two of you been plotting my murder?"

Brady and Mark looked at each other. "Still eating," Mark said. "Where are we going?"

Paul pointed. "About twenty miles that way." He twisted and looked at the highway behind them. "All clear; go now. Hit it."

Brady carefully merged onto the highway and pushed the car up to speed. "Why do we have to go that far?"

Paul opened the glove box and rummaged around. He pulled out a book of matches, then pulled a tiny joint out of his T-shirt pocket. "This stuff is actually grown by the government. For experiments or something. It's so good, it's lethal."

"Put it out, okay?" Mark said. "I don't want to get busted. I can't risk that."

Paul nodded as he inhaled. "Okay. Want just one hit first?" he said after he exhaled.

Mark shook his head. "I smoked enough in Nam to last a lifetime." He shifted slightly, and Brady could tell he was watching her. She clenched the wheel. "A favorite activity over there," he said softly. "It's one of the reasons so many guys go nuts."

She whispered, "I want to hear about everything." She glanced over. "Everything you feel like telling."

"Why are you two whispering?" Paul said. "What are you talking about?"

Mark sat back, stretching his legs out on Paul's side of the transmission hump. "Nothing."

Brady said again, "Why do we have to go so far to eat?"

"Because that's how far it is to where I live. After you put up with my nearly killing you, the least I can do is feed you, right?"

She smiled at the thought of surprising Sally. Mark saw her smile, then nodded. "Right."

10

Brady stood in the middle of the spacious living room as Paul walked around turning on lights. With each switch he flicked, another piece of art or furniture was illuminated. "This house is incredibly beautiful," she said.

"This house is incredibly empty," Paul answered. He unlocked the wide patio doors and pushed them open. Brady heard lake water lapping. "But the Jag's in the driveway, so she must be somewhere."

He disappeared outside, calling his sister's name.

Mark flopped onto a leather sofa. "Everything's perfect in here," he whispered. "Did you know he had this kind of money?"

Brady nodded. "Cooper Flour."

Mark whistled. "That includes Cooper Cupcakes, then, which means I've contributed my share to the family's lifestyle."

"Chocolate or lemon-filled?"

"Chocolate, absolutely. I used to eat them by the dozen. Even when I was on the street, I managed to buy and eat my daily quota."

Brady peeled her gaze from a large abstract painting on the wall and looked at him.

"I think that's why I'm going to like you a lot," he said, rising from the sofa and walking toward her. "Whenever I drop a little bomb about my life, you don't seem to freak. You just . . . get interested."

Brady said, "*Going* to like me?"

Another kiss. Then: "Do you suppose there are bathrooms open to the public?"

He wandered off. Brady pivoted slowly, taking in everything. Paintings, bright glass bowls and vases, pottery, a golden cello. Beautiful things, everywhere she turned. She sat down and closed her eyes, listening to the lake water. What would it be like to sit in this room every day of your life? How could it not calm and soothe?

Or did it make the rest of the world seem uglier and harder to bear whenever you left the cocoon?

Paul returned. "Boat's gone. I bet she heard about a party somewhere."

Brady followed him toward the kitchen. "Are you worried?"

"Not at all. She's a good cook and I was just hoping to talk her into making us something. I can't do much more than eggs and bacon."

"That's what we came for."

Mark joined them in the kitchen. Brady poured him a glass of juice, which he drained.

He sprawled in a chair, a wide smile spread across his face. "It's so great to be alive. You two have no idea. Wasn't that long ago I was humping over jungle mountains and dodging bullets. Somehow I made it through all that shit when so many guys didn't, and then, whaddya know, one night happens and I find myself in a place like this." He turned to Brady. "There's a Van Gogh in his parents' bedroom. I think it's real."

"It's real," Paul said.

"The bedroom?" Brady asked.

"Next to the bathroom door," Mark said. "Can you believe that?"

She held out her glass for him to refill. Who could be so casual about owning fabulous things that a priceless painting would get stuck on any old wall like an afterthought?

Van Gogh. How many families could be fed and housed, how many hospital bills paid? "No one should own—" She covered her mouth. Just once, couldn't she just once leave it behind?

Mark made a noise. She glanced. His eyebrows bobbed and he covered a smile by rubbing the stubble on his chin and cheeks.

"Were you by any chance about to say that no one individual should possess a Van Gogh?" Paul said, his back turned as he dropped bacon slices into a pan. "Then you probably think no one should own the Cezanne and Matisse that are hanging in Dad's study. It's kind of a weird thing, being freak rich.

Sally and I obviously haven't got it all figured out yet. Some problem, hey?" He put a bowl and wire whisk on the table. "One of you beat the eggs, please."

Mark reached for the bowl. "Go look at the painting. It's amazing."

"By the way," Paul said as Brady pushed back her chair, "the paintings are kept out of sight from visitors because about a year ago this part of the house was photographed for a magazine. We have a good security system, but Mom and Dad didn't see the need to publicize the whereabouts of a few priceless paintings, so they moved them to back rooms. Dad decided he liked them there, and that's where they stayed." He dropped bread into the toaster. "The Matisse is my favorite."

Mark said, "I appreciate that you trust us, especially letting me in to snoop around."

"Why the hell wouldn't I?" Paul said. He pointed with the bacon fork. "And I'll trust you with something else, man; why don't you put on some music? My dad's got an incredible collection of seventy-eights, including some mind-blowing old Delta blues."

Mark shot up, nearly spilling the eggs.

Brady rolled her eyes and went to see the priceless painting hanging next to a bathroom door.

The boys were crouched over a stack of albums when she returned to the living room. Mark said something, Paul laughed, they both rose, and each slipped hands into back pockets and continued talking.

The breath caught in her throat.

Will. So many times she had seen him standing like that, talking to friends. He was about the same age as these guys; would they all get along?

Mark saw her and put a hand on Paul's shoulder to quiet him. "You okay, Brady?"

She nodded. "Hungry," she said.

Piano music floated in the background as they sat at the table and ate. The boys launched into a conversation about local musicians and clubs. As they talked, Brady retraced in her head how she had ended up in a fairy-tale house early in the morning with two guys she hardly knew.

"I think my brother's dead," she blurted. The boys stopped talking. They glanced at each other. "Don't panic. I haven't flipped out or anything. You two, talking about music, reminded me of him. That article in the paper you gave me, Mark? He didn't write it." She hesitated, listening to the way the words echoed. A broken record, she thought. I sound like a shrieking broken record: He didn't write it, he didn't write it, he didn't write it.

She stared at the pale yellow eggs on her plate. She could feel the boys lean closer, not certain what was about to happen. "I don't believe he wrote it and I don't believe he cooperated with someone else saying those things under his name. He couldn't have changed that much."

"It happened a lot, Brady," Mark said softly.

She shook her head violently. "Not Will. Not to the point of advocating resistance."

"What paper?" Paul asked.

Mark explained about *Deserter Times*.

Paul said, "So, okay, he didn't write it. Why does that make you think he's dead?"

"If the article is supposed to be the evidence that he deserted, then their case is no good. If he hasn't deserted, he's probably dead. This sounds stupid, but I just feel he's dead."

"But that doesn't explain," Paul said, "how his name shows up in *Deserter Times*. I can't agree, Brady. I think he's alive. I bet I meet him someday. I'd like that. Your family's interesting, and I bet he'd be fun to know."

Brady studied him, thinking about the jackass she'd met at the beach party, the fool who'd nearly driven them to their death. Where was he now? How often did he appear? She said, "A few hours ago I was with Sally. She was trying to convince me of the same thing, that he's alive." The tears spilled out and she reached for a napkin.

Mark studied the slice of toast in his hand, then ripped it in two. He looked at her. "Do you want me to make it worse? Do you want to know more?"

Brady wiped her cheeks. "It's better than not knowing."

"When you told me that he'd last been seen with his squad in Long Binh, I thought it kind of weird that he'd show up in Saigon. That's a long way for a guy on his own to cover. Not impossible, but hard to do."

"That's what we were told. So?"

"He survived an ambush, right?"

"That's what we were told. They didn't find his body."

He stared into middle distance. She said softly, "I'm sorry to make you see it again."

He said, "I see it all the time. Brady, when a guy gets killed, you do everything you can to retrieve the body. But if he was taken prisoner and then killed, or died because of an injury, he might have been left somewhere."

"Just killed and left?"

"A wounded prisoner slows you down."

Did you ever kill a wounded prisoner? Did you ever see it done? She pressed her lips together. She knew there were things she'd never ask him.

"Bodies get stripped. There's a market for tags and other IDs. His could have made it to Saigon pretty quickly while the body . . . " He stopped. "I'm sorry."

She said, "I don't care. Not if it's the truth."

"But you don't know," Paul said to Mark.

Mark said, "Any military court would find the stuff in those articles treasonous. Someone could be hiding behind Will's name."

"What happened to his body?" Brady said.

He glanced away. "That's hard to say."

"Because it's so awful, or because you don't know?"

"Because I don't know."

Paul said, "Well, couldn't the obvious be true? That he deserted and made it to Saigon, where he's writing inflammatory stuff while he has the time of his life in whorehouses and beer joints."

She stared at her plate. "Yeah," she whispered. "Why not. Whorehouses and beer joints—I'll pass that on to my mother."

While the guys cleaned up the kitchen, Brady went to Sally's room to leave a note. Except for books scattered on the bed, the sparely furnished room was neat. She scanned the authors and titles. Dorothy Day, Daniel Berrigan, Teilhard de Chardin, Butler's *Lives of the Saints*. She ripped a sheet from a notebook on Sally's desk and scribbled a message. *We were here, where were you? Another strange night, sad and wonderful. Wish you'd been around for all of it. Brady.*

P.S. Have you decided to reclaim your spiritual roots? Or don't you ever read anything fun?

11

Sally hoisted herself onto the counter. "I guess I missed a good party last night."

Brady looked up from the sink. "Hi to you too. Be careful—that mug you just bumped is Mom's favorite. You did miss a nice time."

"Thanks for the note, rubbing it in and making fun of my books. What was so strange, sad, and wonderful about the night?"

Brady flicked at a mound of soap suds. That it happened at all, she thought. That I survived your brother's driving. That I cried in front of those boys and acted on impulse.

That I let go, let things happen.

Brady said, "It was all so unexpected, to end up at your house in the middle of the night. Nothing like that ever happens to me."

"Make it happen. That's possible, you know."

Brady shrugged. Maybe for some people. "Where were you, anyway?"

"On the lake. Friends called about a party when I got back to the house. I checked it out, but didn't stay too late. That whole spoiled kids scene is so uninteresting. I don't care if I never see any of them again. I left and just cruised around."

"How come you're not up at your cabin? Paul said he was going to make you go back with him."

"He can't force me to do anything. Look, I've only got a moment. I have people waiting, so how about if you stop and listen."

Brady snapped suds off her hands. As she dried with a towel, she looked out the window to the backyard. Cullen and Sam were pounding nails into wood, fashioning God knows what. Her mother sat in a lawn chair, holding the book she was reading at an odd angle, trying to catch the day's last light.

"Go pack a bag and come with us."

"You're being mysterious. I don't like mysterious."

"Some friends and I are headed east to a music festival in New York. You should see the line-up of bands. We're going and you have to come. C'mon, Brady—*make* something happen."

Movement in the back caught her eye and she turned and looked out the window again as two guys entered the yard. Mary rose from her chair, a finger automatically slipping into the book as it closed. Sam and Cullen stopped pounding nails. Brady recognized one of them—the guy who'd been eating pudding at Purple House. "Are those the people you're going with?"

Sally sighed. "I told them to stay in the car."

"You need another girl along, is that it?"

"I don't need anything. I want you to come. It will be an adventure, Brady. It will do you good. Just blow everything and leave." She called out the window. "Avery, Todd, I'm in here."

Brady watched her mother drop back into her chair; saw her hand idly rub a tightened brow; saw her follow the boys with her eyes.

"She's resisting," Sally said as the guys entered.

"That's her problem," the one from Purple House said. He looked at Brady. "Small world, hey?" He helped himself to a clean glass from the drying rack and turned on the faucet. "Did you ever get your hands on Soldier Boy?"

"Todd," Sally said tersely.

Brady said to Sally, "I'm not going."

Todd said, "She doesn't like me. But you still do, right?" As he took a long drink of water, he pressed a thumb against Sally's back and ran it slowly down her spine.

Brady tugged Sally's arm and pulled her out of the kitchen. "You can't have seriously thought I'd want to be some strange guy's date on a cross-country trip. Are you insane?"

"It's not like you're supposed to be Avery's chick for the trip. Nothing's expected of you."

"Speak for yourself," Todd called. "I happen to know that Avery was hoping to get laid."

"Why don't you guys go back to the car," Sally said sharply.

They walked past quickly, their heads turning this way and that as they checked out the house. When they reached the front door, Avery said, "The lower classes are so uptight. Scared of losing what little they've got."

"They've got nothing," Todd said as he opened the door. "They just don't know it."

Before Brady could say a word, Sally held up her hand. "Okay, I don't know Avery so well, but Todd has got this fabulous mind."

"Good. You'll be entertained all the way to New York."

"We'll lose Avery. I'll take them both back to Purple House right now." She lowered her voice. "Don't worry about the money. Don't let that stop you. It's a crazy road trip and it's my idea, so let it be my treat."

Brady said slowly, "It's not the money." She grabbed Sally by the shoulders and pulled her close. "Don't go. Don't go with these guys."

Sally slumped. "I won't if you say you'll go. Just you and me, Brady. It would be so much fun. I'll take them back to the house and come get you. Take a chance. Can you do that? Don't you want to escape, just for a while?"

"Sally, if it's just for a while, it's no escape."

Brady watched the Jaguar pull away.

Her mother came in and stood by her side. "What was that all about?"

"They're driving out to New York to some rock festival. Sally wanted me to go along."

"Sounds foolish. I'm glad you didn't go."

"Well, I wouldn't, would I?" Brady snapped. "Brady Callahan never does anything foolish."

Mary leaned back, almost as if she'd been slapped. Her mouth formed a sound, but nothing came out. Finally she said, "Who were those men with Sally? Do you know them?"

Men? Stupid boys, that's what they were. "They live in a house near St. Bernard's. It's mostly U students there, I think." And one Vietnam vet who likes the blues, she said to herself.

"Should we be concerned about what she's doing? Do you suppose she has permission to go?"

"Sally doesn't seem to factor permission into anything she does, Mother.

Besides, she's eighteen. If her parents trust her and give her plenty of space but don't like what she does with it, that's their problem."

"You have my trust," Mary said softly. "You earned it long ago. And I give you space. There's no money to play with, of course, but you are not bound to me."

Then why did she feel so trapped and squeezed?

She turned and went back to the kitchen. The dishwater was cold and gray. When she stuck her hand into the water to release the drain, she rammed her thumb against something sharp. She gasped and pulled out her hand. Blood flowed down her thumb. Stunned, she held it aloft as she stared at the red. It ran across her wrist, then fell off her arm in steady drops.

She saw an image of Will, wounded and bleeding. He stared straight back, with dark, empty eyes. Blood trickled out of his mouth. He wiped it, and still it flowed.

Sam's scream and Mary's arm around her waist brought her back to the kitchen just as her knees gave away and Brady fell to the floor.

Brady said, "It's supposed to be a bandage, not a club."

Her mother stepped back and said, "Yes, I think that will do."

"I've never seen so much blood," Sam said.

"Can I have that shirt?" asked Cullen. "It would make a great Halloween costume."

The doorbell rang before she could reply. They all looked toward the sound, then looked at one another, puzzled. Brady started to get up from the chair, but her mother put a hand on her shoulder. "Don't get up so quickly. Cullen will go."

Cullen raced to the door, then returned. "It's a boy for Brady," he said. Sam ran out to see.

"Bring him in here, Sam," Mary called.

Brady said, "No, I'll go. I'm fine."

She reached the front door and smiled at Mark.

"Sorry to drop in like this, but I heard about a band that's playing—" He looked at her shirt and said, "Wow. How was your day?"

12

Brady looked at the bandage on her thumb and at the traces of blood still embedded in the lines of her palm. "Were you ever wounded?" she asked Mark.

He set two sweating glasses of lemonade on the table. He pulled out a chair and sat down. "Twice."

"Twice!" Brady's voice cut through the chatter in the café. People at near-by tables turned and looked.

Mark raised a finger to his lips. "Shush, or I take you home." He picked up his glass and drank deeply.

"Badly?"

He nodded.

"Where?"

A smile spread. "No place private. Do you hate being told that you're blushing?"

"I do."

"I'll remember. My second month in-country I was walking behind a guy who triggered a booby trap. I got hit in the shoulder and won some time at the rear in the hospital. Simmons wasn't so lucky."

"Killed?"

"One of many. Over forty thousand to date. My second hit was a little more serious. I was short—"

"Short?"

"Only six weeks left and counting the days. My squad was ambushed. I took a hit on the thigh. A golden hit, I won the jackpot—that's what I remember the medic saying as he wrapped it up. My war was over."

"You were lucky."

Mark nodded slightly. "Oh, so lucky."

She leaned forward and started to speak. He held a finger to his lips and shushed her again. "Turn your chair around. The band is about to kick in."

It was hardly a band—just a two-piece combo, piano and guitar. There wasn't much to watch, which was just as well since her view of the musicians was usually blocked by a large bobbing Afro.

Halfway through the second piece, listening to the cat-and-mouse interplay, she wondered, Is this any good? It certainly wasn't melodic, not like the smooth, dance-inducing music she'd heard last night at the bar. She leaned over and whispered in his ear, "Is this any good?" He nodded, intent on the music. She waited a few minutes more and whispered again, "I don't follow it."

He put a finger to his lips.

She sat back and closed her eyes and saw Will again. He was always there. Whenever she closed her eyes, there he was, at least for an instant.

She remembered when he'd brought home a guitar. Four or five years ago. He'd bought a used one, a beautiful golden brown thing he'd held so tenderly. "A Martin," he'd said proudly.

He couldn't play at first, but in a few days he was pounding out Beatles songs, all the ones he knew the words to. Three chords, he said. Learn three simple chords and you can play any song in the world.

Listening to the duo in the café, Brady suspected she wasn't hearing simple chords and that there were way more than three.

The crowd went nuts when the number finally ended. Mark clapped and cheered with the others. The musicians eased into another piece. Mark sighed softly, sat back, and seemed to drift off into an untroubled sleep. Brady watched him and wondered, What does *he* see when he closes his eyes?

"I didn't get most of that," she said when the musicians took a break. "I mean, I could tell they were skilled, but I just didn't get what they were doing."

"I don't want to force you to listen to stuff you don't like. We can go."

"Let's stay."

He looked pleased, but uncertain. "Sure?"

"I want to figure this out."

At the next intermission she said, "Enough."

Mark nodded. "No problem. It's getting a little weird even for me."

Boldly, she took his hand as they walked from the café. He didn't pull away. "Where to?" she said.

"Do you have to be home soon? It's almost midnight."

Brady laughed. "Setting a curfew is not my mother's style."

"Really? Of course, I only talked with her for a few minutes while you were changing your shirt, but I sure didn't get the impression that she was a flaky hippie mom or anything. Matter of fact, she seemed intent on grilling me. You reappeared just in time."

"What did she want to know?"

"Where we met, for one thing. Your brother's a joker, isn't he? The big one."

"Cullen. What did he say?"

"When I told her we met at the center, he did this buzzing thing and said, 'Wrong answer.' What did he mean by that?"

"She's a very lapsed Catholic. She doesn't like me hanging out with the sort of people she left behind."

"Are you religious?"

"I don't know."

"Is your dad in the picture?"

"He died eight years ago. I'll ask again, Where to?"

"There are things you don't like to talk about, aren't there?"

"Not on street corners."

He said, "We could go to my room, then. We could talk there and listen to music. I've got some albums you might like."

His room. Well, why not. Why the hell not. Like Sally said, Make things happen.

He kissed her on the forehead. She said, "You missed."

He kissed her on the lips, then stepped back, barely. "If it helps you decide, the invitation includes ice cream. I got groceries this afternoon, and I bought peppermint chip."

Brady said, "You're smooth; the answer is yes."

13

Mark did most of the talking as they walked down the street. He told her how he'd gotten interested in music. "A guy in my squad had this incredible voice. Perfect pitch too, and an amazing memory. He knew so much about all types of music. When he wanted to explain something, whether it was about Coltrane or Brahms, he'd sing all the notes, all the parts, until you knew what he meant."

Brady felt a dead weight. "What happened to him?"

"Got out two months before me. Lives in Atlanta."

"Do you hear from him?"

"No. A lot of guys talked about keeping in touch, but it hasn't happened. Guess we all just want to leave it behind." He stopped in his tracks. "Oh, hell. Another party." His voice thickened. "Another goddam party."

Brady looked. From half a block away, she could see the lights and hear the music coming from Purple House. "Don't the neighbors complain?"

"The only real neighbor is the pizza parlor, and it's glad for the business. I can't take it much longer, but I don't know what to do. I hardly ever sleep. I can't read. Can't think. You have no idea how much I crave quiet."

"Move."

"I pay only thirty-five bucks a month for my own room and use of the kitchen. I can't afford any more. Not if I want to start at the U next month."

"Father Tom could help."

"He's the one who told me about this place. I don't think he had a clue. Or maybe he did, but he knew I was desperate. I wish . . ."

"What?" she prompted.

He pulled his arm free. "Nothing. I'll walk you home, Brady, but maybe then we'd better call it a night. I start a new job tomorrow, anyway. I need to be there at seven."

"You should have said something. Will you be able to sleep when you get back?"

"Maybe it will be better."

They turned from the purple house and started walking toward Brady's. Police sirens, squealing car tires, music spilling from open windows filled the lull in the conversation.

Brady thought, Why isn't this easier? We both want to be here, can't we find something to say? Another block passed. She said, "What's the job?"

"Warehouse work. It's only a temp thing for two days, though there's a chance I might get to stay on."

"Are there parties often at the house?"

"Not that many, but even on a normal night, it's not a quiet place."

"You've met my friend Sally. Paul's sister? I guess she's started hanging out there. She came by earlier tonight. She was headed out on a road trip to New York to some rock festival with two guys from your house. I've met one and didn't really like him. I guess that's her business, not mine."

"Who were the guys?"

"Todd and Avery. I don't know their last names." Maybe it was her imagination, the pause was that slight, but it seemed that he held up for a moment. "Do you know them?"

"I know everyone, more or less. That is, everyone who's officially residing there. Todd is official, Avery's an extra."

"Are there lots of extras? Let's turn here; there's a side street that goes through."

"People come and go all the time, like your friend. She's been there a few nights. I thought . . ."

"Thought what?"

"There's this guy, Brian, she seemed to be closer to him. Of course, he's the unofficial property of someone else. Jane, on the third floor. At least, that's what it looks like. I don't really know. I try to keep my head down. That crowd doesn't like me, being a vet and all."

"I met Brian. I went to Purple House before I found you at the Viking."

"They call me Soldier Boy. Brian absolutely refuses to use my name. I guess I should tell you that the other afternoon they were discussing Sally. They were debating whether she was an informant."

Brady laughed. "A narc? I don't think so."

He shook his head. "No, a political informer for the FBI. An infiltrator. They're convinced there are some in all the student groups."

"That's paranoid."

"I guess it goes on."

"She'd be too obvious, though, wouldn't she? A rich girl from the suburbs?"

They stopped to watch a car speed down the quiet street. Mark took Brady's hand. "Yes. More likely it would be you or me. Brian's part of a group that broke off from the SDS chapter at the U about a month ago. He claims they were too middle class and cautious."

Students for a Democratic Society. Brady recalled the piles of books and political literature that had been piled around him in the kitchen, and the cold way he'd appraised her and mocked Mark. "I guess the Democratic Society part might not appeal to him, either."

Mark laughed. "I bet so. There's a light on at your house. Who's still up?"

"My mother. She might be up or she might have fallen asleep with her light on. She does that a lot when she stays up reading."

He walked her to the back door. As she fished in her pockets for the key, she said, "You need to get out of that house, Mark. Even for one night. Why don't you crash here? You can sleep on the sofa. My mom won't mind at all."

"I'll be fine."

"Will it really be any quieter by the time you get back?"

When he didn't answer, she pulled him along as she entered the house. "You're staying," she said.

She switched on the kitchen light. "Hungry? Help yourself while I get things for you."

"I don't need things, Brady," he said as he walked toward the fridge. He studied the clutter of drawings, photos, and notes covering the door. "After we dropped you off last night, Paul and I talked for a while. He said your family was very seductive. Now I see what he means."

"That's an odd thing to say. He hardly knows us."

"It's what he said. Wow, what a picture, Brady. How very brave of you to leave it up for anyone to see."

"I was ten in that picture. I bet you had an ugly stage too."

"Probably so," he said softly. "But there's no record."

She brought bedding and an alarm clock and set them down on a chair. He stood against the arched oak woodwork that marked the living room from the formal dining area. He sipped a glass of milk. "How early do you have to leave for work?" she asked.

"About six. I'll need to walk over to Franklin to catch the bus."

"My mother will be up. She's at work by seven."

"What does she do?"

"She's head psych nurse over at University Hospital. I'll leave her a note so she won't be surprised. Bathroom's upstairs, first door on the left. There might even be a new toothbrush in the drawer by the sink, but I can't promise for sure. Good night." She took two steps toward the stairs, then whirled around. "Want to do something again soon?"

"Come here," he said.

She shook her head slightly. "Much as I'd like a nice long good-night, I need to get some sleep. So do you. Two late nights in a row is not healthy."

"No, this is something else. About Sally. Or, really, about the guys she's with. Oh, maybe I shouldn't. I can't say for sure, and besides, they've taken off, so what difference can it make?"

She walked over to him. "What are you trying to say?"

He looked at the floor, gathering his thoughts. "Todd has the other room in the basement. He had someone with him not long ago."

"Sally? I'm no prude, Mark. And I'm not a policeman for my friend's behavior."

"No. Someone else. I don't know who. It sounded like he was hurting her. He was saying things and slapping. I shouted at them, kind of a 'What's going on?' to let them know someone could hear. Neither one said anything back, and it got quiet, and then pretty soon they left. I haven't heard anything like that since, but the guy has a temper. I've seen it in action."

Brady felt a chill spread, bottom to top.

He said, "Now I've made you worry. I didn't want that."

Brady dropped her head against his shoulder. No one ever made her worry, she did it all on her own. Like breathing. Swallowing. Blushing.

His hand slipped under her hair and stroked her neck. "There's a phenomenal guitar player at Sharkey's Bar the next few nights. Fat Joe Williams, a real legend. Would you go with me? A date, Brady, I want that clear. I'm asking ahead of time."

"I'd love to." She kissed him, a quick graze on his cheek. With one hand he held her from leaving, with the other he reached for the wall switch and turned off the light.

After a nice long good-night, he pulled away. "Please don't forget to warn your mother I'm here."

14

Brady knocked softly on her mother's door before opening it and slipping her arm around to tape up the note.

"I'm awake. Come in."

Her mother was sitting on the floor playing solitaire. Three empty beer bottles stood in a row beside her. "I've won six games in a row. Not this one, though." Mary gathered the cards and shuffled, then briskly laid them out—snap, snap, snap. "I love playing with a new deck of cards."

Brady looked at the beer bottles. She said, "Mom, are you okay?"

"Can't sleep, that's all."

"Mark came back with me. It's so late, I told him to crash on the sofa. I was leaving a note to warn you."

Mary studied the layout of cards. She touched one lightly with her finger, then shook her head. "I hated it when Will did that and didn't call. Please ask him to call his mother, if he hasn't already. She won't mind if he wakes her."

"He doesn't have one. At least, she's not in the picture. There doesn't seem to be any family."

Now her mother was moving in slow motion, thinking long and hard before placing a card. Brady said, "Mom, it's almost one. You need to rest."

Her mother nodded and rose, leaving the cards and bottles on the floor. "What's the story on his family?" she said as she climbed into bed.

"I don't know. He's the one who gave me the *Deserter Times*. He got out of the army a few months ago."

"Older."

Older than you, Brady knew she meant. "Barely. He enlisted when he was seventeen."

Her mother closed her eyes. Her lips moved slightly. If Brady didn't know better, she'd have thought her mother was praying. Brady sat on the bed beside her mother. "Since you're awake, I need some advice."

Mary's eyebrows arched in surprise.

"There's something he said. I don't know what to do about it. Well, there's not anything to do, now that she's gone."

"What is it?"

Brady smiled. Her mother's voice had strengthened, but cooled. Clinical and professional, the nurse was at work. "The guys that Sally's with? Mark knows them, they live in his house—well, at least one does. And he says that the one guy, Todd, is bad news. He knows he . . ." How could she say this to her mother? "He has a temper."

To Brady's surprise, her mother seemed to relax, seemed even to smile for an instant.

"I thought so," Mary said. "The minute they walked into the yard I knew there'd be something I wouldn't like about them."

"Nothing to do, I suppose."

"Except worry, and I'm sure you'll take care of that, so I won't."

Brady rose and turned away, swearing under her breath. Mary lunged and grabbed her shirt, pulling her back. "I shouldn't have said that. I'm sorry."

"I'm such a joke to you, it's such a big laugh, that I care about things? It's just a joke that my friend is with some guy who likes to beat girls?"

"Sit down."

"I want to go to bed."

"Brady, every day, a million times every day, I wish you didn't have to carry so much on your shoulders. I'm so proud of you, but it also breaks my heart that you take so much on. And, believe me: It's no joke at all that Sally might be in danger."

Brady sat on the bed and picked at her bandage. "I should have made her stay, or I should have gone with her. She told me she'd dump them if I went along. But I wouldn't, I couldn't imagine just going. Just taking off for something wild and fun. What's wrong with me that I can never let go?"

"Things are so turned around, because of Will."

"It's not just that. I can never go crazy."

Mary turned off the bedside light. "I think she'll be fine."

"How can you say that?" Brady snapped. She was furious now, fatigue roiling with worry. "Mark heard this guy slap a girl. He *heard* it. The guy could be doing it to Sally."

Her mother's eyes narrowed, focused inward. "Good," she murmured.

Brady gasped, "What?" She stood up. "How can you say that?"

Mary reached for her daughter and took her hands in her own. "Hush, you'll wake the boys."

"I don't care," Brady said loudly. "You think it's good that she's getting beat up? How can you say that?" she asked again.

Mary pulled her down on the bed. "Take a breath and listen. That's not what I meant. That's not what I was saying."

"Then what did you mean to say?"

"That it was good I called her parents tonight."

Brady stood up again. "You did *what?*"

Mary leaned back on a pile of pillows and smiled. "Look at you. I lose either way, that's the lesson here. Yes, Brady. Those boys worried the crap out of me, and after you left I called the Coopers' cabin. I talked with her father. I explained who I was, I said how much I liked his children, and I apologized for intruding on their family business. Then I told him that tonight Sally had stopped by on her way to New York. He didn't know about it. He certainly didn't know that she was taking off in his car and was in the company of two unlikable young men. He thanked me for calling."

"I can't believe you ratted her out."

"I'm a little surprised myself. Like you said, she's eighteen. But it seemed to be the right thing to do. And now, after what you told me, I'm very glad that I did."

"But what can they do? What can anyone do?"

"Don't know." Mary pulled up the bedsheet. "It feels like we may get rain. Hope so. I'd like this heat to break. Does your friend have a pillow and things?"

"He's fine," Brady said absently, her mind still on Sally.

"I'll try not to wake him in the morning."

"He'll probably be gone. He has to be at work early."

"Have him join us for dinner sometime. And don't be so sure Sally's parents can't do anything. Her father seemed determined. He was very polite, but once I'd told him what I knew, he wanted to end the conversation. His exact words were, 'I need to get on this; I need to make some calls.'" She closed her eyes. "I love you. Good night."

As Brady closed her mother's door, she wondered about the calls Sally's father planned to make. Someone who knew generals, ambassadors, cabinet members—whom would he call to retrieve his daughter? What long arm of the law would he twist to ensure her return?

"Oh no," Brady groaned. "She'll never talk to me again."

15

Through the window Brady saw her mother and Cullen glaring at each other. She entered the house, slammed the kitchen door behind her, and dropped her bag on the floor. "I'm home." Her mother and brother held their positions, ignoring her.

Sam sat at the table, peeling leaves off a head of lettuce and dropping them into a bowl. "Don't be so mad at him, Mom. We made twenty bucks!"

Mary's fingers drummed on the table. "I can't believe you made him work. He's eight years old."

"So you'd rather we sat around watching TV when you're gone all day? What sort of life is that?"

"I'm gone all day earning a living. I have no choice, Cullen."

"I get half of twenty bucks!" Sam said.

Brady said, "Go clean up, Sam. You shouldn't be touching food with those hands."

"Twenty bucks and we were done by two o'clock, Brady. Did you make twenty bucks today?"

"Not even close."

"So if you were done by two, where were you coming from now?" Mary demanded.

Cullen leaned against the fridge, arms crossed, still silent.

Sam said, "We were lining up more work. We came back for a while and ate and then went back out and knocked on doors. We've got jobs for every day the rest of the week."

Mary stood in front of Cullen. He put his hands on his hips. Like two gunslingers, Brady thought—each one waiting for the other to move.

"You actually went door to door to strange houses?" Mary said. She took a sharp breath. "You stayed around here, right? Don't tell me you crossed the highway."

Cullen said, "We did. It paid off." He dropped his arms and turned to face Brady. "Your boyfriend called."

Sam said, "Brady has a boyfriend!"

Brady said, "Was there a message?"

"He'll try to call later. But in case he can't, I'm supposed to tell you that he won't be by tonight. He said that Paul has lined up a place for him to live and they're checking it out. How do they know each other?"

"They met the other night," she said, wondering to herself when Paul had returned to town.

Mary took the lettuce from Sam. She ripped it apart in a few violent pulls, then she dropped it in the sink and sighed. "Cullen, I don't want you knocking on doors like that. Do you swear you won't do it again?"

Brady watched him choose an answer. "I guess." He faced Brady. "There was one more thing to his message. He said you two could still go hear Fat Joe tomorrow. He said Fat Joe is playing two more nights at Sharky's."

Out of the corner of her eye, Brady saw her mother react to the comment. "But Sharky's is a bar," Mary said.

Cullen grinned, happy to have shifted the focus of her concern. "That was the message."

Brady opened the door to Paul and Mark. Their arms were loaded with roses.

"Sorry, but they're not for you," Paul said. "Is your mom here? These are from my parents."

"Why?" She knew, though, as soon as she asked. "Sally."

"Bingo. Got vases?"

"Somewhere, collecting dust. Let me get Mom. She's in the backyard with the boys."

"Sally has been caught," Paul said as soon as Mary appeared. He seemed deeply satisfied. "My parents are flying to Cleveland to drive her home. They didn't have time to call you themselves, so they asked me to deliver these and the news."

Mary hesitated before holding out her arms for the flowers. "This was not necessary. They're gorgeous, though. I don't think I've ever seen so many roses in my life. Cullen, Sam—there are vases in the closet next to the laundry room. Bring several." The boys raced each other into the kitchen and down the basement stairs. Someone hit the bottom with a thud.

Mark said, "Why don't I go help them." He handed his armload to Brady and followed the boys.

Brady said, "You seem pretty happy that they found her, Paul. Sally will be furious."

"I don't care. Mark was telling me about the guys she's with. It's good she's coming home."

"Where is she?"

"I'm not sure. Being detained by a sheriff somewhere in Ohio."

"And the guys?"

"That's all I know."

Mark and the boys returned with several vases.

Cullen said, "Pretty dusty, Mom."

Paul said, "Whose fault is that, man? Don't you ever buy your mother flowers?"

Cullen wiped his hands and put them in his back pockets. He looked down, thinking about it.

Mark was in the same pose. Sheepish, feeling guilty about something. Brady moved to his side. "What's the story on the new place?"

He tipped his head. Other room? She nodded, suspecting he really wanted to be in some other world, at least somewhere other than where Paul was winning the hearts of her brothers and mother.

"It's not for long," he said as soon as they were alone in the living room. "I'll have to look for another place pretty quick, but at least I'm out of Purple House. I'll be house-sitting for friends of his parents. A retired professor and his wife. They live at their lake cabin until October. Someone broke into the house last week, so now they want someone there. I'm sorry I didn't show up or call last night."

She took his hand and led him to the sofa. "Cullen gave me your message. It's fine. How was the job?"

"Two days of warehouse work. I put price tags on boxes of nails all day yesterday and today I marked nuts and bolts."

"Tired?"

He shook his head. "Furious, that's what I am. I want to punch a hole in a wall. It's not the job, though. I got a letter from the VA today telling me about some new forms they want filled before they'll approve my tuition. Jesus, I spend fourteen months in their lousy war and they still squeeze me bloodless and make me beg for the money they promised for school. I am not in a good mood, Brady."

"You have a new place to live."

"I'll have the house all to myself," he said. "Well, there's a cat. The person who's supposed to be watching it discovered she's allergic, so she's bringing it back. Paul thinks that's the real reason they want a house sitter. I'll have to move out in about six weeks, but this gives me a chance to look for a place."

"Invite me over."

She sensed something was coming—a question, an invitation, a kiss, but before he could make the move, the others burst into the room, everyone carrying vases full of roses.

Paul set his on the coffee table. He flopped down onto the sofa next to Mark. "Ready to go?"

Mark nodded. "We're moving my stuff out of Purple House," he said to Brady.

"We can use some help," Paul said to the younger boys. "You would not believe the books he has. He's been out of the army for only three months and he's got a room full of books and records. You two want to come along?"

Brady said, "I'll help."

Mark said, "Let the guys do it. It's fine."

"Besides," Paul said to Cullen and Sam, "what if a suitcase or something falls open and it's full of his underwear and she sees it?"

Sam giggled. Cullen, always too cool, only smiled and said, "Yeah."

After they left, Brady, trying not to feel dumped and sorry for herself, went to the kitchen to clean up the rose mess she was certain was there.

Yes, indeed. There were snippets of stems, torn leaves, thorns, and soggy florist's paper all over the counter, sink, and floor. She cleaned, getting angrier every time a thorn pricked her. The image of Mark's darkened face popped into her mind. *Furious.* "We're a helluva pair," she said.

"You and who else?" her mother asked.

"Don't sneak up on me."

"Walking into my own kitchen is not sneaking up on you."

"I was talking to myself. You should at least pretend you didn't hear."

"True. And I probably would have with anyone but my daughter. Mark didn't look happy tonight. I'm not sure he liked Paul's idea of the boys going with them."

Brady didn't want to talk about Mark's mood, or Paul's generous brainstorms, or the silence that was left behind when all the boys left the house. She said, "I'll clean this mess up."

"You're not getting rid of me that easily. Do you want to hear what I did today?"

Brady said, "I know what you did today. You listened to suicidal teenagers or maybe it was psychotics or flashers or depressed housewives. You saved the world. That's what we do, Mom, the two of us. You know what the last thing Will said to me was? The very last thing, our good-bye?"

Her mother fell back into a chair, looking stunned.

"He said something about you and me and how we're always searching for wounded animals to love. Why do you think some people do that—go looking for burdens and unhappiness, while others just seem to turn lights on everywhere they go?" She sat down. "Will could turn lights on, couldn't he?"

"In an obvious way, yes. Your father too. When he entered a room, everyone there felt better. He . . ."

Brady held still, wanting more, wanting to see and hear whatever it was her mother was remembering. She watched, knowing her mother had fallen deep into memory and was once again seeing a tall laughing Irishman enter a room.

Mary Callahan resurfaced, breathed deeply, and faced her daughter. "I went to the FBI today after work. I saw Agent Blake. I showed him Will's letters. He made copies of them for me to keep while they studied the real ones. God knows what they think they need to find. I told him we don't think Will could have written that article. He showed me another one they just received. It called for more combat refusals. It called for a soldiers' strike. It was signed with my son's name and I know in my heart he didn't write it. Now I agree with you, Brady. I believe someone's using his name and I believe that means Will is dead."

Missing in action, Brady wanted to say. Or a prisoner of war. "Maybe . . ." she whispered, then halted, unable to finish.

Her mother shook her head. She tapped the calendar hanging on the wall. "Today's August sixteenth. Until I know differently, I'll think of this as the day he died." She stared at the calendar a bit longer, then said, "Do you know the real reason I had to accept this? It wasn't those articles, though I think you're right about them; he couldn't write like that."

"Tell me."

"If he's alive and in Saigon, why hasn't he called home?"

Brady waited too long to follow her mother out of the kitchen. By the time she stirred—mad and swearing at herself for staying frozen in place as her mother walked away—Mary had gone upstairs to her room.

"Mom," she said as she turned the corner of the hallway. Her mother's door was ajar. She held up, looking in. Her mother was asleep, sprawled fully clothed across her bed. Her breathing was steady and peaceful.

Brady pulled the door closed. She too felt exhausted by sadness.

16

Brady had just finished cleaning the kitchen when the phone trilled. She leaped toward it, wanting to catch it before it rang again and roused her mother.

Mark said, "You'll hate me." Her heart sank. "Would you mind if we don't go out tonight? I want to settle in. Paul and the guys have left. They were great, by the way. Didn't complain once about hauling boxes. Not that I have that much. I just want to be here tonight, Brady. If you're angry, I understand."

"It's fine, Mark. I'm in a lousy mood anyway."

"Tomorrow, for sure?"

"For sure."

She waited on the front steps, wanting to catch Sam and Cullen before they burst into the house and woke their mother.

She greeted them with a threat: "Mom's asleep. If you wake her up, I'll kill you."

They seemed to know she was serious and immediately slowed down. They crept past her to enter the house.

Sam paused. "Mark has a huge place all to himself."

Cullen, halfway into the house, said, "I didn't see any Viet Cong trophy ears. He got kind of pissed when I asked."

Before she could release her wrath, he'd escaped inside. She heard his footsteps pounding up the stairs to the second floor and the refuge of the room he shared with Sam.

"You're so human around your brothers," Paul said.

"Human?"

"Imperfect."

"I'm imperfect all the time, Paul. Was Cullen rude to Mark?"

"Not at all. And I don't think he really asked him about trophy ears. I didn't hear it happen, and he stuck pretty close to me the whole time."

"It was a sweet thing to include them. You and Sally are amazing, the way you jump in and find the right thing to do and say." Both of you, she thought, turning on lights.

"Did Mark call?"

"Yes."

"Are you mad? He was worried you would be."

"I'm mad, but not at him. It's perfectly reasonable that he'd want to settle in."

"Mad at me for interfering with your date?"

"Are you kidding? Not only have you found Mark a place to live, you got my brothers out of the house for a few hours. I owe you big time."

"Then why be mad?"

"It's sort of a state of mind these days. And today was . . ."

Ordinary. If your ordinary day includes holding the hand of a pregnant fourteen-year-old who's been beaten by her father, being kissed by a sobbing grizzled man who was starved and grateful for the sandwich and glass of cold lemonade you've handed him, rocking the infant daughter of a woman being hauled off in an ambulance to county detox.

"It was a long day. I was looking forward to tonight. I wanted to . . ."

Paul sat on the step. His knee dropped against hers.

Oh, God. Such soft brown eyes.

What did she want? That was easy: to get out, evade the sadness, crawl into Mark's arms and rest. Yes, she'd thought about that all day, crawling into his arms.

Oh, God. Such a smooth, square jaw.

Anyone's arms, maybe. "Work was tough today. My mother's sad. I'll catch hell from your sister when she gets back in town. Our lawn needs mowing. I guess I wanted Mark to show up tonight and help me escape."

He rose and held out a hand. "I'll help you. Let's go out to my place."

Those paintings, the music, the lake.

"We'll take the boat out. I won't drive fast."

Stars, the moon, space to breathe.

Brady said, "Yes."

The well-kept two-story Victorian stood out from the other houses on the street not far from St. Bernard's. Brady eyed the lace curtains, opulent flower garden, white picket fence. "Why are we stopping here?"

"Groceries," Paul said. "I'll just be a minute. Of course, you could come in with me, Brady. This place is a trip. It's like a farmer's market for dealers. Closest thing to an opium den that you'll ever see in Minneapolis. You really should check it out."

"No, thanks."

He leaned over and undid the tie that bound her hair. "I love it when your hair is loose. The first night I saw you, it seemed like you were walking out of the bonfire and your hair was a ball of flames. You blew me away, Brady."

She refastened the tie. "I've been thinking of getting it cut."

He sat back, sat still, then got out of the car and walked toward the house.

Brady watched him climb the steps. She opened the door and called, "Wait!"

She wanted to escape, didn't she?

Let it happen.

The front porch was enclosed with new windows. The frames gleamed with fresh varnish. A neatly dressed man with a long gray ponytail sat on a chair, reading a book and sipping from a delicate teacup.

"Good evening, Professor," Paul said cheerfully. The man looked up and looked them over. His eyes were red-rimmed and watery. Brady jumped back when he suddenly reached and banged on the front door three times before returning to his book.

A lock clicked, the door opened, and they walked in. "It's his place," Paul whispered. "He used to be a chem professor at the U 'til his brain fried. That's the story, anyway."

A tall, muscular, tattooed guard stood near the door. Only after they'd moved through the foyer did Brady realize the guard was female. She turned for a second look and was met by watchful eyes.

The interior of the house was dismal: scuffed walls, stained carpeting, sour smell. Music, so soft it was more of a suggestion than a sound, came from somewhere. A few people sat in the large living room on old sofas, everyone staring at a spot on the floor, their heads bobbing to the faint music.

"Upstairs," Paul said, and he took the steps two at a time.

The second-floor hallway was crowded with people and piles of books. There was a different smell here, not any more pleasant. Incense and dope, certainly. Old food, maybe. Animals? Brady wrinkled her nose and made a face. A girl wearing only a muscle shirt and underwear walked past, looked at Brady, and laughed. "Who let in the schoolteacher?" she shrieked before disappearing into a room.

Brady said, "Make it fast, Paul."

He knocked on one of the many closed doors, then pulled her along when he entered. The only occupant was a short guy with a full beard and hair pulled into a thick dark braid. He was perched on a plaid sofa, rolling joints on a coffee table. "Paulie!" he cried. He stood and they hugged. "Who's your lady?"

Brady tugged on Paul's arm. "Make your buy and let's go."

"Her name's Brady," Paul said. "She's not mine."

"Lady Brady," the guy said, sitting back down. "Well, pal, maybe she'll be yours before the night is over. Until then, cheer her up with one of these." He held out a skinny joint. "Compliments of the house for the friend of a good customer. Government issue, spiced with a little fairy dust, my very own recipe." He shook the joint at Brady, then shrugged when she didn't take it and lit it himself. "Terry's back from Boston," he said to Paul after exhaling. "Got some mean shit from an MIT lab. They're absolute geniuses out there. And Tyrone's got some bad-ass hash. Should we go sample?"

Brady didn't think she'd made a sound, but Paul looked at her for a long moment, then shook his head. "No thanks, Carl. Just load me up with what you've got." He pulled some bills from a pocket and set them on the table.

Carl counted the money, then cleared his table into a brown lunch bag and handed it to Paul. "Looks like I can take the rest of the night off. I love you rich boys. I'm going down the hall to Tyrone's and treat myself to a pipe. If you can shake the leash, join us."

"I'm the leash?" Brady said as soon as the door closed.

Paul sat on the sofa and looked into the brown bag. "He's a jerk. Christ, I think he screwed me."

"Complain to the Better Business Bureau. Can we go?"

"Can we relax?"

"Don't you worry about getting caught in some raid?"

"I don't worry at all." He lit a joint and took a long hit. "Oh, yes. This is his own recipe." He held out the joint. "Don't worry, I can drive on this stuff. It's only booze that turns me stupid. C'mon. You wanted to escape, didn't you?"

She sat. He fished in the bag and pulled out another joint. "One for each of us, then we go. Promise."

She'd been high before. Will liked to smoke and hated to smoke alone. But nothing he'd ever brought home was like this stuff, not even close.

After the joint was half gone, it was enough to watch it burn.

Watch it burn.

Paul said, "Wow. I think maybe he souped up the recipe tonight. Maybe we should let it wear off a bit." He dropped back and pulled on her arm. "Lie down with me."

"Only. If." She sighed and fell over. Only if you kiss me, she'd meant to say. She lay alongside Paul. He cradled her neck. Found the buttons on her shirt.

Seconds later? Minutes later? She heard the door click open. She looked over and saw Carl grinning in the doorway. "Rich boy always gets what he wants." The door closed again.

She pushed Paul. "Stop."

He moaned and dropped his head against her chest.

She combed her fingers through his hair. "Let's go."

He pushed up on an elbow.

"Your house."

He smiled and sat up. He slowly buttoned her shirt. "I'm not sure I got them right. Better check." He stood. "Hey, look what I found." He picked up a smoldering joint from the floor and brought it back to life with a long draw. He passed it over. "Yeah. Let's get out of here." He held up a hand. "Wait. I need to see a guy. For something." He pointed toward the door. "One more stop down the hall. I'll be right back."

"Bathroom?"

He opened the door and looked. "That way, I think. No. That way. Shit, I can't remember. It's dirty, I never use it. I'm going down this way. Room with the red door. Come get me when you're ready. Those buttons are crooked. Sorry."

She finished the joint, got as far as the open door, then leaned against the doorjamb and slid to the floor. What was in Carl's fairy dust?

How long did she sit there, looking at patterns in the peeling paint? Someone's foot nudged her until she moved slightly, and the door closed behind her.

Paul will come, Brady thought. How long could it take?

She rose unsteadily and walked toward the red door, one hand sliding along the wall.

Paul was one of several bodies lying on a mound of pillows. Heads turned when she opened the door and let in light from the hall. Paul looked around as he passed a pipe to the girl next to him. "Oh, shit," he mumbled, sitting up. "I wasn't gonna stay." He fell back. His shirt was unbuttoned and it flopped open. The girl to his right rubbed his bare chest as she passed the pipe to her neighbor. Paul patted the pillows. "Brady, come here. We can do the boat tomorrow, right?"

As she walked back down the hallway, Brady heard someone say, "She's mad at you, rich boy."

The professor looked up from his book and watched her navigate the front door, the porch, the steps. He made a noise, and Brady turned around. The suddenness of her movement threw her off balance, and she gripped the handrail. The tattooed guard appeared, holding out a foam cup of steaming coffee.

Brady sat on the steps and drank. She drank slowly, but still Paul didn't appear.

Above the treetops she could see the lighted spire of St. Bernard's. Bernie's After Dark—was someone still there? She patted her pocket, felt her keys. She finished her coffee and started walking.

She was alone on the streets until she hit Riverside. At the corner, two men leaned against the lamppost across the street. They straightened when they spotted her, then started walking in the same direction, matching her speed.

St. Bernard's was dark. The men watched from across the street as she fumbled with her keys at the delivery door. A nearby bush stirred as she swore at the lock. She looked and saw legs. A shadowy figure sat up. An arm reached out.

She closed the door behind her, locked it, and stood panting in the kitchen hallway as she leaned against the wall, swearing at Paul under her breath.

Someone pounded on the door, then tried the knob. She hurried across the room. Just as she reached the phone, she looked over her shoulder and saw two silhouettes outside the kitchen window.

17

Brady slid into the front passenger seat of the car and slumped down. "I'm sorry I woke you. Thanks for coming."

Mary Callahan looked over her shoulder as she pulled out of the church parking lot. "Where's Mark?" she said tersely. "Why did he leave you?"

Mark? "Oh, Mom, no, you went to bed, and he called and . . . I didn't go out with him tonight. I . . . Never mind."

Her mother touched her shoulder. "You sounded scared to death."

Brady pressed her forehead against the cool window glass. "I'm okay. Mark has nothing to do with this. I don't want to talk about it."

Mary said, "In the morning."

Brady closed her eyes. Yes, avoid it all until the morning. But then what should she offer up—truth, lies, or silence?

Brady hadn't taken two steps out of her room the next morning when she ran right into her mother. Flushed with guilt, she went on the attack. "Why aren't you at work? It's nearly ten."

Mary said, "I'm not going in until noon. Neither are you. I've already called the center and told them."

"You shouldn't have done that."

Mary cocked her head and narrowed her eyes. "So, do I get the story or not?"

Brady brushed past her and went downstairs.

"Brady, I've given you so much freedom, and you've earned it, but now I'm worried."

"Mom. Don't."

"Don't what? Don't worry? Brady, would you stop me, then? Please, I'd love it if you could stop me from worrying."

Brady sat on the bottom step and looked at the wood grain pattern in the floorboards under her feet. Waves and loops, waves and loops. She wanted to sink into the waves and loops.

She wanted to say, Help me.

"Brady," Mary said softly as she sat beside her, "you were scared to death last night and you were obviously on something. What happened?"

Truth, lies, or silence?

Was evasion the same as a lie? Worth a try. "Mark called to cancel. I didn't feel like hanging around the house. They have stuff going on at night at the center. I was the last one there. Some neighborhood guys, or bums, saw me and tried to get in. Yes, I was frightened, so I called you."

Mary studied her; after a long moment, Brady had to turn from those scary green eyes. "If that's all you're going to tell me," Mary said, "I think I'm free to fill in the blanks. I also think I'm free to demand that either you observe a curfew or you call me at midnight on the dot whenever you're out. I don't care if you're eighteen. I can't handle you disappearing at night. It's been twice this week." She pointed an accusing finger. "Don't think I don't know how late it was when you came in after being out with Sally the other night."

Again Brady had to turn away from those green eyes.

Silence, Brady decided, was almost the same as a lie.

Mary rose and walked toward the kitchen. "By the way, you might want to go see what Paul wants. He's been out front in his car all morning. I couldn't get him to come in. He looks like hell." She held up a hand as she walked away. "Don't worry, you don't have to feed me half-truths about him either. Like I said, I'll just fill in the blanks."

Paul got out of the car as soon as he saw Brady. As usual, she thought, her mother was dead right: He looked like hell.

"I am incredibly sorry." He walked toward her in a rush. "I don't remember half of anything, but I'm sorry for all of it."

"Lucky you; I wish I didn't remember. How long have you been here?"

"I don't know exactly. I've been dozing. I woke up at the professor's and came over. Your mother was getting the paper when I parked. You got home all right?"

"Must have, because here I am, talking to you."

"I am so sorry, Brady."

"You already said that." She closed in on him. He averted his eyes. "You have no idea what it was like for me getting away from that place. I was followed, Paul. Two guys came after me. I was so scared." She raised a hand. "Do not say you're sorry. It's not enough, so I don't want to hear it."

He looked at the ground.

"The really scary thing about it all? Until you deserted me in that hellhole, I was ready to let anything happen between us. As much as I like Mark, I was still going to let anything happen."

He looked up. "Did we?"

"*We* didn't. I don't know about you and anyone else." She turned to leave, then spun back around. "I've seen you split apart into two different people, Paul. I only like and trust one of them."

18

Mark was in the yard tinkering with a lawn mower when Brady pulled into the driveway. He looked up, startled, then smiled broadly when he spotted her behind the wheel.

"You found the house," he said when she got out of the car.

"Mom used to know some people who lived around here. She'd haul us to meetings at a house up the street. Health Workers Against the War, or something like that. Another lifetime."

"Same war, though," he said. "May I kiss you, or are you mad about last night?" When she didn't answer, he kissed her. "I'll show you around," he said after he stepped back.

"Are the neighbors watching? Should you be taking a girl inside?"

He waved at whoever might be looking. "Why not? I'm living here. And it's not like I'll be throwing parties."

The house was smaller than she'd expected from Sam's description. It was filled with clutter. "Are they old?"

"Pretty old, I think. He's a retired botany professor, she's still teaching part-time at Macalester College. I guess they know Paul's dad through some conservation group. They've called twice today from their cabin with things they want me to do."

"That could get annoying, even if the rent's cheap."

He shook his head. "The rent's zero, and even if it weren't, I'm happy to help."

He did look happy. Rested, relaxed, happy. He washed his hands in the sink and chatted about the projects he'd done during the day.

Brady listened, watched, and wondered.

That T-shirt looked so soft. It would be nice to slide a hand across it, lift it up, and—

"You haven't been listening, have you?" He seemed amused. "What were you thinking about? You're kind of pink. Sorry, I wasn't ever going to mention that."

"I was too listening. I was also wondering what you'd look like with your shirt off."

"I don't know what to say." Mark drummed on the counter and looked down at the floor for a moment. "I guess I could show you."

"You . . ." She paused, and he raised his eyebrows and waited. "You're in your 'Great to be alive' mood, aren't you?" She walked over and rested her forehead against his shoulder. Yes, the T-shirt was very soft. "I hope it's contagious," she whispered, her voice breaking. He wrapped his arms around her. Crawl in, she thought. Crawl in and erase last night.

After a moment, Brady pushed away. She picked up her bag and started going through everything that was jumbled together. "I brought you something."

She took his hand and placed in his palm two condoms she'd taken from the Help Yourself! bowl at the free clinic. "I want to do this, Mark. I know it probably seems really soon, but I want to be with you. For at least a little while, I want to be as close as we can and forget about everything else."

PART THREE

Brady made a face at the images on the television. "Why are you watching this, Sam?" she said as she turned off the TV. "You'll have nightmares."

Sam didn't protest. He stared at the blank screen for a moment, then looked up at his sister. "You and Mom used to watch the war news all the time. Now you never do."

She sat alongside him on the sofa. "I guess it makes us both feel sad. Mad too, but mostly sad. So much of what they show is combat film, and it's like seeing Will get shot, over and over."

"But you don't know he's been shot. You two are just guessing about that."

"True."

"It was a good show. It was about the helicopters and bombers they use. And I don't ever have nightmares anyway."

"I'll turn it back on."

Sam tipped his head, listening. "Better not. Sounds like Mom's home from the grocery store." He jumped up and ran toward the kitchen. "Hope she got donuts."

Hugging three brown grocery bags, Mary kicked the kitchen door closed behind her. Brady took a bag just as it threatened to slip from her mother's arms. She set it down on the table, and immediately Sam started digging through it.

"I thought you were going out with Mark," Mary said.

"He got called in to work."

"Again? That's two nights in a row."

"Someone needed a last-minute sub. He gets time and a half and he's the new guy on the job, so he didn't want to say no."

"Still, it's not a fun Saturday night for you."

Brady looked over the groceries Sam had spread out on the table as he'd searched for donuts. At least she hadn't spent her night at the grocery store. "What would you and Dad do on Saturdays?"

Mary seemed startled by the question. "Not much," she said after a moment. "With all of you, we couldn't get out often." She reached into a bag and pulled out a container of ice cream. "Sam, put this away."

"Chocolate?" he whined.

"We had vanilla last time; this was Cullen's choice." She looked around. "Where is he, anyway? He was supposed to watch Sam."

"Some kid came over," Brady said. "They went out for pizza. A guy named Kyle. I wasn't going anywhere, so I told him it was okay. Didn't you and Dad ever go out?"

Mary shrugged. "Too poor and too swamped with kids. But your father loved being with people, so sometimes we'd entertain at home. Nothing fancy. People would bring wine and beer, we'd play cards and talk. It was usually faculty or students from whatever school he was teaching at and some of the girls I worked with." She crossed her arms and leaned against the kitchen table. "Your father was an incorrigible matchmaker. He loved trying to set up my friends with his grad students or unmarried colleagues."

"What's a colleague?" Sam asked.

"Someone you work with," Mary said. "And don't eat more than two donuts, okay? I'm counting, Sam."

"Did any of the matches ever work?"

"No, but he kept trying. He was a hopeless romantic." She shot Brady a look. "I doubt, though, if he'd be so romantic once his own daughter was old enough—barely old enough—to—"

"Who's that?" Sam said as he bolted to the front when the doorbell chimed.

Mary watched him leave. Brady said, "Old enough to what?"

Mary, leaning to look toward the front door, said, "Be in love. Oh my goodness. It's Sally."

Brady reached Sally two steps ahead of her mother. She stopped short and set her fists on her hips. "What are you doing here?"

Sally said, "Hi to you too. Did you see what we missed, Brady? Did you read about Woodstock? Half a million people and the best music ever." She shrugged off her backpack and set it on the floor.

"I thought you were being held captive up at your cabin," Mary said.

Sally turned to Sam. "At least *you're* glad to see me, aren't you?"

He beamed. "Want to hear a joke? It's Mom's favorite. Of course, she loves any nun jokes." He made a face. "Darn. I gave it away."

Brady hugged Sally. "I am glad to see you. Just surprised."

"Do your parents know you're here?" Mary said suspiciously.

Sally sighed and ran a hand through her hair.

Mary gasped and grabbed the hand. "Sally—" She stopped herself, then turned to her son. "Sam, would you go and finish putting away the groceries and then maybe bring us some lemonade? I bet Sally's thirsty."

"That would be nice, Sam," Sally said.

What's going on? Brady wondered as her friend and her mother stared at each other, one tightly holding the hand of the other.

As soon as Sam was making noise in the kitchen, Mary said, "These are cigarette burns on your hand, Sally. Almost healed, but I can still tell. I've seen plenty. Who did this?"

Brady felt her heart drop. She stepped forward to look just as Sally freed her hand and stuffed it into a pocket.

"I'm fine," Sally said. "Nothing much happened."

"Did one of those guys do it?" Brady asked.

"Let's just say that even though I spent one night in an Ohio jail, and even though I missed the musical and social event of the century, and even though I have spent the last week a prisoner of my very pissed-off parents, I'm not all that sorry you ratted me out. Can we leave it at that?"

Brady tipped her head. "*She* ratted you out."

"I don't really care who did. I just need to know if it's okay if I crash here for a night or two. I can sleep on the sofa."

Mary said again, "Do your parents know you're here?"

"They don't. They went sailing with Paul this afternoon—taking all the car keys with them, the sly devils—and I left. Hitchhiked. Made it all the way from the cabin in just three rides." Sally pasted on a smile. "Feel free to call them. You probably want to try the house first, though, because I bet as soon as they realized I was gone, they packed up and came home."

Mary stiffened. "There's an extra bed in Brady's room. As long as she agrees, you're welcome to stay with us. But, Sally, please don't put me in the middle of whatever is going on between you and your parents. You call them. Excuse me now; I'm going to help Sam."

Brady waited until her mother was out of sight, then she led Sally out the front door.

"Are you kicking me out?"

Brady said, "Sit down." They sat on the top step.

Sally hugged her knees and dropped her head on her arms. "I screwed that up, didn't I? She's steamed."

"Yup. But she'll cool down."

"Is it okay if I stay for a while?"

Brady thought, It's probably the last thing we need. Things are upside down already. Would having her here send them out of control? "It's fine. But why us? I'm sorry, that sounds like I'm whining."

Sally straightened. "I know what you mean. I have other friends, but their lives, or their parents', are all tangled up with mine. I'm not running away, you know. You've got to understand that much. I'm leaving my old life behind."

"Not possible," Brady said.

"We'll see. At the very least I'm leaving the house and letting go of all the plans that have been written in stone since the day I was born."

"You're not going to college in Connecticut?"

"That's the first thing I'm not doing. Maybe I'll go to the U. I can't say for sure what will happen next, but what's wrong with that? I'm so glad, though, that you were home. It would have been too scary getting here and finding just your mom." Her eyes narrowed and a slight smile appeared. "So what's up with you and Mark-man? Paul said you two were in deep. Well, okay, that's my interpretation of what he said."

"Why does Paul think he knows anything about Mark and me?"

"He called him a couple times. They've got plans to hear some bands before Paul leaves for school. My brother was also trying persuade him to take a break and come up to the lake for a couple of nights. Mostly I think he wanted help cutting and stacking firewood."

"Mark's working two jobs; he can't afford to take any breaks." She watched a bird land on a nearby birch tree. "By the way, just so you don't think I'm entirely hopeless," she said, pointing, "that's a cardinal."

Sally patted her hand. "The evil teacher would be proud. What was her name?"

"Mrs. Bronson. So, how is Paul?" She furtively glanced at Sally, trying to read on her face any sign that her brother had talked about the night at the professor's.

"Fine. Busy ingratiating himself with my parents by playing the perfect son. You're very good at changing the subject, Brady, but I'm just as good at changing it back. Why is Mark working on a Saturday night when he could be chasing you around the Willoughbys' house?"

Paul must not have said a thing. "You are spoiled, Sally," she said cheerfully. "A lot of people in the world work weekend nights. He's marking stock at a warehouse most mornings, which he thought gave him time for a second job until classes start. He got a campus job—parking lot attendant. There's a big concert at Northrop tonight; he gets extra pay."

"Two jobs. Must cut into your social life."

"We have no social life." Brady felt her breath slow. Don't do it, don't say a thing, she thought. She blurted, "Just a sex life."

Sally drew her breath in sharply, then let it out in a high-pitched sound. She pounded Brady's shoulder. "I am astounded."

"That was a really weird noise. You sounded like a demonized cat," Brady said. "And why should you be astounded? We're human. We like each other."

"Oh, stop. I bet you're wild about each other. No, Brady, I'm not astounded by the fact it's happened." She pounded on her again. "Just that you actually told me!"

"That might have been a mistake."

The screen door creaked. Brady turned around slowly and saw her mother.

"Sam's got lemonade set out. And I think he wants to tell Sally a few jokes."

How much had she heard? "Okay."

Sally said, "Sounds great. We'll be inside in just a second. I'm getting details of all the stuff I missed when I was gone."

Mary looked from one girl to the other, then said, "In that case, I'm headed to my room to read. See you both tomorrow."

"I'll call my parents in a minute," Sally shouted after her. She waited until Mary was out of sight, then whispered to Brady, "That was weird, the way she appeared at the wrong moment."

"Believe me, she has this sense about things. Mostly she uses it to detect BS; she is the best in the world at doing that." Brady rose, pulling Sally with her. "You've been warned."

2

Brady was rinsing dirty dishes when everyone in St. Bernard's dining hall went still and quiet. She couldn't see the change in activity because her back was turned to the diners. Nor could she hear the change because she had the spray gun going full blast. But out of the corner of her eye she saw that Sally—who'd been loading the large commercial dishwasher—had stiffened and was staring across the serving counter toward the far side of the dining hall.

Sally said something. Brady turned off the spray. "What?"

"I can't believe he did this. We had a deal. I can't believe he did this."

"Did what?" Brady wiped her hands on her apron. Sally's face was pinched and dark with rage.

"When I called them last night, they said they'd leave me alone, but now they've sent someone after me. I know that guy, the one who looks like a cop. I'm sure he's one of my dad's errand boys." She pulled off her apron, flung it on the floor, and charged out of the kitchen.

Brady watched her race into the dining hall. When she spotted Sally's target, Brady took off. She caught up just as her friend was about to accost Special Agent Blake. Brady grabbed Sally's arm and said, "Cool down. He's probably here for me."

As she led the agent from the dining hall, Brady said, "I was hoping you'd forgotten about us." The door closed behind them, and the lunch hour noise returned to normal volume.

"That would be hard to do. Your mother is persistent. Unusual, really.

Most families in your situation avoid contact with our office. Your mother initiates it."

Contact? More like harassment, Brady thought, recalling her mother's belligerence on the phone whenever she hounded the FBI for information. "Why did you come here?"

"To see you, Miss Callahan."

"Why couldn't it wait? I'm working and, as you probably saw, it's disruptive to have the FBI walk into the middle of things. It's intimidating."

"You don't seem the least bit intimidated, Miss Callahan. You're a lot like your mother."

Brady shook her head. She hadn't meant herself, but others. There were a number of people in the dining hall with reasons to be scared of any type of cop. "I don't mean me." Hearing a door open behind her, she turned. Sally peered around the dining room door.

"Everything's cool," Brady said. "I'll be back in a minute."

Sally walked forward. "It just hit me why you were so familiar. You're the same guy who came to the lake to tell them about Will. Now you bust in here while she's working. Do you enjoy ambushing people? Do you get off on intimidating teenage girls?"

"Stop, Sally," Brady said softly. "If you want to help, go finish in the kitchen."

Sally glared, but left.

"Miss Cooper is protective, isn't she?"

When and why had he bothered to learn Sally's name? Had he been curious after seeing her with the family last summer at the resort? Or had she come into view once she'd started hanging out at St. B.'s? Either way, Brady knew she didn't dare tell Sally that she'd been mentioned by name. "Miss Cooper," she said, "doesn't like strong-arm tactics."

Agent Blake opened his briefcase and pulled out a sheaf of wrinkled papers. "I'm not here to strong-arm anyone. I brought you something. It arrived in our office yesterday and I thought you and your mother might like to see it."

Deserter Times. Brady took the newsletter. There was another article on the first page with Will's name. She scanned it silently. "The dynamics of Hegelian philosophy require—" She shook her head. "You have to believe me, Mr. Blake—thoughts about Hegelian philosophy never entered my brother's head. He's not writing these articles. My mother doesn't think so either." She offered the *Times* back.

"She might want to see it."

"Then you'll have to give it to her, because I won't."

He dropped it into his briefcase. "Perhaps I'll stop by your house later and do that."

Brady said, "It's a free country."

Two volunteers had taken over in the kitchen. Brady went looking for Sally.

"Upstairs," Dee said. "Tom opened the library for some people. About time, don't you think? I mean, there's no reason we can't have Bernie's After Dark during the day too. Say, can you help with Bitch and Gripe this afternoon?"

Brady nodded. Of course. She always helped when asked. Always said yes, always showed up.

Halfway up the stairs she leaned against the wall. Closed her eyes and slowed her breathing into a steady rhythm. Why didn't she have a normal job? Waitress, babysit, work in a library. Yes, shelving books in some library would be simple and nice. She pressed her cheek against the cool wall.

A piercing shriek shot up the stairwell. It was followed by the ringing clatter of dishes hitting the dining hall floor.

It would be quiet in a library.

Sally and several others were seated around a table in the church library. Brady recognized Brian from Purple House. He tapped two fingers to his forehead in a mock salute.

A young woman shouted, "Come join us." Brady shook her head and waited in the hall as Sally excused herself from the group. She heard Brian say something to the others, who all laughed.

"What's up?" Sally said.

"I was just wondering where you'd gone to."

"Is the FBI bastard gone?"

"Calm down. He was just doing his job. Look, I've got a couple more hours I have to put in here, then I could go check out those apartments with you."

"I don't think I need to." Sally tipped her head toward the group in the library. "They say there's room in Purple House."

Brady groaned. "You don't want to live there."

"It's not the same as before. They threw out the hard-core partiers. They're turning it into a real cooperative." She crossed her arms. "I don't need your approval, Brady."

"I'm not saying you do. It's just that Mark hated it there, that's all."

"It's different now."

Brady sincerely doubted if a party house could change character in two weeks, but she swallowed the thought. Sally seemed so defiant. "When are you moving in?"

"A day or so. I need to get stuff together."

"Will you be staying with us tonight?"

"If it's still okay. I'll wait around and go back with you."

"Fine. If you're hanging around all afternoon, though, there are things you could do to be useful." Right away she wished the words back.

Sally's face hardened. "On second thought, I'll just see you back at your house, okay?"

Brady resisted the impulse to grab her hand and pull her away from the library. As she turned to leave, she glanced back at the people around the table. Brian caught her eye and he shot her a final victorious smirk. His hand slid across Sally's shoulders as she sat down at his side.

Brady worked late. There were people waiting for hours at Bitch and Gripe, there were questions to answer and letters to write, and when she and Dee finally said good-bye to the last person, there were vegetables to clean and peel.

She tore at them angrily—five pounds, ten pounds, twenty and more. Volunteers came in, started to speak, and she cut them off angrily: "Does it look like I need help?"

Father Tom came into the kitchen, pressed his hands on her shoulders, and said, "Go home. I only pay you for six hours a day, not nine. Go home."

"I can't. There's stuff to do, Tom, there's so much work to do."

"Of course there are things to do; more than will ever be done. Go home."

Two doors from her house Brady stopped walking and stared. There—the aging Volvo planted in their driveway, solid and square, chosen after her father's death for its promise of safety. There—her mother's bedroom window, dark now but in a few hours the light would be on and would stay on late into the night. There—Cullen's bike lying on the grass, left in haste or indifference before he charged noisily into the house. There—the three hydrangeas her mother had planted last fall as Will paced behind her, joking and smoking and making Mary laugh as she put the plants in the ground.

There—home.

A car, a window, a bike, plants with pink blossoms. Mundane details in a snapshot: *American Street, 1969.*

Why did everything, *everything,* tear at her heart?

3

Brady slipped off her sandals, leaving them by the pile of shoes just inside the kitchen door. "I'm shocked."

"Don't be," Sally said "You told me to make myself useful, so I have. Cullen, the moment you get it all in the water, start the timer; fresh pasta shouldn't cook for too long."

Brady made a slow reconnoiter of the kitchen. Cullen was dropping funny-looking noodles into boiling water, Sam was carefully slicing cucumbers for a salad, her mother was studying the label of a wine bottle.

Mary said, "We almost didn't wait for you. It's going on seven."

"Sorry. It smells really good. I can't believe you did this, Sally."

"What I can't believe, Sally," Mary said, still transfixed by the wine, "is that you were able to walk into a liquor store and buy something."

"It's all in the attitude," Sally said. "Open it."

Mary shook her head. "I don't like to drink by myself."

Cullen whispered to the two girls, "So why is there all that beer in the fridge?"

Brady said to Sally, "Your brother said you were a good cook. To be honest, I'm kind of surprised."

"Why? Only half of me is spoiled Midwestern Wasp princess. The other is pure east coast Italian. Oh, yes, Miss Ireland, I can cook. Cullen, stir the sauce, please, and lower the heat under the pasta." She stepped behind Mary and rubbed her shoulders. "Go ahead and live dangerously, open the wine."

Brady thought, How easy it is for her. She touches, she talks, she makes us laugh. And all I can do is stand here with my hands glued to my sides. Not even one day in the house and she's lifted more weight from my mother than I have in years. All I ever do is think of new things to worry about. All I—

Doorbell. "Oh damn," Brady said. "It's Agent Blake. He came to the center today to talk and said he'd probably stop by here tonight."

Sally turned from Mary's chair. "The guy is such a prick." The boys giggled until they saw that she was furious. "You should have seen him play the intimidator this afternoon."

Brady said, "Sally, please don't get so riled."

Mary saw the same thing in Sally's face that Brady did. She rose from her chair and grabbed her just as she was about to rush to the door. "You're a dear, but this is our business, not yours."

"It's all of our business," Sally said angrily as she broke loose and walked out of the kitchen. "I am so tired of thugs and their intimidating power plays. This time I'm going to tell that son of a bitch what I think of him."

Brady rushed past her mother, wrapped her arms around Sally, and tried to hold her in place. Sally plowed forward, towing Brady behind her until they tumbled to the floor and rolled, wrestling all the way to the door.

Mary walked past them, shaking her head. She pushed them out of the way with a foot, unlocked the door, and pulled it open.

Sally looked up and said, "Oh, shit."

A woman peered in through the screen. She saw the girls on the floor and said, "Hello, dear."

"Is that your mother?" Brady said to Sally.

Cullen called from the kitchen, "Timer went off!"

Sam shouted, "How do you cut up an avocado?"

Mary said, "Good, another adult; now I'll open that wine."

They called each other Mrs. Cooper and Mrs. Callahan for about two minutes, then something clicked, and Brady and the others sat back while Mary and Sylvia got acquainted.

This can't be happening, Brady said to herself for the hundredth time as she ate. She tried catching Sally's eye, but either she was avoiding contact or she was off somewhere in her own head. She must have been partly tuned in to the chatter, though, because once or twice Brady saw her grimace at something her mother said.

Childbirth, breast-feeding, neighbors, the war, sons, daughters, gardening—the women covered it all in a landslide of conversation, making no effort whatsoever to be discreet or include anyone else.

Brady noticed Cullen furtively watching Mrs. Cooper, who was shapely, beautifully dressed, and drop-dead gorgeous. Sally's mother radiated va-va-voom, and Cullen was trying his best to take it all in without being spotted.

Sam was oblivious to everyone; when they'd first sat down, he'd told his newest joke and then focused on shoveling in food.

Brady saw her mother tap Mrs. Cooper's hand as they laughed about something. How did she do it? One of the richest women in the state, maybe even the country, drops in for dinner and her mother was totally cool about it.

Sally, however, wasn't feeling cool about anything. She obviously needed cheering up. Brady said to her, "This pasta is incredible. I can't cook anything that comes close to being this good."

Cullen made a noise in agreement.

"And the sauce is nothing like what we're used to." She spoke in a whisper, but Sally's mother picked it up and started telling a story about when she was nineteen and went to work in an uncle's restaurant.

"Oh, the drama!" she exclaimed. "We all have to rebel, of course, and that was my shot. A pretty good one too. My parents were dour academics and they were appalled that their only child would drop out of college and go to work in a place with red-checked tablecloths and candles in wine bottles. The shame of the stereotype!" She sipped wine. "My husband's rebellion trumped mine, though. He's the first Cooper to vote for a Democrat."

"I can top you both," Mary said as she refilled their wineglasses. "I ran away from a convent." Brady sat back and watched them convulse in obnoxious laughter.

When they tapped glasses—To rebellion!—and drank, Sally pushed away from the table and left the room.

Brady also rose. She said to the women, "Don't let us stop you. You're having such fun."

She joined Sally on the front step.

"Rebellion," Sally snapped. "What a trite word. It doesn't even come close to what I'm thinking and feeling."

"It sure got weird in there," Brady said. "Not that your mom isn't nice."

"She is nice, that's the sad thing. She's an incredibly good person who's been sucked into a way of life that's thoroughly corrupt. Our life is so seductive, so soul-sucking seductive."

Brady closed her eyes and recalled the comforting warmth she'd felt in the luxurious house, surrounded by the paintings, the music, the lapping lake water. She opened her eyes. Sally was turned toward her, face tight with anger. "I'm sure it is," Brady said. "I'm sure that it can suck you into the wrong place and make it easy to do the wrong thing."

Sally nodded. "All the material stuff that strokes you and woos you and numbs you. All of it designed to make you forget that the life you lead and the people you live with are slowly raping and destroying the world."

"Sally, you're talking like . . ." Like a freshly-minted radical. "Like you're angry. Like we all are."

"I'm not just goofing off at the center, Brady. I talk with the people who come there for help. I've met so many interesting people and heard so many sad stories." She lifted Brady's hand and kissed it. "As if I need to tell you. Know who I talked with today? Maybe that's why I'm so nuts tonight."

Brady shook her head. Let her go, she thought. Let her get it all out.

"A couple of sisters from North Dakota. The Blumens, you must know them. But did you know that their family farmed the same two hundred acres for three generations until they couldn't compete with the huge corporate wheat farms? Do you know who owns those corporate farms? Do you know who sets the low grain prices that bankrupt the small farms? Do you know who then comes in and pays rock-bottom dollar for the land when the families are forced to sell? Cooper Ag International."

"But you said your family, your dad at least, wasn't part of the company anymore. Don't take on guilt that's not yours."

"He's not involved, but that doesn't mean we aren't guilty, because there's still a direct pipeline from the company to our pockets." She watched a mosquito land on her knee and totter around looking for a place to tap in. She slapped it. "It's not just the family business that I hate. Do you know what else comes with the seductive, diseased package? People. Have you ever heard of Harry Wilcox? Three-star army general and Dad's best friend in the world. Harry was one of JFK's top advisors. LBJ listened to him too. Harry is one of the geniuses who came up with the idea that if we fight communism in Vietnam we save the world. My dad's prep school roommate, Paul's goddam godfather, is one of the reasons there are half a million guys in Vietnam. One of the other reasons is my father, of course. All the spineless congressmen who rolled over and let the war happen? My dad finds the money that gets them elected and reelected. That's what he does, you know. He's a lawyer who never opens a law book. He arranges things. Elections. Wars. Finding his daughter on the interstate highway."

"You make him sound so evil, Sally."

Sally snapped off the tip of a branch. She brushed it against her palm, then peeled it in two and tossed it on the grass. "He's not. He's like my mom: basically good, but sucked in so deep, he can't tell right from wrong anymore. It's their acceptance of the corrupt life they lead that drives me crazy. Their silent complicity." Her head dropped. "My grandmother, Dad's mother, has a winter place in Florida. You know who has the estate next to hers? The chairman of Dow Chemical. Napalm, Brady. Every Easter I'm expected to dress up and have brunch with Mr. Napalm."

"Jesus," Brady whispered.

"I have to do something to break free before it sucks the soul out of me. That's what's happening to Paul. I know that's why he's drowning himself in drugs and alcohol the way he does. I'm scared of what might happen to me. I can't be part of it. I have to escape." She turned and faced Brady. "With all that's gone on in your life, how can you be so rock solid?"

"You really think I am? I must be a pretty good actress."

"I should go apologize to your mother."

"Why? Because you bought a ton of groceries and cooked an amazing meal? And if she passes out from drinking all that wine you bought illegally, it's still nothing you have to apologize for."

"No one's passing out," Sally's mother said as she pushed open the screen door. "We only drank one bottle."

"Hi, Mrs. Cooper," Brady said. "Leaving?" She stood. Sally remained sitting on the step, staring out at the street.

"Yes. I never meant to stay this long. I certainly didn't mean to ambush the family at dinner. But as it turned out I'm glad I did and I'm very glad I've met you, Brady. Both Sally and Paul have spoken so highly of you. And please, call me Sylvia."

Oh no, Brady thought. You're not making me into a buddy. She held the door, ready to slip inside.

Sally's mother wasn't finished. She smoothed the front of her dress and smiled. "I've meddled plenty already tonight, but I can't stop myself sometimes, and here I go again."

Sally made a noise. Brady prodded her with a foot.

"When I left home to come here, the boys were debating how much trouble Mark would be in for not calling you tonight. Apparently it's his first night off in some time."

"The boys?" Brady said slowly, not quite getting the picture.

"Mark and Paul. Your young man's a very nice person."

My young man, Brady thought, her eyes frozen on the woman, her mind spinning.

Sally made another noise, then said, "Her young man's gonna be a dead young man." She stood before Brady's foot reached her.

Mrs. Cooper said, "Paul picked him up earlier today. They've been helping Sally's father with some projects around the house and then they planned to go out. I believe they're going band-chasing tonight in St. Paul." She smiled brightly. "As a favor to me, please don't be mad at Mark. Paul leaves soon for school. Mark seems to be good company for him." She turned and peered back into the house, then she took Brady's elbow. "One question," she said softly.

Brady held her breath. What else could the woman possibly spring on her now?

"Does your mother date? We have this friend—"

Brady gasped. "What?"

Sally swatted the bush near her. "Holy crap, Mom, I don't believe you!"

Brady said, "Date? My mother?"

Mrs. Cooper smiled. "Don't be so shocked, dear." She turned to Sally. "You calm down too. I think Mary and Jed Webster would be perfect together, don't you? Still, I know things aren't too settled right now, so before I rushed in, I thought I'd ask."

"You never stop and think before you rush in and mess with people's lives," Sally said. "I can't imagine what made you want to start now."

Brady said, "She doesn't date. Hasn't ever since my dad died, at least that I know about."

Sally turned away from her mother. "Really? That's weird. You'd think the guys would be swarming over her."

Brady ignored her. "And with all that's going on now, I'd be surprised if she wanted to."

"Not even once?" Sally said. "It can't be because guys haven't asked."

Brady sighed. "You two probably want to talk. I'll disappear. Good night, Mrs. Cooper. And don't worry about Mark. I don't keep him on a leash."

"Please," Mrs. Cooper said again, "call me Sylvia."

Brady closed both doors when she went inside.

"Are you locking them out?"

Brady glanced over her shoulder. Her mother, full wineglass in hand, stood smiling in the kitchen doorway. "No. I just think a girl should be able to yell at her mother in private. Where are the guys?"

"Backyard."

"Do you think Mrs. Cooper should be driving?"

"Maybe not, but that's okay because she isn't. She called a cab. She's meeting her husband at his office and she'll go home with him."

"How did she get here?"

Mary pulled a chair out from the never-used dining room table and sat down. "We should eat in this room more often."

"Right, Mom—we're so into being formal. And where would we put all the junk that we dump on the table?"

Mary ran her fingers across the spines of a stack of library books. "Your room, for starters." She picked up the top book. "*Masterpieces of the Louvre*. I didn't know you were interested in art." She dropped the book back on the table. "Sylvia is leaving a car for Sally. She doesn't want her hitchhiking, so today she bought one for her and drove that in."

"Oh, no," Brady moaned. "She'll be so pissed."

"That doesn't make sense. She's getting a new car. If that pisses her off, she's nuts. I wish I could piss you off that way. Would you mind cleaning up the kitchen? I'm going to take a bath and go to bed."

"It's only eight-thirty."

"I have an early meeting."

Just as her mother reached the stairs, Brady said, "Mrs. Cooper has some guy she wants you to meet. She thinks you and he would be perfect together."

As her hand was about to grab the banister, Mary froze. After a second she started laughing. "Those two are so obviously alike. Sweet meddlers, both of them. What did you say?"

"That you don't ever date. And I guessed that because of stuff going on right now you probably wouldn't feel like it."

Mary sat on the bottom step, looking amused. "Oh really? 'Stuff going on' hasn't stopped you, has it?"

Brady flushed. "I'm sorry, Brady. That was the wine talking." Mary dropped her head and rubbed her brow. "And you're absolutely right. I couldn't possibly date now. Not the way I am these days. Not with things the way they are."

Voices outside rose to an audible level. Mary said, "Either we intervene or disappear completely. I vote for the latter."

Brady stepped closer to the large front window. Her mother followed. They both peered out just as a cab pulled up to the curb and Sally flung a set of car keys across the yard.

Brady put her arm around her mother and said, "I told you so."

4

Brady propped herself up on an elbow and watched Sally undress. "Use the car for good and not evil," she said.

Sally wiggled her hips. "So now you're interested in my body? What's happened to change that?"

"I'm not interested." Brady rolled onto her back and stared at the ceiling. "You turn everything into sex. I figure you do it for the shock value. Are you trying to get attention or are you trying to deflect it?"

Sally pulled on a T-shirt and sat on the edge of the spare bed. "Have you figured out yet what you want to do with your life? I think you'd be a very good psych nurse. Whoa—is that an angry blush or an embarrassed blush? Never mind—I think I know."

Brady pressed her lips, holding back all the things she thought she might spill out.

I haven't figured out a single damn thing.

I almost slept with your brother.

Shut up, Sally.

She said tersely, "I plan to go to medical school. Want a beer? I feel like a beer. I don't think Mom would mind."

By the time Sally caught up with her in the kitchen, Brady had opened two beers and was sitting at the table, scratching the label off an already half-empty bottle.

"Med school?" Sally said. "Really?"

Brady shrugged. "That's the plan. So tell me about this guy who would be perfect for my mother. She's not interested, by the way; I was right about that. Still, I'm curious."

"I have to hand it to Sylvia; she's absolutely right on this. Jed's one of the good people in their life. He's not a political or country club friend. He's an architect, he designed our house. Ah, now you like him, I can tell. He's divorced. He teaches at the U part-time. Very sexy, in a rumpled sort of way. Your mom should at least meet him."

"She said no." She blinked away an image of her mother embracing a faceless, rumpled man. "I think she means it. I wonder where Mark and Paul are."

"Hey, that's an idea. It's early. We could take my new car and go find them."

Brady rolled the bottle between her palms. "There must be dozens of bars or clubs with live music in St. Paul; we'd never find them. I don't really want to, I was just wondering. And even if I did feel up to it, we couldn't because you threw away the keys. I saw you do it; it was terribly dramatic."

Sally turned on her heels and left the kitchen. Brady heard her go upstairs. After a couple of minutes she heard her brothers tear down the steps and go out the front door. Just as it slammed, Sam shouted, "I don't want to hold the flashlight."

When Sally returned, Brady said, "If they wake up my mother, I'll kill you all."

Sally paled. "I didn't think about that."

Brady pointed at the second bottle. "Are you going to drink that?"

"Help yourself."

"She's probably awake anyway. Most nights she stays up playing solitaire. Did you bribe them into getting out of bed and hunting for your keys?" Sally nodded. "How much?"

"Five bucks."

"Don't you realize what you're doing?"

"What am I doing, Brady?"

"Paying other people to do your unpleasant work." She blew twice across the neck of the bottle. The hollow noise was loud in the still kitchen. "Your personal revolution might be harder than you think."

"Small steps."

"Some backward." Brady rose and stretched. Too damn tired, she thought. I want to sleep for days. Fat chance, though. St. B.'s will be crazy tomorrow.

"You're a clear-eyed soul, Brady."

Brady looked at the two empty bottles. Not at the moment.

"I'm the owner of a brand-new car that cost more money than some people have to live on for an entire year. How, exactly, do I use it for good and not evil?" Sally's voice sounded as hollow as the bottle noise.

Brady heard the boys come back into the house. She quickly tossed the bottles into the trash. "Well, for starters, you can drive me to work in the morning. Let's leave at nine."

5

Something about the way they were standing. Secrets, Brady thought as she spun around and tried to leave the classroom without being seen by Sally and the other girl. Back in the hallway she set down the box of flyers on a chair.

Dee raced by. "Ambulance is coming," she said to Brady as she passed. "Mrs. Salisbury went nuts during the crocheting class. I left seven senior volunteers in the kitchen. Could you go show them around?"

"I was supposed to be out of here an hour ago. I have to go buy textbooks before the store closes."

Dee waved her arms over her head. "Thank you!"

"I thought I was saying no," Brady muttered.

The classroom door opened and Sally and the girl came out. The girl turned abruptly and walked away. Sally called, "Jane, I need the keys." A set of keys came flying past Sally's head. Brady caught them. "Come back here," Sally said. "I want you to meet Brady."

The girl looked over her shoulder as she kept on walking. "Hi." She turned the corner and disappeared.

"One of your housemates?" Sally nodded. "You loaned her the car?"

"I'm not possessive. She was doing errands for the house."

"Are you settled in? It's been a week."

"More or less."

"Feels like I haven't seen you in ages. I keep hearing you're around, but it's like you're a phantom."

"Father Tom has had stuff for me to do. Running errands, mostly."

"I told you the car would be useful."

"If escorting old ladies to the foot doctor is useful, then yes."

Brady picked up the box and carried it into the room.

"Are we still on for dinner?"

"Yes, but can we go to the U first? I have to buy books."

"When are you done here?"

"An hour ago."

"Let's go now."

Brady imagined the seven senior volunteers waiting patiently in the kitchen. Surely someone would eventually find them. She shook her head. "I have to do something first."

Sally made an impatient noise. "They take advantage of you here. They pay you next to nothing and expect way too much. Jane says the church oppresses—"

Brady held up a hand. "Two things, Sally. First, apparently Father Tom now has his charismatic claws in you and you're serving the church for no pay whatsoever, so you can hardly talk. Second, I don't want to hear what your pal Jane says. I'm not interested in secondhand revolutionary chatter. Give me ten minutes. I'll meet you in the parking lot."

Sally was talking with Brian and Jane in the parking lot when Brady finally escaped the kitchen and the seven volunteers. Jane held out her hand to shake as Brady approached.

"Sorry I was such a bitch back there. I spoke to a group over at Macalester College this afternoon and it turned into a ridiculous scene. I spent the entire afternoon getting hassled by some privileged eighteen-year-old morons. I was letting off steam with Sally and didn't feel like being nice right then. But it's good to finally meet you."

Eighteen-year-old morons. Brady shook the girl's hand. What was she—twenty, twenty-one?

"I wish you'd join us at the house sometime. I've heard a lot about you. We're planning a few actions for the fall and I'd love to have your input."

"Actions?"

"Civil disobedience. Civil disruptions."

Brian said, "Bring Soldier Boy. I sort of miss the old killer."

Brady pivoted, took a step, and slapped him. She turned back to Jane. "I don't think so." She walked around to the passenger door and got in. She drummed on the dash and stared at the threesome. Brian and Jane walked away. After a moment, Sally followed, saying something in a low, angry voice. Then she pulled money out of her pocket and handed Jane a wad of bills.

"What was the bet?" Brady asked when Sally got in the car. "Whether or not he could make me turn violent?"

Sally clenched the steering wheel. "We're having pamphlets printed to give out on campus when classes start next week. That money was to pay the printer."

"They're going to suck you dry."

"That's my choice, isn't it? Look, I'm furious about what he just said." She put the car in gear, and raced out of the parking lot. Car horns blared as they sped onto the street.

"Sally, I have to tell you that if you're sleeping with the bastard, I don't ever want to know about it."

"I'm not. Never have. I was kind of attracted to him at first, a long time ago, but my eyes are open now. The others in the house aren't like him, Brady; you have to believe that."

Brady touched Sally's arm gently. "Slow down."

"He and Jane are sort of together, I'm sad to say. Though Jane says—" She caught herself. "We aren't into exclusive relationships in the house. You can't be committed to a purpose if you're hung up on a person."

Sounds like a bumper sticker, Brady thought. "She doesn't seem very happy."

"What's there to be happy about these days? Forty thousand American dead in Vietnam, famine in Biafra—"

"And so on. I get your point."

Sally floored the accelerator and Brady rocked back and forth as the car sped along. "Your brother's a bad driver too. You'll kill me before I even start college."

Sally slowed down. "I'm glad I'm not starting college. I'm learning tons just by living at Purple House."

Brady said, "If you could promise I wouldn't run into the SOB I just slapped, maybe I would stop by."

Sally tapped the steering wheel. "You could meet Jerome, then. You'd like him. He's premed at the U too. A junior. He'd probably tell you to study something else. Sometimes we . . ." She shrugged.

"Nothing exclusive, though."

"No. We just keep each other company at night. In a way he reminds me of a grown-up Sam."

"How so?"

"He's happy and sweet." She turned into a U parking lot. "And he tells really bad jokes."

6

As she wrote out the check, Brady felt her stomach knot. Seventy-five dollars. She was definitely broke. Two weeks until the next payday, Mark's birthday was tomorrow and she hadn't bought him a present, she had maybe ten dollars in her wallet, and there was no way she'd ask her mother for money. At least Sally was treating her to dinner.

Sally stood beside her at the counter. She picked up the small maroon and gold pennant lying on the stack of textbooks. "I wouldn't have guessed you'd be such a rah-rah freshman."

"It's for my grandmother. Pretty corny, but she'll get a kick out of it. She's thrilled I'm doing premed. She could only be more thrilled if I were entering a convent or getting married and producing good Catholic children. Given the circumstances, she's making herself feel happy about her only granddaughter becoming a doctor."

"Brady, I don't figure you for a doctor."

"Why not?" She nodded at the clerk and took the bag of books.

"Well, okay, maybe I can. It's just that the few times you've mentioned it lately, you haven't seemed happy."

Brady said, "I'm happy."

Outside, Sally paused to read the leaflets and posters stapled to a bulletin board. She tapped one. "This talk tomorrow looks good. Want to go?"

"'Military Draft: Modern Slavery,'" Brady read. "Thanks, but no. It could be interesting, but it's Mark's birthday." She pointed at a different flyer.

Sally said, "No way. I've seen one Ingmar Bergman movie and it was so depressing. Mom dragged Dad and me. He didn't like it either; we have that in common, at least. Besides, it starts at seven and we still have to eat."

Brady shook her head. "What I was going to say is that our mothers are going to it. Together. And it's not their first date. They had lunch on Saturday." She smiled at Sally's stunned look. "Maybe you should check in at home more often." She tugged on Sally's arm. "This way."

"The car's in the other direction."

"One stop before we eat. It's time I show you my favorite place in the world. It's not a hidden lake or a leechy bog, but I love it."

"Isn't this a great view?" Brady said. "Especially now that the campus is so deserted. I bet there are more squirrels than students."

Sally sat at one of the study carrels and looked out the third-floor window. "Your favorite place in the world is a dusty corner in the stacks of an old library. Doesn't that seem a little weird to you?"

Brady gazed out the window. "I love this place. Even if I had the money to go to a different school, I don't think I would. The high school I went to last year is near here, and I'd walk home through the U. It was like a refuge after getting out of that nightmare school. I'd stop here before I went home or to work." She pointed again. "That's the building the students took over last winter for three days."

"Jane was part of that group. She thinks they gave in too easily. She says they should have just blown the place up. Look at all the stuff people have written on this carrel."

"It's fun to read. Some of it's pretty raunchy."

"Whoa—you're right. Must make it hard to study."

Someone had left a leaky Bic pen on the desktop. Brady searched for a clear space and scribbled: *See SC for your revolution's $$ needs.*

Sally grabbed the Bic and went to the next carrel. *BC loves MW.*

Brady grabbed it back. *SC prefers bogs to boys.*

Sally jumped to another carrel. *Canonize BC. She helps the needy and performs miracles with TVs.*

Minutes later a librarian tracked down the laughter and asked them to leave.

7

Sally pushed a mound of potato peelings off the counter into a garbage can. "Do you realize that if we spent half the time and effort working in your kitchen that we put in here, I could turn you into a decent cook?"

Brady smiled as she dumped a handful of sliced carrots into a huge pot. "It's possible. Of course, what we do here isn't exactly cooking because this stuff hardly qualifies as edible."

"Ah, but it's food for the soul," said Father Tom from the doorway. He looked far too cheerful.

"Run fast, Sally," Brady said. "I know that look on his face. It's his 'I need a small favor' look."

"Not so small, I'm afraid, Brady. We've just had confirmation that we're about to receive some visitors and we're having an impromptu meeting tonight. Could I prevail on you to stay and do some extra tasks?"

"Such as?"

While he ran down the list, her heart sank. She wouldn't get home until at least seven.

"She has plans, Father Tom," Sally said. "Mark's taking her to a movie. Classes start Monday and she says it's their last chance for fun. Even I couldn't talk her out of it."

"What's wrong with wanting to keep a date?"

Father Tom said, "Let me tell you what's happening, and perhaps that will persuade you. But it's not to go past these walls, not for a few hours at least."

"Should I leave?" Sally asked. "I'm not staff."

"No, please stay. I'll need you for something else. You're both aware, I'm sure, of St. Bernard's draft counseling efforts. What is not so well known is that part of those efforts is to assist any young man who—like your brother is alleged to have done, Brady—decides he can no long acquiesce to military activity. A small group of army deserters will be arriving later this afternoon. Separately, they've been on the run for several months. But for the last few days they've been traveling together. Some will move on, but others will stay."

Brady stared impassively.

"We're giving them sanctuary in the church. They'll be safe here from the military police. For a few days they'll be free to meet with family and friends and speak with the press before they turn themselves in and face the courts. Tonight is a welcome reception."

Brady said, "I'll do what I can, but only until it's my regular quitting time."

"I'll stay and help," Sally said. Before Tom could answer, Dee burst into the kitchen, surrounded by a noisy band of teen volunteers.

Tom said to Brady, "Don't you at least want to talk with them? They might know something about Will."

"Tom, I think it's great you're doing what you're doing. And I wish them well. But I'm going home. I have a date. I made a promise. Besides, there's nothing those guys can tell me about Will. If you don't mind, I need to finish this soup."

Tom started to say something. He scratched his beard, then smiled. "Sally, let's step outside, away from . . . " He tipped his head toward the volunteers.

Tom and Sally stood for a while outside the kitchen. Sally nodded as he spoke. What now? Brady wondered as she watched them through a window. What not-very-small task was she agreeing to do?

Beyond them was an apartment high-rise. On one high-up floor, tenants had put peace signs in all of the windows. At the far end of the display was a bold-lettered sign: *Stop the killing*. Another not-very-small task.

Father Tom and Sally shook hands. Sally looked toward the kitchen. She blew a kiss to Brady, then jogged toward the parking lot.

The priest met Brady's gaze for a moment. What the hell's going on? she wondered. And why does he look so guilty?

• • •

It was a lousy evening. She hated the movie and hated that Mark loved it. Worse, when they returned to her house, everyone was still up. She hated that he talked to her mother more than to her. He'd bought textbooks that afternoon and was excited about his classes; Mary listened to him patiently, glancing every now and then at her daughter.

When had the evening gone bad? With the movie's opening credits? Mark's first comments? Or when they got back and he'd been, once again, folded into the family?

Why did she suddenly hate that?

When she'd heard enough about his classes and plans, she went to the kitchen for car keys. "Time to go, Mark," she called.

Sam whined. "We were going to watch the weather. Mark said he'd take us hiking by the river Saturday."

Her mother came into the kitchen. "I'll send them to bed after the news," she said softly. Brady sighed and went back into the other room. Cullen turned on the TV. Sam whined again, and told him to change to a different station. Brady spun the keys around a finger and sat on the sofa. Mark plopped beside her, made an apologetic face, and she felt herself melting.

Cullen, changing channels, made kissing sounds. Brady was about to toss a sofa pillow at him when she saw the picture on the screen. "Hold it, that's St. Bernard's."

The reporter was announcing the end of the welcome meeting for the army deserters. He explained the historical background of church sanctuary for lawbreakers, then said that four deserters would be taking sanctuary for an undetermined time at St. Bernard's before giving themselves up to military police. Two others, choosing to flee to Canada, had been spirited away earlier in the evening, driven by person or persons unknown.

Suddenly Brady knew why Tom had looked so guilty that afternoon. She knew why Sally had disappeared, and she knew where she was now: at the wheel of her car, shepherding the two fugitives to safety.

8

Brady peeled off from the stream of students rushing along the campus side-walks between classes. She ran up the library steps, her heavy book bag thumping against her thigh. A badly thrown Frisbee hit the top step just before she did. She grabbed it on the bounce and turned around to loud cheers. Several boys, shirtless in the warm October sun, waved their arms. "Sorry!" someone called. She sent the Frisbee to him, making a long bull's-eye shot above heads, between trees and straight into his hand. A few students lounging on the steps applauded lazily.

"I should be out there, not in here," she said as she walked through the library. But she didn't dare, not with two tests the next day and a chem lab to write up.

The stacks were mostly deserted, and she headed for her usual spot. She hesitated when she spotted a dark head bent over a book in the corner carrel. Sally.

Where the hell have you been? Brady thought. Haven't seen you in over a week and now you pop up here. What have you been up to?

Three days after the deserters had disappeared from the center Sally had shown up at Brady's house. Brady had confronted her.

"Did you have anything to do with them getting away from St. Bernard's?"

Sally sat at the table with the evening paper. She folded it open to the movie section. "Harboring fugitives? That would be a federal offense."

"Of course it would be. I'm glad you know that. Did you do it?"

"Let's go to a movie. Have you seen *The Sterile Cuckoo*? This D. H.

Lawrence thing might be good, but maybe you want to see it with Mark. Supposed to be steamy. How's his new place, by the way?"

"Sally, answer my question."

Sally looked up and Brady sat back, startled by the cool anger in her friend's eyes.

"Don't ask, Brady. That way you don't have to disapprove of my life and, even better, neither of us has to lie about anything."

Don't ask. Now Brady watched Sally read and thought of the deeper meaning in the warning: That way we can still be friends.

She pulled the book from Sally's hand and dropped it on the carrel. "*A Frontier Teacher's Diary*. Interesting?"

"Interesting enough to kill time until you showed up. I figured you'd come sooner or later. Your mom said you had a heavy test schedule and that you planned to study late."

Brady nodded. "Psych and bio tests tomorrow and I also have to write up a chem lab. When did you talk with my mom?"

Sally looked out the window. "About an hour ago."

"She should still be at work."

"She and my mom were going to do something, so she took off early. A yoga class, can you believe that?"

Brady laughed. "That's right. I think it's great. Hey, if they can go nuts, so can I. Screw the studying. Let's go get something to eat. There's a new pizza joint on Como that supposedly doesn't card—Sally, what's wrong?"

Sally's jaw clenched, then relaxed as she sighed. She turned away from the window. "It's beautiful outside. Almost seventy; that's so weird for October. What are we doing in this dark place?"

Brady said, "I came to study and you came to find me."

"I found you. Let's go."

Outside, Sally linked her arm through Brady's and led her across the mall to a huge oak tree. They passed the Frisbee players, who all shouted at Brady to join their game.

"Friends?" Sally asked.

"Fans," Brady replied.

They sat under the tree. "I'm not getting any less hungry," Brady said. "But I guess you want to talk."

Sally looked out over the mall. "You're right. This is a great place."

"Enroll."

She shook her head back and forth, a wide, slow arc. "No school. That would tie me down. I've been traveling."

"I wondered."

"But you weren't going to ask."

"We agreed."

"Mostly I've been going around and meeting people who . . . help people." She shrugged. "I've been giving away some of my money."

"Nothing wrong with that."

"I saw my brother. I was in New York for a couple of days. He came down from New Haven and met me. Paulie may be juiced up most of the time, but even so, he's a lot smarter than I am."

Brady plucked a blade of grass and carefully split it in two. Sally's stalling, she thought. Something's about to happen. I just have to wait.

"I bluster and rage and whine, but my brother, well, he does something."

"What's he done?"

Sally picked up an acorn and tossed it at a nearby squirrel. It looked up from the cracker it was gnawing. "Before he went back to school, he asked our dad to find out what he could about your brother."

"What could *he* find out?"

"I guess that's what Dad said. But, still, his son had asked, so he made some calls. Got his buddy Harry working on it. One of their ideas was to press army intelligence for any information on the Will Callahan in Saigon."

"And?"

Sally shook her head. "Nothing. Then he started pushing . . ." Her eyes were bright with tears. "Will's dead, Brady. They've got his body . . ." Her voice caught.

"His body?" she whispered.

"It will take some time to get it—him—back to Minneapolis. Your mom is getting the official notice, but not until tomorrow. They told my father first, of course. That's how it works between the old boys when they do favors for each other. Dad didn't want your mom to have to wait even one day longer. He told my mom, she found me at the house, and we went over to your place. I'm so sorry, Brady. God, look at me and look at you. I'm a wreck and you are . . . you."

"You haven't told me everything, have you?"

The Frisbee whizzed by. Both girls turned their heads at the sound.

Sally wiped her cheeks with her palms. "It's not very pleasant."

"I don't suppose it is."

"They think he's been dead almost as long as he's been missing. Last month a couple of Vietnamese civilians led some U.S. soldiers to a grave with a lot of bodies. I guess it wasn't very far from where Will was last seen. Brady, all this will be in the letter your mom gets tomorrow."

"Tell me."

Sally exhaled. "There was nothing left with the bodies to identify them. American soldiers, that's all they knew. Probably captured, then shot. I guess there's some evidence that makes them think that."

"They found the grave a month ago? Why did it take them so long to identify Will?"

"They were convinced he was a deserter, because of those articles. So they didn't try to match his records with . . . what they had."

"My mother tried to convince the Army that he was missing, not AWOL. They wouldn't listen to her. But they listened to your father."

"Yes. Which is outrageous that only insiders get treated right."

Brady squeezed Sally's hand. "No. It's so good he did it. Sally, all that matters is now we know. Oh, God. Did you bring any Kleenex?"

"I didn't. How stupid was that."

"Lucky I wore long sleeves. Would you mind driving me home? We'd better go before our audience gets any bigger. Do you suppose people think we're breaking up?"

Sally rose and held out a hand. "Come on, honey," she said loudly.

Brady took her hand, then fell back. Her head dropped against the tree. Beyond the canopy of oak leaves she saw a single powder puff cloud in the wide blue sky.

This place, she thought. This moment, this friend. Etched forever.

"Oh," she whispered. "Will."

9

The spot where they buried Will was on the side of a hill in a cemetery near one of the city's lakes. As an uncle read a blessing and her younger brothers each read a poem, Brady watched a solitary sailboat skim across the lake, its skipper braving the cold water for a last-chance outing.

Sam finished his reading. Brady fingered the paper in her pocket. Her turn. She shook her head and whispered, "Can't," when her mother looked at her expectantly. Mary nodded. Brady felt Mark's hand rub her back. She leaned against it.

"Well, then," Mary said, "I guess that's it. We should get back to the house. People were invited for one o'clock, and—"

"Mary Rose," Brady's grandmother said sharply. "The flag. They've got to fold the flag. Go ahead, gentlemen."

Brady watched as her mother and grandmother glared at each other across the flag-draped coffin. Grandma Casey, furious that there was no possibility of a religious ceremony, had wanted her grandson at least buried with full military honors. Mary hadn't wanted a military ceremony and had even resisted the presence at the cemetery of the gracious army officer who had escorted Will's remains to Minneapolis. It was Brady who had negotiated the private, poems-and-blessing, one-soldier burial, and had established a tentative cease-fire between her mother and grandmother. "Please," she prayed silently to the chilly October air, "don't let it blow up now."

As Sergeant Nichols and the man from the mortuary stepped forward and began the precision flag-folding, Brady felt her mother stiffen. She took her hand and whispered, "Almost over."

When Sergeant Nichols stood before them offering the folded flag, Mary, grim and unmoving, simply stared at it. Brady reached for the flag and smiled at the soldier. "Thank you, sir," she said. She dared a glance at her grandmother, who gave her a satisfied nod.

Mary dropped her head on Brady's shoulder. "Thank you," she echoed softly.

By the time they returned home from the cemetery, the street in front of the house was lined with cars. Someone had blocked off the driveway with a rope strung between two lawn chairs. Brady pulled up to the rope and stopped. "What's that for?" Sam asked.

"So we'd be sure to have a place to park," Mary said. "Sylvia's idea, I'm sure. She said she'd take care of everything."

"Who's Sylvia?" Grandma Casey asked. "I don't know her."

"One of Mom's friends," said Brady. "A bunch of them are fixing the lunch today. Sam, get out and take down the rope, would you?" She looked toward the house. She could see a crowd in the living room. Two classmates of Sam's ran out the front door and started tossing a football. He hopped out and raced to join them.

Brady rolled down her window and shouted, "Sam, get the chairs." He cleared the driveway for her, then raced across the lawn, waving his arms and calling for the football.

"He'll ruin that lovely new suit," Brady's grandmother said.

"What does it matter, Mother?" Mary said. "He'll outgrow it in a month, anyway."

"He could change."

"We could eat," Brady said cheerfully. "I'm hungry." She got out and opened the back door. "C'mon, Grandma, let's get some food."

"Where is the other car?" her grandmother said. "It was behind us. Do you suppose your uncle's gotten lost again?"

"He was going to let Mark drive, so no, I don't think they're lost. I heard Cullen say they should take the river road. It's beautiful now, with all the fall color."

"I'd like to have done that." She said it matter-of-factly, but her eyes as she looked at her daughter were accusing.

"I had to get home, Mother," Mary said. "We're so late as it is. We'll do it tomorrow."

"I leave tomorrow," Grandma Casey called out as Mary walked toward the house. She rose from the car seat and took Brady's arm. "She knows that, Brady. She's being so difficult. We came all the way from Cleveland, and she's being difficult."

"Grandma, she buried her oldest child today. Go easy on her."

"I'm trying my best."

Brady counted to three, then said, "I know. I'm so glad you're here."

She installed her grandmother in a comfortable spot in the living room. With a surge of relief, she spotted Father Tom in the corner, surrounded by several of the center volunteers. She waved to them all and signaled him over. "This is Father McGann, Grandma. He's the parish priest at St. Bernard's, where I work." Her grandmother beamed and held out a hand.

Brady began to make her way through the crowd. It wasn't a large house, but it was filled with more people than she would ever have believed they could possibly know. They all came at her. She waded through a tar pit of handshakes, hugs, soft murmurs of sorrow, shrieks of grief, words of anger about the senseless war. Neighbors who'd been chilly when they thought Will Callahan was a deserter now shook her hand; a few even wept.

She finally gained the relative calm of the kitchen. Loud chatter and laughter stopped when she walked in. Her mother sat at the table, sipping a glass of wine as a friend from work massaged her shoulders. Another friend poured fresh coffee from a percolator into a silver pitcher. Sylvia struggled with the cork in a wine bottle. Sally stood at the sink washing dishes.

Brady said to her mother, "Can I hide out here too?" She walked to the sink, leaned against the counter, and sighed.

Sally shook suds off her hands, looked around for a towel, then said, "What the hell," and gave her a soapy hug.

"This is so sweet that you and your mom are here doing all this work. It means a lot, Sally."

"My mother," Sally said loud enough for all to hear, "never misses a chance to be in charge of a kitchen, especially someone else's kitchen."

"Oh, hush," said the woman pummeling Mary's shoulders. "If it hadn't been for her the rest of us would never have stopped talking long enough to get anything done."

A cork popped loudly. "Thank you, Dixie," Sylvia said. "Who's for trying this Burgundy?"

Brady lowered her voice. "Did you see the flowers Paul sent? Your family has been so terrific, Sally."

Sally's face darkened. She turned back to the dishes and plunged her hands into the water. "My father should have come today. Claims he had one of his big-deal meetings in Washington. I know he could've cancelled, but he wouldn't."

"He's already managed a miracle for us, Sally. That's more than enough. Besides, he doesn't really know us. I'd like to meet him, but he absolutely didn't have to come today." She glanced up and saw that Sylvia was listening, watching over the rim of a glass that she held to her lips.

"I asked him to. He refused."

"Sally, just for today—just for me—would you not hate him?"

Sylvia said, "Thank you, Brady. I appreciate that. Now if you could persuade my daughter to—"

Brady raised her hand and shot Sylvia a silencing look.

Sally said, "Neat trick. I didn't know anyone could make her—"

"Shut up," Brady said.

"Brady!" Mary said. "I think—" Whatever she thought, no one would hear, because the moment her daughter turned and faced her, Mary went mute.

Brady said to her mother, "All morning—no, for nearly three days—I have been making peace between you and Grandma." She looked at Sally and Sylvia in turn. "Then I get home today after burying my brother and it appears that I'm supposed to fix things between you two." She lifted her hands and pointed at herself. "Keep staring, people. This is what it looks like when you can't take any more."

"Darling," Mary said. "Let's go outside."

Brady brushed past her on the way out of the house. "I'm going, all right." Just as she reached the door, she turned back, opened the fridge, and scooped up a few beer bottles. When she reached the door a second time, she paused and said, "Don't anyone dare come out to talk unless it's to tell me that the last guest is gone." When the screen slammed behind her she paused again. "Thank you, everyone, for all the help with the lunch. It's not the sort of thing Mom and I could pull off."

She sat in a lawn chair, facing away from the house. She put her feet up on a second chair, dropped her head back, and looked up at the sky. High clouds veiled the sun. A single leaf spiraled through the air on a manic journey from tree to ground. She closed her eyes. An animal rustled through leaves.

What would happen next? Would they really leave her alone? All those veteran psych nurses—could they possibly resist this?

No. She heard the screech of the screen door spring stretching, heard the soft thunk as the door closed.

Who's the emissary? Had they pointed fingers, or—more likely—eagerly drawn straws? Maybe they'd found someone else to come make the peace. Mark, perhaps. Yes, that's who it would be, a very good choice.

Something fell into her lap and tapped against a bottle.

"I'm not here to bug you," Sally said. "Your mom thought you might want that."

Brady looked down. A bottle opener. "Has Mark made it back yet?"

"I'll go look."

Brady reached behind the chair and grabbed Sally's skirt. "Stay," she said after a moment.

"Are you sure?"

Brady nodded. After her friend had settled into another chair, she said, "I guess that was a pretty good exit."

"Even I couldn't have done better. And coming from you—wow."

"Things have been building. And it just sort of blew."

"That's how it happens."

Brady pulled up one foot and turned sideways in her chair. "I can't keep grinding along, Sally. Obediently, quietly grinding along. Always being the good girl. Always fixing things."

"Who said that you have to?"

"True. No one but me." Brady opened a bottle, took a drink, and made a face. "Mom buys the lousiest beer." She poured it onto the grass.

"I'm sorry for that scene with my mother. I'm sorry I've pulled you into our family soap opera."

"Any other day but today I'd have played along." She added to herself, I'd have fixed it.

Sally drew up her knees and hugged them. "Brady, I have to tell you something. I wish it didn't have to be today, but things have happened and I don't have a choice."

Brady raised a hand to silence her. She closed her eyes.

Was this what it felt like to stand at the edge of an abyss, waiting for the fall?

She opened her eyes. "Yes?"

"I might be going away soon. No—I *am* going away. I'm almost certain."

Brady buttoned her sweater and tugged it down over her hips. "Where?"

"That's just it; I can't tell you where. I'm not entirely sure myself at this point. But the reason for leaving is to be out of sight, so even if I knew, I wouldn't say."

"Sally, what have you done? Why do you need to hide?"

"I don't need to, not exactly. At least not yet."

"What are you planning to do?"

"It's beyond planning; it's started. Did you see the news yesterday?"

"Things have been so nuts, I have no idea what's going on in the world."

"There were some protests down in Chicago. Days of Rage, they've been calling it."

Brady nodded. "I did hear. My uncles were talking about it. Lots of broken store windows and smashed cars. Not a great way to change the world, if you ask me."

"Several people from the house went down to participate. They were arrested and charged with trespassing at a federal courthouse. I wired money for their bail and they were released."

"Posting bail isn't illegal. Why should that be a problem?"

"Jane and the others have decided that they're not going to subject themselves to a sham of a trial. They don't trust the system to give them a fair hearing. Right after they were released, they slipped out of sight and went underground."

"So you lose all that money because they want to evade trial and jail?"

"Money's not the point. I'm thinking about slipping out of sight too. As soon as the police and FBI realize they've gone, there will be questions."

"So? You're not accountable for their actions."

Sally took a deep breath. "I've been involved in a few things. We haven't talked about it, but I know that you suspect something. It's why I've been traveling. It's work I want to keep doing, and that will be impossible with the cops and FBI breathing down my neck when they start looking for Jane and the others. Please, you look like you're about to explode. I'm not funding violence; I'm not interested in that. I bailed out Jane and the others only because they're friends. Brady, I've been involved in other stuff *they* don't know about. There are people connected to that who could get found out and maybe sent to prison if the cops start following me too closely. Good-hearted people."

"Is Father Tom involved? I know he must be. I bet he's behind all of this. Do you have any idea how furious that makes me, that he sucked you into something?"

"I have my own mind, Brady. I do my own thinking."

"But he's the one who's gotten you involved, isn't he?"

"We agreed before: You wouldn't ask questions I can't answer. Brady, I didn't want to say this much, except that if—when—I do go away, I wanted you to have an idea why."

"If you go, when will I see you again?"

Sally smoothed her skirt. "It might be some time."

"You mean never, don't you?" Brady whispered. "Please, no."

"I don't mean that. I could end up somewhere else. Another country." Brady gasped. "You could visit. I don't know. I don't have it all figured out, okay? I'm getting pushed too fast to a decision and I don't have it all figured out."

"Sally, how can you possibly think about leaving forever? It'll kill your parents. Have you told them?"

"I probably will, but I'm not sure when or how. Don't you say anything yet. Please? Would you do that much for me?"

"I won't lie for you, Sally."

"I don't expect you to lie, Brady. You'll be true."

"True to you?"

"True to you, to who you are. Why do you think I haven't told you anything about where I've been and who I've seen these past few weeks? If you knew anything, you'd speak up."

"You mean you expect me to betray you."

"If it's expected, I don't think it's betrayal."

Brady crossed her arms and dropped her head. "Don't go. Stop it all, whatever it is you're doing, and don't go. Oh, I wish we could back up, I wish we could go in reverse and just stop all of this from happening. You wouldn't be doing this if you hadn't met me. I wish I'd never gone to that party, that horrible party."

"I'm glad you did. I'm so incredibly glad you stormed into the boathouse that night. Not only did I get a new best friend, I learned something about TVs and tinfoil."

Brady lightly punched her friend's shoulder, then let her hand drop to hold Sally's. "You know what's so strange? That party wasn't even three months ago. And now it's so hard to think of a time when we haven't been friends."

A V of squawking ducks flew high overhead, and both girls looked up. The ducks flew out of sight, but Brady and Sally still stared, each finding something to study in the deepening color of the late afternoon sky.

I could sit here all day, Brady thought. If I refuse to move, nothing else will happen. The screen door opened and closed. "Damn," she whispered.

Sally twisted around. "Mark looks really good in a suit."

"I know. Thinking about it is what's kept me from going insane all day."

He called from the steps. "Father Tom's going to leave soon, but he wants to say something first. Your mother asked me to tell you."

Sally said, "You don't have to go in. I'll stay here with you."

"It's all right. I think it must be some sort of peace offering, either to my grandmother or me. Probably both." They sat a moment longer. Brady sighed. "Okay. I'll go." She hooked her arm through Sally's and they walked back across the yard. At the steps she stopped. "Please, don't go away," she whispered.

Sally said, "Look at me."

Brady wiped away tears and looked.

"I can't live in this world. I don't know what else to do." They hugged, then Sally ran up the steps into the house as Mark held the door open.

Brady sat on the bottom step, head resting on her knees.

After a while Mark said, "Brady?"

She looked up. "You don't plan on deserting me, do you?"

He shook his head and held out a hand.

She took a deep breath and rose. "I'm ready," she said.

Everyone had crowded into the living room. People parted for Brady, who pulled Mark along. Passing Sally and Sylvia, she paused long enough to kiss Sylvia on the cheek.

She found a spot behind her own mother and brothers. She let go of Mark and straightened her mother's collar, then she rested her hands on Mary's shoulders. "I'm here," she said softly.

Father Tom nodded and smiled at everyone. "Will's grandmother asked if I'd say something, and his mother has graciously allowed me to do so." He held up a book. "I was snooping around, I confess, and came across the very thing. And, while my Irish is rusty, I think it will do. Why don't we say farewell to Will with one of his father's poems?" He riffled the pages, searching for something. He looked up. "Would that be all right, Mrs. Callahan?"

Brady heard a noise form and stick in her mother's throat as she nodded. She thought her own knees might buckle.

Sally called out, "Better make it a short one, Father Tom, otherwise I don't think any of us can hold it together."

People laughed. Brady felt her mother relax. She turned and saw Sylvia kiss the top of Sally's head and pull her into her arms.

Father Tom was still searching. "Short it will be, Sally. Here we go, this is the one I thought would do. Only sixteen lines. I wouldn't do it justice if I attempted a translation. Ah, but it's a lovely piece of writing. The title, perhaps. I can translate that much. Kieran Callahan called this one 'Sky at Sunrise.'" His head bobbed as he read it over once to himself, absorbing the rhythm, recalling the sound of the language. Then he cleared his throat and began to read.

Brady closed her eyes and listened to her father's poem. Word by word, line by line, the lyrical language worked its magic, gently brushing back her sadness and, for a moment, lifting the nearly unbearable weight of saying good-bye.

PART FOUR

I

The Sunday after Will's funeral Brady was roused by the sound of sirens. By the time she was completely awake, she realized they'd been screaming for a long time, a constant stream of wailing emergency vehicles on the nearby streets and highway.

Her mother was leaning against the kitchen counter, drinking coffee and frowning as she listened to the radio. "Have you heard all the sirens?" Brady said as she rushed in. "What do you think it is?"

Mary switched off the radio. "There's been an explosion at the U. The administration building is on fire."

Jane says they should have just blown the place up. "A bomb?"

"That's what they're guessing, but no one's saying for sure."

Brady ran back to her room. She pulled on the clothes she'd dropped on the floor just a few hours earlier as she'd crawled into bed right before dawn.

Mary was at the bottom of the steps when she came back down. "Where do you think you're going?"

"Sally's house."

Mary's arms spread out, one hand on the wall, one on the banister. "Do you think she's involved?"

"That's what I need to find out."

"Don't go."

"Please move."

"Why do you think she's involved? What has she told you?"

"I haven't talked to her since the day of the funeral. I think her housemates might have been planning something. She swore she wouldn't be involved in anything violent, but I don't know about the others." Brady started to push past her mother.

Mary held fast. "If she's involved, she'll be gone and there's nothing you can do. If she's not, she'll know that you'll be worried and she'll get in touch."

"I want to find out."

"Brady, please, no. If those people are involved, the police will know soon enough and then the house will be crawling with police. If it's truly a bombing, then the FBI will be there too. When they hear you went rushing over to the house, they'll want to know why. I can't bear it to have all that questioning start again."

Brady sat down on the steps. She reached for her mother's hand and pulled her down beside her. "If Sally's involved, or even knows people who are involved, it's too late to stop that from happening. They'll want to talk to everyone who knows her."

Mary sighed. "Then all we can do is wait. Please, Brady, stay here with me."

"There's more, Mom. She was talking about going away, going underground. She hadn't totally made up her mind, but if her housemates have done this, she may have no choice. She asked me not to say anything. She was working it out, so I thought I'd give her time. I wish I had talked to someone. If this bombing involves her, maybe I could have stopped it."

They turned on the TV. All the stations were broadcasting church services, so they returned to the kitchen and listened to the radio. By mid-morning the police had confirmed it was a bomb that had started the fire in the university building. The announcer seemed almost joyful to have something concrete to report, and his voice punched out the words. "Sources now confirm that just prior to the explosion the FBI was in contact with one of the bombers, a woman protesting university involvement with military weapons development. They are not releasing her identity at this time."

"It can't be Sally," Brady said tersely.

Someone knocked on the back door and they both shot out of their chairs. Brady reached the door first. "You," she said when she saw Mark. "I'm sorry, that was awful. Come in. Have you heard about the bomb?"

"I heard it go off. The sirens started right after. It's a zoo all around campus. I went over to the mall but I couldn't get very close to the actual scene. They've got it blocked off. There was a mob of gawkers, but all any of us could see was smoke. What do you suppose it's all about? Have you been listening to the news?"

"It's a protest against the university's involvement with the military."

Mark swore.

Mary said, "I bet you need some breakfast."

"I'm sorry, Mrs. Callahan. I just . . ." His hand bobbed in the air and then froze. "Some coffee would be nice, thank you." He turned to Brady. "Do you want to go for a walk later?"

"She's not going anywhere," Mary said as she took a mug from the cupboard. "For the first time in her life, she's grounded."

The phone rang. Brady lunged toward it, but Mary was faster. "Callahans'." After a moment she glanced at Brady and shook her head. "Mrs. Tollefson, hello. No, Cullen's not up yet."

Brady sat back down. One of the boys' customers. No doubt the woman was calling to see when she could get her leaves raked.

Mary handed the mug to Mark as she talked on the phone. He filled it with coffee and sat next to Brady. "Why are you grounded?" he whispered. "Because you were at my place all night?"

"I'm not grounded. She just doesn't want me going over to Purple House."

"Why not?"

"On the chance that someone in the house is connected to the bombing and the police might be there. Because of the chance they'll be interested in me if I show up right now looking for Sally."

"I find it hard to believe she'd be involved in something like this."

"You know the people she lived with, Mark. The radio said there was a female involved; it could be Jane."

"You're jumping to conclusions, Brady. And, sure, they're pretty good candidates, but they're not the only radicals in town. The campus is crawling with them."

"I'm worried about Sally. I wish we knew more."

Just as Mary hung up the phone, Cullen appeared. "What's going on?" he said sleepily. Then: "Are there any donuts?"

Mary said, "The Tollefsons wondered if you could do their yard today. It's supposed to rain later and they'd like the leaves cleared before it does."

Cullen made a face. "It's a huge yard. Sam's no help. I wish I hadn't taken the job."

Mark said, "I'll help you, Cullen. We'll get some donuts on the way."

"I'll help too," Mary said. "When we get back, we can do our yard. I'd love a nice, normal chore after this hellish week."

Brady said, "I'm staying here."

The others got Sam up and dressed and they headed out. Brady moved the radio to the living room and stretched out on the sofa. The news came in dribbles between commercials and terrible pop music.

Extensive damage to the top two floors . . .

Smoke could be seen as far away as . . .

The FBI is assisting campus police . . .

When the station announced it was about to begin coverage of the afternoon's Viking football game, Brady sat up. "The hell with this," she said aloud. "I'm going over to campus. I want to see it myself." But just as she reached to turn off the radio, the pulsing notes of the station's special-report theme sounded.

Two bodies have been recovered . . .

2

Sylvia Cooper spread her hands on the kitchen table. One by one, the fingers rose and fell, as if she were rippling piano keys. Brady thought she'd never seen such perfect nails.

Sylvia said, "I love this room, Mary. It was a marvelous space to cook in the other day. Sally had told me it would be. I adore my house, of course, but sometimes it feels like there's no life there."

Mary set a teapot down on the table. Sylvia leaned forward and held the plump pot between her hands. "Let me pour you a cup," Brady said gently.

Sylvia smoothed hair off her forehead with both hands and took a deep breath. "Did you know the two who died in the explosion?"

"I'd met the woman, Jane, but not the guy. Sally had mentioned him. I think they were—" Keeping company at night. "—sort of close." Sylvia winced. "I didn't visit her at the house very often. There was one guy I absolutely hated, so I stayed away. Brian."

"His name was mentioned. He's disappeared too. Are they together, do you think?"

"I don't know. I don't know any more than what I've told you. I've spent the two days since the bombing going over it all, thinking about what she told me and what I could have done to keep her from going away."

"I wish you'd told me what she was thinking about. I would have locked her in the trunk of my car and taken her home instead of leaving her at that house."

Mary sat down. "Brady's not to be blamed, Sylvia."

Sylvia reached and squeezed Brady's hand. Brady stared at the perfect red nails. I'm going nuts, she thought. I'm sitting in the middle of a nightmare and I'm obsessing about someone's manicure.

"I don't blame you," Sylvia said. "Do you understand that? I do not blame you, Brady. Once Sally has her mind set about something, no one can stop her. She's always been that way." She pulled back. "And evidently now she has chosen to be involved in this horrendous act and is a fugitive."

"She knew them, yes, but—"

"Lived with them," Sylvia said sharply.

"But that doesn't mean she was part of this."

"They've found her car at the airport and they found traces of explosives in the trunk."

"People borrowed it. Sometimes she had no idea where it was."

"They've got fingerprints from the car, Brady. Those deserters that were here, the ones who have been traveling and evading arrest, they know that they were in Sally's car. They believe she helped them get to Canada."

"I think she probably did that, but I can't believe she'd have helped plan the bombing. I especially don't think she'd have allowed anyone to kill herself by staying with the bomb. Sally must not have known what was going to happen."

"The FBI doesn't think the boy who died knew what was going to happen, not until it was too late. They think he had gone back in to get her, to see why she hadn't come out. There were chemical bombs on two other floors. Glorified stink bombs. They've told Rob that they think the others who were involved placed those and then got out. But the one that the girl had was real, and she knew it. She'd called campus police so they could listen to the explosion. They heard the boy come in the room and scream and then . . ." Sylvia shook her head sharply, chasing away an image.

Brady thought, What they heard was two people dying.

Sylvia stood. "I keep thinking, what if Sally had run back instead?" She smoothed her sweater and picked up her purse. "I need to get home. There will be a lawyer from Rob's firm with you tomorrow."

"I don't need a lawyer. That makes me look guilty, or at least like I'm hiding something. I'm just making a statement. And I can't afford a lawyer."

"Rob says they might try to implicate you, so of course you need one. And there's no expense, so don't be concerned."

Brady felt her mother's hand grip her shoulder. "The lawyer is a good idea. Thank you."

"You didn't have to come all the way into the city to ask me to do this, Sylvia. I'll do anything to help."

"We want to cooperate fully. We think it means the best chance to find her. We told them all that we knew, which meant we gave them your name. It seemed only fair to warn you and ask for your help. I couldn't do that by phone. We're asking you to betray a friend, Brady. That's asking a lot."

Brady laughed, startling herself and both of the older women. She said, "It's not a betrayal."

3

The lawyer motioned Brady to take a seat, then she opened a briefcase and pulled out a yellow legal pad. "At the request of the Cooper family, my client is here to answer any questions pertaining to her conversations with Sylvia Ann Cooper."

Sylvia Ann? "I probably won't be much help," Brady whispered to the lawyer. "I didn't even know her real name. She's Sylvia Junior?"

Julia Taylor scratched her scalp with the eraser end of a pencil. The coifed gray curls barely moved. "No. Mother and daughter have different middle names."

The door of the interrogation room opened and Agent Blake slipped in. He stood at the back of the room. Brady turned to the agent sitting across the table from her. "I can't think of her as Sylvia Ann. I'll need to call her Sally, if that's okay."

He nodded. "Of course. When did you meet her?"

"Last summer. July twentieth, the night the astronauts walked on the moon. Easy to remember."

"When did you last speak with her?"

"October twelfth. Which is also easy to remember because it was the day of my brother's funeral."

That shut them up and stilled their pens. Would they ask about Will? They no doubt already had a thick file on that subject. They probably even already knew how and when she'd met Sally. Maybe even knew—

"Miss Callahan?"

"I'm sorry. Please repeat the question."

"Do you know where she is?"

"No."

"So the last time you saw her was one week ago?"

The last time I saw her, Brady thought, she was coming down the stairs in my house. I was at the front door with Mom, saying good-bye to some neighbors. Sally was carrying an armload of coats. She'd brought them down because everyone was leaving. She was on the stairs and then she was gone. We didn't say good-bye.

Brady said, "Yes. One week ago. I'll tell you what she told me the last time we spoke. You don't have to ask." Brady closed her eyes and talked, lifting the last conversation they'd had from where it was seared on her memory. As she talked, she heard the clacking of the steno machine, the scratching of pencils.

She finished and looked at her hands. The nail of an index finger was rimmed with blood, its cuticle picked raw.

"And you really have no idea what she was doing during the time she said she was traveling?"

"No. Just that she was giving away some of her money."

"No names or places?"

"I've told you everything she said. She knew I wouldn't lie for her. That's why she didn't tell me anything."

The two agents consulted quietly for a moment before Daniel Blake slipped out of the room. The one who remained said, "Thank you, Miss Callahan. If we have more questions, we'll be in touch."

"Through me," Julia Taylor said.

The agent and his assistant gathered their things and left the room. Brady said, "That was so short. They hardly—"

Julia Taylor murmured, "We'll talk outside."

Brady looked around. Were there hidden cameras and microphones?

"Ready to go?"

Brady nodded and rose. She was glad it was over, but she wondered why they hadn't asked anything about St. Bernard's. That's where Sally had first met the Purple House people.

Why, she wondered, hadn't they asked about Father Tom?

They paused on the sidewalk to button coats. "Bloody hell," Julia said, looking up at the sky. "I think it's going to snow. It's not even November."

"I expected them to ask a lot more."

Julia slipped her briefcase under her arm, put her hands in her pockets, and started walking. Brady, long-legged and quick, had to hustle to keep up. "Rob's pretty sure that they had an informant close to the group. He doesn't have a name, though."

An informant? "Oh my God," Brady said. "I bet it's Brian. That son of a bitch. That mean, loudmouthed son of a bitch. He was always provoking things. He was always pushing. And now he's disappeared. *He* didn't die."

Julia said, "I have no idea who it was, but I absolutely trust Rob and his sources. Yes, that's often what informants do—provoke. It's not just about gathering information. One of the ways we suspect that the FBI uses them is to have people in place in these groups who push others into behavior that the general public finds reprehensible. A lot of people make no distinction at all between these radical groups and the peace movement."

Brady stopped walking. "But what they did at the U has nothing to do with the peace movement."

"Of course not, but lots of folks, lots of voters, don't see a difference. Nixon and his cronies would love to discredit the peace movement; while it's doubtful that they'd actually plan something like a bombing, all this plays right into their hands. Brady, if you do hear from Sally, it's very important that you call me or Rob Cooper."

"Why, so *he* can decide if it's something the FBI should know?" God, listen to me, she thought. I sound like Sally.

"He intends to cooperate fully with the investigation. He also intends to use what connections he has to ensure that she's apprehended safely. That will be easiest to do if he has any information first."

A bus roared past on the street, leaving behind a burst of exhaust. "She's in danger?"

"This administration believes it has nothing to lose by a show of force against the radical groups. Whatever Sally may in fact have done, it appears they've decided to go after her as if she's guilty of the worst. They'll track her down, Brady. They'll corner her. Rob wants to make sure that they don't go in firing."

4

Mary emptied her mug into the kitchen sink. "How was it?"

"Kind of weird, Mom, but at least it didn't last long. I had nothing to tell them. The lawyer was nice. She said one reason they didn't ask too many questions was that they already knew stuff. Sally's dad is certain there was an informant close to the group. What's Mr. Cooper like?"

"He seemed very nice. He was quiet. He looks like Paul. Or vice versa."

"He wasn't there today." Pulling strings offstage, she could almost imagine Sally saying.

"Oh, Lord, how I want this to be over," Mary said. "I thought with Will buried, maybe it was. But no, the nightmare just moved on to the next person in line. I'm so glad they weren't tough on you."

"Not with a high-priced lawyer at my side. Look at all this food in the freezer. We'll be eating hot dishes for months."

"I just want to get on with a normal life," Mary said.

"And what would that be?"

"Schoolwork is normal. Are you horribly behind in your classes?"

Brady pulled a small Tupperware container out of the freezer. "That pretty well describes it. I think I can salvage comp and psych. I've been debating dropping chem and bio. If I do it this week, I'll still get most of the tuition refunded. I could start over winter quarter. I should tell you, though, that I've been thinking of not doing premed. Do you suppose this is tuna noodle?"

"What do you mean, no premed? You've talked about med school for years."

Brady played a trick, a favorite new trick, one she'd used more and more as the days and news grew grimmer. If she closed her eyes and held very still, she could put herself back in the Coopers' house, where she was surrounded by soothing sounds and priceless art. For five seconds or five minutes, she could be somewhere else.

"Brady?"

She put the casserole back in the freezer. "Mom, I get so blue at the center. It's like nothing I do there makes a difference. It's like I'm piling up sand at the edge of the ocean and then the very next wave takes it all down. I don't know how you do what you do, day after day."

"I love it far more than it hurts. I believe that I do manage to help."

"I don't think I can handle a lifetime of fixing and helping, not if I don't love it. Problem is, I don't know what I do love. I know I need to stop going to the center, but how can I? What if everyone gave up?"

"You're eighteen. Taking time to figure things out is not giving up. I think . . ."

Brady watched her mother pull her own disappearing trick. She let her go, let her stay away as long as she needed.

Mary said finally, "Darling, there's no hurry. As bad as it seems, the world's not ending. Explore everything, Brady. Find something to love."

5

Police barriers still blocked the administration building. Plywood covered the windows on the second floor. A huge sheet of plastic repeatedly billowed and collapsed over a hole in the wall. Students stood and stared at the wreckage.

Brady, hurrying past on the way to the temporary registrar's office in the building across from Administration, heard someone say, "Maybe it will be haunted now. You always get ghosts where there's been a violent death."

Someone else replied, "Do you suppose there are still pieces of them in those piles of bricks?"

It was the last day to drop classes and the registrar's office was crowded. Brady stood in line for ninety minutes, most of it spent with her eyes closed, using the memory of Sally and Paul's house to block out images of ghosts, bricks, and body parts.

It was sprinkling when she finally escaped. The campus mall was nearly deserted; even the squirrels had taken shelter. She heard the snap of the plastic from the damaged building. She turned her head to avoid seeing piles of bricks.

As she passed the library, she debated going inside to study. Why hadn't she just dropped all her classes? She hadn't opened a book since the day Sally came and got her out of the stacks.

Brady stopped in her tracks and stared up at the third-floor windows. Then she ran.

The corner carrels on the third floor were occupied. Brady found a footstool in the stacks and sat down to wait.

A girl in the second carrel from the back was the first to leave. As soon as she started packing up, Brady moved. The girl looked up, startled. "Sorry," Brady said. "Didn't mean to rush you." But she did, of course. She wanted to throw everyone out.

She scanned the forest of scribbled musings. After a minute they blurred, jumped around, twisted in shape. Brady rubbed her eyes and started over. She read methodically, going over one small section at a time. After several minutes she came across the scribble they'd left the first time they'd been here.

BC loves MW.

There. Just below.

BC, She said it would be only smoke and stink. She lied, B, she lied. SC.

A book slammed closed and a boy cleared his throat in the carrel behind her. When she heard his chair push back, Brady stood up.

This message was easier to find. First she spotted *See SC for all your revolution's $$ needs.* Just above that—almost invisible, part of the dense weaving of scribbles—

BC, I didn't know what she was going to do. SC.

The other two carrels emptied at the same time. Now the whole section was deserted. Brady glanced at her watch. Yes, almost supper time. She took off her sweater and laid it on the chair of the last carrel so no one would sit there. She sat at number three and searched.

BC, I don't trust Brian. I'm on my own. SC.

The next carrel was the messiest yet. Someone had rubbed out and crossed over much of the graffiti. "Please," Brady whispered as she searched for a message, "please let it still be here."

Yes. There.

All the other scribbles faded as she sat back and stared.

BC, Sky at sunrise. Love you. SC.

6

By the time Brady met Sally's parents inside the library entrance, the light rain had turned to a persistent downpour.

"It took us forever," Sylvia said as she shook water off her umbrella. She wiped her brow and kissed Brady. "A good thing I was already headed to Rob's office to meet him for dinner when you called Julia Taylor. Traffic was a bitch. But here we are at last."

As Sylvia talked, Brady sensed Mr. Cooper's steady gaze on her. Was she being evaluated? When his wife caught her breath, he said, "I'm Rob Cooper."

"Oh my God," Sylvia said, "of course you two haven't met. That seems so unreal."

He shot a sideways glance at his wife. "Especially since you've been friends for so long," he said dryly.

Brady led them to the third floor. She'd saved the carrels with stacks of books and pens and paper. "Start in the corner," she said. "I think she meant that to be first. She knows it's the place I usually sit." She pointed out the two messages on the corner carrel. "I did the first one a few weeks ago. That's when I told her I liked to study here. We got kind of silly and scribbled lots of things. I have no idea when she added the new ones. After the explosion all the buildings on the mall were closed until Monday morning, so it had to have been sometime after then."

When she had finished pointing out each of the messages, she again sensed that Mr. Cooper was studying her. She faced him and said, "I didn't fake these."

He said, "While I was waiting for Sylvia to get to the office, I talked with Julia. I asked her if she thought you might try something like that."

"Rob," Sylvia snapped. "How ridiculous."

"She said no. And now that I see these, I recognize my daughter's penchant for drama."

Sylvia rose from one desk chair. She bumped her husband as she moved to sit in another. "It's not drama. Read these again. She's scared, Rob. She's in shock and she's frightened. Are you sure you found them all, Brady?"

"I think so."

"You said you thought one gave a clue to where she is."

"The last one."

Sylvia was already sitting there. " 'Sky at sunrise.' That's the title of your father's poem that the priest read."

"Yes, but that's not all it is. Sally and I met last summer at your cabin. It was the night of the moonwalk. The next day she and I went hiking. She took me to a floating bog."

Sylvia groaned and rolled her eyes. "Lord, how my family loves that place."

Brady looked at Mr. Cooper. "We walked to a little lake, to a shack she said was yours. She called it your hiding place. She didn't think you knew that she knew about it."

Hint of a smile. "I knew. Sally is about as subtle and careful as a charging bull. She always left some trace when she was there. We're having the cabin watched; we know she's not there. Why do you think she's gone to the shack?"

"Because we sat on the beach and she talked about how perfect it was at sunrise. She said I should see the sky in the morning. She said we'd go back sometime. I think this means she wants me to go there." Brady turned to Sylvia. "I think you're right. She's scared and in shock. I bet she wants to talk."

Brady wasn't sure if she'd been heard. Sylvia's face was frozen in open-mouthed wonder. Mr. Cooper faced his wife and sighed. "I had assumed she'd told you and it was one of the many secrets you two shared."

Sylvia said, "You have a hiding place?"

• • •

The Coopers argued about calling the FBI. Mr. Cooper wanted to wait until they'd gone to the shack to look for Sally. Sylvia was vehement about calling immediately.

"I'm calling," Brady said after listening to them for a while. "I told them I would if I got a message and now I'm going to." She used the pay phone in the library lobby. It was late, almost seven, but Agent Blake was working. When she said the magic words, "I've heard from Sally Cooper," she could almost see him snap to attention. She gave him the details and promised to wait. "I'm calling the Coopers too," she said before hanging up. Not exactly a lie.

Sylvia came over when Brady hung up the phone. "What did they say?"

"I talked to Agent Blake. He's on his way."

Just then, a cluster of students came out of a reading room and chatted noisily nearby. Mr. Cooper turned and watched them, his hands shoved into the pockets of his topcoat. Observing his weariness, Brady thought about all the vagrants, tired vets, and lost souls at the center. She realized she'd never seen a grown man look so sad.

His eyes followed the students as they left. After they were gone, he faced her and smiled slightly. Brady caught her breath. She said, "Mom was right. You look like Paul."

That wiped off the smile. He started to say something, couldn't, and instead shook his head. Finally: "I'm not sure things are going well for him either this fall. He doesn't seem to be studying very much. Have you or Mark heard from him?"

"Mark maybe has, but I don't know, he hasn't said. Paul sent flowers last week before the funeral. My brothers adore him, Mr. Cooper. He was so incredibly nice to them last summer. They're crazy about Sally too. This is probably hard to believe now, but both of them have a way of brightening things up for people."

He touched her lightly on the arm and said, "Thank you, Brady."

They waited for Agent Blake on the library steps. The rain had stopped and the air was cool. After an extended silence, Sylvia pointed and said, "My daughter did not blow up that building." She made a noise, and her husband took her arm. "God rest their troubled souls," she whispered. She fumbled in her pockets for a tissue, blew her nose, and exhaled. "They're predicting only a few hundred people will be here for the peace rally next month because everyone's headed to the big one in DC. I may come, Rob. I should have come to the others. I should have done more, I should always have done more." She walked to a trash can and dropped her tissue in. "Brady, Sally's not hiding in her father's secret place." Sylvia returned to her husband's side and slipped an arm through his. "You don't need to go after her tomorrow, Rob. I'm sure you will, but you won't find her there. She's gone somewhere else. Be practical, you two. She had no idea when or if you'd find the message, Brady. She wouldn't dare risk staying there and waiting. And how would she get to such an out-of-the-way place like the bog? She doesn't have a car anymore." Sylvia shook her head. "That's not what the message means."

"Then what does it mean?" Brady said.

"Where were we when she heard the poem?"

"My house."

"At the funeral lunch. It's not a clue, Brady. She's not asking you or us to chase her. She's saying good-bye."

7

With the Coopers beside her, Brady watched the posse of FBI technicians scrutinize and then dismantle her favorite place in the world. As the study carrels were carted away toward the library's freight elevator, Agent Blake said to Brady, "We'll need a more complete statement tomorrow."

Mr. Cooper put a hand on her shoulder and gently squeezed a warning. "My office will be in touch," he said. "I'm sure Brady will continue to cooperate."

The Coopers drove her home. When they reached the house, Brady saw her mother on her hands and knees in the front yard, digging. Sam, wearing rubber boots on his feet and a sweater over his pajamas, held a flashlight for his mother.

"She's gone nuts," Brady said.

Mary rose and brushed dirt off her hands as Brady and the Coopers got out of the Jaguar. Sam waved the flashlight, then held it under his chin and made a face.

"What are you doing, Mom?"

"Planting tulip bulbs."

"In the dark?"

"They're predicting more rain tomorrow."

"Are you Paul and Sally's dad?" Sam asked Mr. Cooper. "I'm Sam."

"I am their dad. I'm Rob." He offered his hand.

Sam shook solemnly. "Would you like some French toast? My brother and my sister's boyfriend are making some in the kitchen. They were supposed to call us when it was done, but I bet they went ahead and started eating."

Rob Cooper said, "I'd love some. I didn't have any supper."

Brady said, "Mark's here?"

"He came by for you," Mary said. "He thought you had plans to see a movie."

Damn. "I forgot."

"He took us to the park," Sam said. "We played football with some kids that were there. We got really muddy and Mom didn't even get mad at him for letting us do it."

Sylvia said, "Sam, why don't you give me that flashlight? Your mother and I can finish these bulbs while you go have a snack. Make sure Rob doesn't use too much syrup."

Sam handed over the flashlight. "Come on," he said to Mr. Cooper, taking him by the hand and pulling.

"You go too," Sylvia said to Brady. "Go in and see Mark. I'll tell the story to your mother."

"In other words," Brady said, "get lost."

"Something like that. Just give us a minute."

They didn't come inside for nearly fifteen minutes. All that time Brady sat with the guys in the kitchen, picking at her food and pretending she was amused by their jokes. Every now and then she noticed Mr. Cooper glance toward the front of the house.

She heard the front door open and close. He must have heard it too, because he rose and said, "Time for me to leave. Cullen and Sam, it was nice to meet you. Thanks for the supper. Mark, good to see you again."

Brady followed him out of the kitchen. In the living room, they stopped in their tracks. A soft pained sound escaped from Rob Cooper.

Mary and Sylvia stood side by side, staring out the front window. Brady wondered what they hoped to see. A change in weather? A prodigal child's return?

"Sylvia," Rob whispered, "it's time to go."

She nodded, but then moved no further except to slip her arm through Mary's.

Brady realized then what they were doing: Waiting together for the inevitable arrival of the next bad thing.

8

Mark lifted a grocery bag from the floor of the car. "I have something that might cheer you up. Why don't you come in?"

"Is that a lewd invitation, Mark? And who says I need cheering up."

"It's a musical invitation, Brady. I bought a great album yesterday—Hadda Brooks, some crazy boogie-woogie piano. You'll love it. And yes, you do need cheering up. What a day you must have had, to find those messages and then deal with the FBI. You looked so sad when you walked into your kitchen. You still do. Drives me nuts to see you like this."

When wasn't she like this?

He opened the car door. "Not that you don't have good reasons to be blue. Are you coming in?"

"I can't stay long."

"I know; I saw the look your mother gave you when we left."

Mark's room was on the second floor of a large house that sat at a noisy corner in Dinkytown, the student district at the edge of campus. Several people greeted him cheerfully when they entered through the back door into the clean, always busy kitchen. A few even remembered Brady's name and called out a welcome.

Tonight's kitchen crowd included a trio of girls making cookies. Brady helped Mark initial and put away the groceries they'd bought on the way over. She was quiet as he chatted and joked with the bakers.

They didn't need cheering up. They lived right under the same roof.

Their mothers weren't around to give warning looks. So why did he put up with her?

One of the trio was an older girl. She offered Brady a spoonful of dough. Brady blinked, trying to remember her name as she took the spoon.

"I need your help," the girl said. She dropped a glob of dough onto the cookie sheet. "Mark's been giving me trouble and I want you to fix it. I know you can."

"Cut it out, Grace," Mark said sharply.

Grace, that was it. Brady looked back and forth between them. "What are you talking about?"

"I'm trying to persuade him to do something he'd be really good at, but he won't listen. I think he's scared."

Mark made a noise as he folded the empty grocery bag and slipped it with others stored in the narrow space between the fridge and a cabinet. "Let's go, Brady."

Grace followed them out of the kitchen. "Ask him about it," she said as they climbed the stairs to his room. "Then tell him I'm right."

Mark's room was small—barely large enough for a boards-and-bricks bookcase, a four-drawer dresser, a chair, a floor lamp, his stereo, and a twin bed. He took off his shoes and kicked them into a corner. He peeled off his muddy sweatshirt and tossed that into a laundry basket in the closet. Brady said, "Wait. If you're taking off any more, I want to watch." She smoothed the blanket on his bed, arranged the pillows into a pile, and sat against them. "I'm ready."

He wasn't amused.

"Now *you* need cheering up," she said. "What was all that about with Grace?"

He changed records on the turntable and handed her the headphones. "It's after ten, you have to use these."

"I've been here before and I know the house rule. What's the story with Grace?"

He sat on the bed, looked at the floor, and shook his head. She reached and scraped dried mud that was caked on his arm and brushed some off his hair. "You guys really got dirty playing football."

"You should have seen us when we first got back to the house. Your mom made us wipe off in the backyard. The Coopers are nice, aren't they?"

"I like them. But I don't want to think any more about Sally and her family tonight, so tell me about Grace."

"It's not that big a deal. She's being way too dramatic. She has the room across the hall. We talk a lot about music. She's a journalism major and an editor at the *Daily*. She thinks I should write for the paper, review bands and albums, that sort of thing."

"And you don't want to do it?"

He breathed deeply. "She's right; I'm scared."

"Well, of course you are. It would be like putting your opinions out for the whole world to shoot down, but how can you not do it? She's absolutely right about the other part: You'd be great. You'll at least try it, won't you? I know you can do it."

He nodded slightly. "I want to, I admit."

She caught him between her feet and rocked him back and forth. "I'm so excited. *This* has cheered me up." She tipped her head toward the stereo as she put on the headphones. "I'll listen to the new album. Go take a shower."

She sat back against the pillows, closed her eyes, and let the boogie-woogie drown out what remained of the sadness of the day. Mark was right. It was crazy piano. She loved it.

9

Brady rushed from the center toward the bus stop. She couldn't see the number on the bus, but it didn't matter. Any bus would do, as long as it took her away.

Away from the long line of people waiting for Food Day to officially open. Away from the bum sitting by the kitchen door who was spouting obscenities about his mismatched socks. Away from Dee and the disbelieving No! she'd shouted when Brady told her she was quitting, effective immediately.

Away from Father Tom and his knowing smile, his calm, his patience, his daily welcome. And away from what she believed had to be his lies:

I don't know where she could be, Brady.

I don't know where she'd been or who she'd seen when she was traveling.

There's nothing I can tell you.

She was on the Franklin Avenue bus, but she didn't get off when it passed the stop nearest her house. She rode past the co-op café, through the Indian neighborhood, over the highway. Away.

"No regrets," she muttered. "It was the right thing to do. After today, life is different." She snapped her fingers. "Like that; I changed it."

The lady next to her got up and moved to a different seat.

Brady called after her, "Nothing I did there helped, anyway."

She spotted the small sign on the street corner too late and had to get off at the next stop.

Minneapolis Institute of Art.

A few blocks south of Franklin the massive stone museum towered over a hilly park. She walked past stone lions to enter.

The building was crowded with schoolchildren. She drifted from gallery to gallery, trying to avoid the clusters of noisy kids, but there were so many, she couldn't escape.

Wait for me. Look at that. Stop it. When's lunch? I don't feel good.

She'd quit the center to clear herself of noise and need. Why did it follow her even here?

One group left a gallery and she slipped in. The guard eyed her, then tuned out, apparently confident that she wouldn't play with the sculptures or smear chocolate on a canvas. Brady made a slow circle, taking in the canvases one by one. Madonnas, angels, chubby baby Jesuses, wrathful Gods.

And naked frolicking nymphs. When Brady made the final turn of her circle, she faced a huge painting depicting some sort of wild gathering in a lush forest. She counted the naked and near-naked bodies: over a dozen voluptuous nymphs, a few leering satyrs, a few exhausted women peeking out from behind trees.

"What sort of crazy mind thought this up?" she said, turning to the guard. "I love it. And isn't it great how they hung it opposite that one of the angry God?" The guard shrugged, but didn't comment. "You know," Brady persisted, "I've been to a party like this one." The guard pulled on a stone face and looked away.

Who was the artist? She stepped to the wall to read the small explanatory plaque. *Midsummer's Gathering, French, 1830–35. Artist Unknown.* "I bet," she muttered. No way the artist dared go public with this canvas, not when all the other painters were toeing the line with saints and angels.

She spotted a tiny line of print at the bottom of the plaque. She leaned closer to read, then let out a loud, choked gasp. By the time the guard had reached her side to offer help, Brady had stepped back and collapsed, laughing, on a gallery bench.

Gift of Robert and Sylvia Cooper.

10

"I had no idea what to wear to a peace rally."

Brady held open the door. "Hi to you too, Sylvia. And I'm sure you can't go wrong with suede; that's a beautiful jacket. Is it warm enough? Come inside; we're letting in cold air. Mom's in the kitchen. Where's Mr. Cooper?"

"He's here. We saw Mark up on a ladder and Rob had to go check it out. He's like a moth to a flame when he sees another male doing outdoor chores. Why is Mark on a ladder, Brady?"

"He's cleaning the gutters. Mom was doing it when he got here and he made her stop."

"Rob's in heaven, then. He probably won't go with us now. I had a hard enough time convincing him to come along, and cleaning gutters will be all the excuse he needs to stay behind."

"Mark too. He knows guys who are still fighting in Vietnam, and he's not clear in his head that he wants to be doing this today."

"They can stay behind and get some work done. I'm going." Sylvia peeled off her gloves and stuffed them into her jacket pocket. "I hear you quit your job. I'm glad. I think that center must be a dangerous place. Sally would still be here if she'd never gotten involved with the people she met there."

"Sally would still be here if she hadn't met me. Do you think I'm dangerous?"

Sylvia kissed her. "No." She fell back against the wall and whispered, "She's been gone a month."

Brady pulled her in for a long hug. "You'll find her."

Sylvia lifted an end of her scarf and wiped her cheeks. "This will be a long, tough day. I'm glad to be going through it with friends. Mary!" she shouted as she marched toward the kitchen. "I hope you have coffee. I need to talk."

"There must be a million people here!" Sam said, hopping up and down. "All I can see are legs and butts."

With one swift motion Rob Cooper hoisted Sam onto his shoulders. "Wow," Sam said. "Two million people."

"Not that many," Brady said. "Maybe a few thousand."

Sam shook his head. "Two million."

She looked around. The space immediately in front of the student union was packed with people and signs. A stage had been set up on the steps. A folk trio was performing, but no one seemed to be listening.

"There's someone with a bunch of balloons," Mr. Cooper said. "Let's go get one, Sam."

"This is wild," Cullen said. "Like a huge party. I hope they don't ruin it with speeches. Hey, there's a guy from school. I guess I'm not the only one whose mom made him ditch." Before Brady could stop him, he'd pushed through the crowd and disappeared.

She started to go after him, but Mark held her back. "Let him go."

"We'll get separated."

"Big deal. He's fourteen now. He knows the way home. Let him enjoy this."

"You're not enjoying this, are you?"

"Not a whole lot. Want to know why?"

"Because you feel guilty about the guys you know who are still fighting. You feel disloyal."

He shook his head. "I think I'm okay with that, finally. I think it's important for vets to speak out."

She covered his cold red ears with her mittened hands. "Because you're the only young guy here with short hair?"

"No, what bugs me most is that being squished together with all these people has made me extremely aware that I'm shorter than my girlfriend."

Brady tousled his hair and kissed the top of his head. "Not a lot. I had to

199

stand on my toes to do that." She slipped a hand into one of his pockets. Something sharp pierced through her mitten. "Ow. What's that?"

She pulled out her hand and took off her mitten. No blood. Carefully, she reached back in. She pulled out a medal. "One of your Purple Hearts."

"I had it on, but I changed my mind and took it off. It seems so showy."

"You should be wearing it. People should know that you fought and you were wounded in the goddam war and today you're here trying to stop it. I've spotted a lot of these today, Mark. You won't be the only one."

He sighed. "Did you hear what Nixon said about the veterans joining the demonstrations? He called us cowards." He looked over the crowd. "Okay, go ahead."

Brady pinned it to his jacket. Before she'd even secured the clasp, a nearby man stuck out his hand to Mark. "Me too. Where were you?" Mark shook his hand and they began talking. Soon he was part of a cluster of men, all sharing stories.

Brady couldn't take her eyes off the crowd. What if Sally was here? It would be a perfect place to blend in. Sylvia too seemed to be searching. Their eyes met. "You don't suppose . . . ?" Sylvia said.

Brady shrugged. Maybe, probably not.

The speakers began talking. Attention dwindled. Balloons started rolling over the top of the crowd to greater cheers than were earned by the speakers. Sam, now on Mark's shoulders, refused to let go of his.

Brady felt an arm slip through hers. "Too many ghosts on this campus," her mother said. "Your father taught here. Will went to school here. And now that." She nodded toward the administration building. Peace signs had been sprayed on all of the plywood patches. "I don't think I can take much more of this. I certainly can't march all the way downtown. Oh, Lord, Brady, I'm missing Will."

"Let's leave now." Brady tugged on Sam's arm. "Do you see Cullen anywhere?"

Sam pointed. "He's with a friend. They're ripping flyers off a post and making paper airplanes."

"Go get him." Mark and Sam pushed their way through the crowd.

Mary was talking to the Coopers. Rob nodded. "I say we cut out and go grab something to eat." He turned to his wife. "I'm sorry, Syl. It makes me think too much about Sally and the kids who died. It's too soon to be here, especially with that building right there."

Sylvia nodded and shrugged. Then she rose to her toes. Her eyes widened and she said, "There! Rob, over there!"

Sally? Brady looked, but all she could see was a sea of faces, most of them energetically repeating a chant: *Out now! Out now!*

"It's Jed Webster, Rob. He's with one of his daughters. Go bring him over here."

"Sylvia," Rob said sternly.

"Make me happy, Rob."

He sighed, then pushed through the crowd.

Sylvia spun around, laughing. "Well, I'm cheered up."

"I thought you'd seen Sally," Brady said.

Mary said, "Sylvia, I know what this is about. I've told you repeatedly: I'm not ready. Don't."

Sylvia waved. "Here they come. Don't what? What am I doing? This is a happy coincidence, running into a friend." She turned, tucked a strand of Mary's hair back up under her beret, and kissed her cheek. "Just relax. He doesn't know a thing; nothing's at stake. And by the way, you look absolutely beautiful."

No, she doesn't, Brady thought. She looks scared to death.

11

The *Daily* newsroom was crowded, loud, and smoky. Brady settled into the chair at the desk the receptionist had pointed out and opened her book. It was hard to concentrate. How could people get anything done in here?

Her throat seemed to be lined with claws, and even breathing hurt. She touched her hot skin with the back of her hand. She'd started feeling warm during the psych lecture and now she was burning. A girl carrying an armload of yellow paper paused. "Are you okay? You don't look good."

She didn't really want to talk, but the girl seemed concerned. "I'm waiting for Mark Walker. I think maybe I'm getting a cold, that's all."

The girl nodded. "There's some stuff going around campus. Lots of strep. My roommate missed a week of classes. The arts staff is in a meeting—hey, here they come."

Several people emerged from a corner room. Everyone was laughing. Mark put a hand on a guy's shoulder, said something, and the laughter got louder.

Ah, his great-to-be-alive mood. Usually it cheered her up, but today, already burning with fever, she felt suddenly weak as something else rushed through her while she watched him. The girl with the yellow paper—Brady now saw that she was very pretty and very blonde—said something to Mark and swatted him lightly on the arm. He spun around, spotted Brady, and waved. He hurried over.

God, she thought. I think I'm jealous.

"Sorry you had to wait," he said. "But I need five minutes more."

"I need to go. I don't feel right, Mark." It wasn't just the cold—she didn't feel right being in the room. After only one week on the staff, he obviously belonged here. It was his place and she was intruding.

"You do look like crap," he said. He pulled up a chair and sat on the other side of the desk. He set the paper he'd been holding in front of her. "Could you check this over? I had to do a really fast rewrite and it's not quite where I want it."

Her groan was loud enough to stop newsroom traffic.

"What are you doing to that poor, sick girl, Mark?"

Brady looked up. "Hi, Grace."

Grace laid a hand on her shoulder. "You look like crap."

Brady whispered, "So I've been told." She took the paper off the desk and took the pencil from his hand. "You're a good writer, Mark. You don't really need me to do this." She made a few marks and changes as she read the review. When she was done, she held it out. Grace lifted it from her hand.

"Hey, let me retype it," Mark said.

Grace scanned the yellow sheet. "No, it's fine. It's good. Huh. Better than good. On her deathbed and she does an impressive one-minute edit. Now get her out of here before we all get sick."

Brady let Mark zip up her coat, knot her scarf, carry her books. "Let's get you home," he said tenderly.

"Let's get me to a doctor."

Mary pulled a blanket up to Brady's shoulders. "What did they say at the clinic?"

"They're guessing strep. They did a throat culture and gave me some pills. Where are you and Jed going for dinner? Never mind, tell me tomorrow. I need to sleep."

"I'm staying home with you."

"Don't be nuts. Just leave a note for the boys to be quiet. Where did Mark take them?"

"Bowling."

"I met Mark at the *Daily* today. I got so jealous when I was there. I need to sleep. 'Night."

"Not so fast. Jealous about what? I can't believe he's interested in someone else."

"No, though there was this pretty blonde there. I wonder what it's like to be a pretty blonde who's never had a broken nose. Don't make me talk anymore. It hurts."

"Why were you jealous?"

Brady looked at her mother. The black hair was shot with white, but the green eyes didn't look so sad. "He's been working at the *Daily* for about a week and it's like he already belongs. That's the only thing I miss about St. B.'s. I'd like to belong somewhere, and have people to joke with. You must be late. Don't make Jed mad. Did you bring up the ice water?"

"Right here on the table. You had some mail, so I brought that up too."

Brady closed her eyes and rolled over to her side. "What'd I get?"

"Something from Grandma. Looks like an early birthday card."

"She's neurotically punctual, your mother." Brady sighed, feeling her own mother's hand rub the back of her neck. She could feel herself drifting into sleep at last.

"You also got your bank statement, a postcard from one of your old teachers, a flyer from the center, and the new *Rolling Stone*."

Brady nodded into her pillow. So hot. She heard the rattle of the pills as her mother looked at the medicine. Mary rose from the bed. "Don't you dare break your date," Brady mumbled. "I want you to go for the record. Three dates in five days must be some kind of record."

"It hasn't been three. That first time we simply ran into each other after work and ended up having a quick drink. Hardly a date. And I'm not going tonight."

"I'm sleeping now. Go away."

Mary shut off the light. Brady heard the door unlatch, but nothing else. "Still here?"

Her mother returned to her side. "They told you about these pills, didn't they?"

"Told me what? They just said if I have strep, they'll clear it up. If I don't have strep, nothing will help."

"They'll clear it up, all right. You'll feel better tomorrow. But they also interfere with oral contraceptives. You won't be safe for an entire cycle after you're done with the antibiotic."

Brady groaned into her pillow. What hell was this—a mother who knew everything.

"Just so you know," Mary said softly.

The door finally closed. "Mom!" Brady called, then pressed her hand against her neck. When would it not hurt to talk? Mary rushed back in. Brady said, "You be careful too."

Sleep came in feverish fits. In between them, she heard the boys return noisily from bowling, Mark's low rumble of a voice, a ringing phone, her mother's laugh, the distant scraping of snow being cleared from sidewalks.

She woke from a dream about Will. Her eyes opened wide. How strange, she thought. That's the first time in days. Was he fading already?

She tried to recall the dream. What had Will been doing? Had he said anything? How much longer would she remember the sound of his voice?

Wide awake now, and not feeling so feverish, she checked the clock. One in the morning. She sat up and switched on the light, turning her head from the sudden brightness. Ah, *Rolling Stone*. Perfect. Just as she reached toward the chair where the magazine lay, she could again hear her mother. . . . *bank statement, a postcard from one of your old teachers, a flyer from the center* . . .

What old teacher?

Brady poked through the mail. The postcard was lying picture-up. A bird on a tree branch. *The American Robin—Michigan's State Bird,* according to the caption. She picked up the card and flipped it over. She read the signature first.

Your very favorite science teacher, Mrs. Bronson.

Her heart threatened to pump its way out of her chest.

Brady, dear, I'm busy traveling this holiday season. I hope your birthday finds you well. I hope too that you continue to nurture your interest in wildlife and the great outdoors. Such a fine student you were!

"Mrs. Bronson," she whispered as she read it again. She started laughing and her raw, swollen throat squeezed, fought, and twisted the sound into a cackling rasp. Within seconds, her mother had burst into the room.

"Mom, why are you still up? Or did you just get in?"

"I didn't go out. I was playing solitaire. Are you okay? My God, Brady, that sounds like a death rattle."

"It's not," she whispered, her throat screaming at every breath. "I'm laughing. I've heard from Sally."

12

Sylvia lit a cigarette. She whipped the match in the air until it was out, then tossed it into an ashtray. "Thank goodness my kids don't smoke. At least I don't think they do; of course, they've both surprised me about a lot of things."

Brady dropped down on the sofa and stared at the large painting on the wall.

Sylvia followed her gaze. "My Frankenthaler. Gorgeous, isn't it? Keeps me company. The last few days I've just hated leaving the house. What if Sally calls and I miss her? We've even put in a new phone line to use so the number she knows is always free. So, here I stay, waiting. Thank God for your mother. She calls me every day, did you know that? Most of my old friends have been acting so distant. I guess they don't know what to say."

"Sylvia, what haven't you told me? I showed Agent Blake the postcard. He took it to make a copy, but he didn't seem too excited. All he said was that I should talk to you. What's going on?"

Sylvia stared at the burning tip of her cigarette. "The FBI has a picture from a demonstration in Ann Arbor. It was on the same day as the one we went to here. Apparently there is thorough surveillance of these events. No doubt *we're* now in some FBI photo. Sally showed up in one from Ann Arbor. Rob saw it on Friday and verified it was she. He brought home a copy." She pointed to the coffee table.

Brady leaned forward and picked up a large photo showing a sea of people. She had to search for Sally.

"Left side," Sylvia said. "She's standing next to the nun, in front of the guy holding up the poster."

Yes, there she was. It could have been any demonstration anywhere. Such a public place, why had she risked it? Did she want to be found? Were these people her friends? Were they hiding her? Taking her money?

"The Ann Arbor police already knew the names of some of the people with her in the photos. Names and addresses, so I guess it was easy enough to find her. They watched her for a few more days. Then she slipped out of sight again."

"Why didn't they grab her?"

Sylvia took a deep pull on the cigarette. As she exhaled, she smashed it out furiously in the ashtray. "They hoped she'd lead them to bigger fish."

"What bigger fish?"

"Maybe that's the wrong term. They're pretty certain Sally is funneling money into various groups. When she turned eighteen, she gained control over part of her trust fund. She's cleared it all out."

"Already?"

"Emptied her account and put it elsewhere. What the FBI wants to do is track the money and learn how it flows between these groups and the people in them. The agents are much more interested in that, Brady, than they are in Sally. Not only did they spot her in Ann Arbor, but they confirmed the name she was using and have traced it to a bank account she opened. Her name—the alias—was on it along with three other names. Those were also fakes. The people behind them all had access to the money in that account. Fifteen thousand dollars, most of it gone. They traced some of it to two legal defense funds. One for the Chicago 7, another for black students on trial for some campus takeover. They didn't say where. They think there must be several such accounts that she's opened around the country."

"You knew this when I called you about the postcard last night? Why didn't you tell me?"

"As far as Rob and I knew, last night she was still in Michigan. The agents asked us not to say anything while she and the others were under surveillance. They didn't want to jeopardize their little stake-out. Last night we didn't know they'd already lost her."

"They don't trust me, then. They thought I'd have a way to tip her off. You don't trust me either."

"Now you're angry. Paul is too. He's so angry with us for cooperating. He says that if he hears from her, he'll never tell us. He'll help her and do what she asks, and no one will know. He said he'd even help her get out of the country. He's so furious, he won't come home for Thanksgiving. He's going up to Boston. He thinks it's possible she's there blending in with all the students. He thinks he'll find her, or she'll spot him and make contact. Can you believe that? I think we're all going insane. Oh, I suppose I should feel lucky I have children so loyal to each other."

"Why does the FBI care if she gives money to those defense funds? It's legal to give them money."

"Not when you use phony names to set up accounts and transfer funds. That's bank fraud, yet another federal offense they can hit her with. Brady, the longer she stays out there, the more damage she does to herself."

"I don't like this, Sylvia. It's one thing for me to cooperate when it's just Sally we're trying to find. But this is something else. Now it's like we're helping to implicate, even entrap, others. I don't want to do that. I'm with Paul. If I hear from her, I'm not talking anymore. Not to the FBI, and maybe not even to you and Mr. Cooper."

"You might not have the choice. They'll surely be watching your mail now, if they haven't been already. Clever girl, my daughter, to get something past them to you. I imagine the challenge of that amuses her. I'm sure she'll try it again."

"Sylvia—" Brady stopped when the woman slashed the air with her hand.

Sylvia's eyes were fierce, sharp points. "They will find her, Brady. Next week, or next year, or in ten years or twenty—they'll find her. And then she'll go to prison. I will do anything to limit the time she has to be in prison. If you have political concerns or personal scruples that make that difficult, fine. Good for you. I don't. None whatsoever. I just want my daughter back."

Sylvia barely acknowledged Brady's leave-taking. As Brady walked to her car, she glanced back. Through a window she saw the woman sitting on the sofa, smoking again and staring at the painting on the wall.

13

Brady finished her second cup of coffee and glanced again toward the front of the café. Where was he? She sighed and resumed looking through the inch-thick book of listings for winter classes. Nothing much grabbed her. Irish, yes, but that was only one class. More psychology? Art history, maybe? She closed her eyes, riffled pages, stopped, and put her finger down. Erotic literature of the nineteenth century. Well, okay.

Mark slid into a chair across the table. He took off his stocking cap and jacket. His cheeks were red from the cold, and his hair was smashed flat. "Sorry I'm late. Did you order?"

"Not yet." Brady sat back and studied him. She wasn't sure what mood he was in, but he obviously wasn't feeling great about anything. "You look down, but I've got something that will cheer you up. I think I found a class we should take together." Nothing registered. She closed the course bulletin and waved it in front of his face. "Hello there."

He mustered a smile. "You're in a good mood."

"I am. I turned in two very late midterm papers today and took an exam I missed when I was sick. I am finally up to date on everything."

"Are you up to date on the news?"

She sat back, sobered. "Of course." Impossible not to be. The whole campus was on fire with the revelation of a government cover-up of a U.S. army massacre of civilians in a Vietnamese village called My Lai. "It's all we talked about in both my classes."

Mark pushed back from the table and looked out the café window.

Outside, cars waited for a traffic signal to change, their turn lights blinking in the dark. "I'm sure that was fascinating," he said. "Especially in your psych class. I mean, hey, what's more relevant to the subject than discussing human behavior in war?"

Brady picked up her water glass and sipped. "What's going on? Did someone say something today?"

The window was steamed over, and he cleared a spot with his arm. "I've never hid the fact that I'm a vet. People in my classes know, people at Purple House knew, they know at the paper. Everyone I met today, I could see it in their eyes. The question. No, the accusation: 'What did you do in the war? Didja kill any women and babies?'"

"Look at me, Mark." As he continued to stare out the window, she watched his chest rise slightly and sink with each breath he took. When he finally faced her, she said softly, "Not in *my* eyes."

He shrugged, picked up his cap, and pulled it on. "This has not been a good day, Brady. Do you mind if I take off? I need to get to the library." He lifted his arm to rub another spot on the fogged glass.

"Would you quit looking out the window?"

He faced her, yawning and rubbing his chin. She knew he shaved every day, knew that for some reason the whiskers grew back fastest on the right side of his chin—one of the spots she loved to kiss. "What happened today? There must be more."

His face darkened. He played with a spoon. She waited. Finally he said, "One of the editors at the *Daily* insisted that I allow them to interview me for a local angle on the massacre."

Brady sighed. So that was it.

"He wouldn't leave me alone. He wanted a story and there I was: a real, live Vietnam vet, right in the newsroom. I didn't want to talk. He actually threatened me, Brady. He said I should cooperate or *maybe* I wouldn't get to write any reviews. *Maybe* I'd be stuck compiling sports scores. *Maybe* I wouldn't be on the staff at all. What was I supposed to do—give up the chance to do something I love, give up my place there? So, yeah, I talked. Nothing they hadn't heard already, but that didn't stop them from pushing. Man, did they push." He put on his jacket. The Purple Heart was gone.

He rose, took a few steps, then returned and dropped back into his seat.

"I was never involved in anything even close to what they've uncovered at that village. It sickens me more than you can imagine. But my hands are bloody, Brady. It's a war, and I spent fourteen months in the middle of it. I set booby traps. I used my weapons. Yes, I have killed other human beings." He dropped his head. "I just want it to be over," he whispered.

She leaned across the table and grabbed his hand. "Stay with me now. I'll go home with you tonight."

He rose, shaking his head. "I don't want to talk anymore, not even to you. I have a paper due tomorrow. Sorry about dinner. I'll call you."

Brady sat back. "'Call me'? That sounds like I'm getting dumped."

"Don't be silly. I just need a little break—don't look like that. Not from you, just everything else."

"How long a break? Thanksgiving's Thursday—you still plan on helping at St. B.'s community dinner, don't you?"

He looked pained. "I don't know if I'll be up for it. All those people talking about My Lai and the war—it's exactly what I don't want on a holiday."

"I don't know if *I'm* up for it. I'm not sure I want to go back so soon after quitting. It was your idea to volunteer, and now Cullen and Sam are psyched to help."

He shrugged.

"Mark," she said softly, leaning forward and touching his arm. "I understand if you don't want to go to the center, but please tell me you still want to come to our house for Thanksgiving dinner after we're done at the church. You promised my mother."

Outside, a car horn beeped insistently. Mark turned toward the window and stared, looking for something in the dark, blurry cityscape. "Of course I'll be there," he said. "Even if I didn't want to be with you and your family, where the hell else would I go?"

14

"It's Paul! I see him getting out of his car." Sam raced to the front door and opened it wide. He hopped from bare foot to bare foot as the cold rushed in.

"Close the door, Sam," Brady said. "He's taking forever."

"He's getting something."

Paul leaned into the backseat of the car. He pulled out a covered pan. He kicked the door closed with a foot and walked toward the house.

"Sam, close the door," Mary said, coming from the kitchen. "My goodness. What are you doing here, Paul?"

Brady was startled by the coolness in her mother's voice. But then, why be surprised? Mary had probably long ago filled in all the blanks concerning that frightening night last summer.

Paul obviously sensed the chill too. "Happy Thanksgiving," he said tentatively as he entered the house. "I come bearing a treat: one double recipe of my mother's deserves-to-be-world-famous *zuppa inglese*."

"I'm surprised to see you," Mary said. "I had dinner with your parents the other night and they said you weren't coming home. Let me take that. She didn't need to do this."

"Of course she didn't, but she's on a one-woman campaign to save the world from apple pie."

Mary smiled. "I'm glad you changed your mind and came home."

Paul finally relaxed. "Not much choice, Mary. When a boy gets a late-night long-distance phone call and someone rips into him for breaking his mother's heart, what can he do?"

"She didn't want Rob to call you about that. I'm glad he did."

Paul looked at Brady, then back at Mary. "It wasn't my father. So, how goes the thing with Jed? I hear—holy cow, you blush like your daughter."

Mary turned toward the kitchen. "You are getting a little fresh, young man. I'm going to put this in the fridge and then I need to baste the turkey."

Paul turned to Brady. "Oops, I guess. She's obviously still pissed at me and I think I just made it worse." He turned to Sam. "Oops, again. You didn't hear me say that, right? Where's Cullen?"

"Sleeping," Sam said.

"Go get him, man, and tell him to get his ass out of bed. You didn't hear me say that either, in case your mother wonders the next time it slips out of your mouth. Both of you guys should get dressed. We've got to get down to the center and start serving turkey dinners."

Sam raced up the stairs.

"Should I go apologize to her?"

"No. I doubt if she's really upset, at least about the Jed comment. That exit of hers was pure technique. She's a pro at conversation control."

He looked around. "Where's Mark?"

"The center, I suppose. I haven't seen or talked to him since the night I called you."

"I called him right after we hung up. Don't panic, I didn't mention that I knew anything about him being freaked over the My Lai thing. I just said I was going to be in town after all and that we should do something. We agreed to meet here by"—he checked his watch—"now, or meet at the center if he was late. Are you going to invite me in?"

Paul unzipped his parka and followed her to the sofa. As they sat, Mary appeared in the doorway, holding a fork. "This zuppa-whatever is delicious."

"It's Jed's favorite," Paul said. Mary rolled her eyes and disappeared again.

"Conversation control," Paul said softly. "I can do it too. Brady, I was so glad you called the other night. I've wanted to talk to you a million times this fall."

"You could have called."

"We didn't exactly part on the best of terms. The last time I saw you, you couldn't get away from me fast enough. You were so mad. Are you still?"

Brady took a deep breath and glanced at the kitchen. Awfully quiet in there. "No," she whispered. "I want to be friends."

"We are."

"I want to forget about that horrible night." And how close she'd come to a mistake.

"There's not a whole lot I remember, anyway." He kissed her. "Forgive me?"

She nodded.

"Can we come down now?" Sam said.

Brady looked over Paul's shoulder. Her brothers were both watching from the steps.

Sam ran past to the kitchen. "Mom, Paul was kissing Brady."

Her mother appeared in the doorway, looking concerned.

"It was a friendly kiss," Paul said. "A cheer-up kiss. On the cheek."

Mary said, "Okay, then." She disappeared again.

Paul turned to Brady. "It's obvious whose side she's on. Hey there, Cullen. Man, have you grown in three months, or what?"

"Yeah, I guess."

"Go get some shoes on, then we're out of here." As soon as Cullen was out of sight, Paul whispered, "He told Mark he had a girlfriend. Mark told me. I'm being a rat and telling you. Don't worry, Mark's talked to him about stuff. You should see your face."

"Why hasn't he said anything?"

"He has, just not to you or your mom. Leave him alone about it, okay?"

"I will, if you promise to talk to Mark. He needs a friend, Paul."

"That's why I'm here."

She leaned over and put her arms around him. She felt his head drop against hers.

Paul whispered, "I wonder where she is tonight." Brady squeezed him tighter.

Sam shouted, "Mom, now they're hugging."

15

Deanna came running when Brady walked into the dining hall. "We've missed you," she said as they embraced. "Tell me you've come back to beg for your old job."

"I'd heard you'd hired someone else."

"We have, true." Deanna nodded toward a petite girl in the kitchen hauling a huge pot from stove top to counter. "That's Barb. She's great. Social work major at St. Kate's. She's also over twenty-one, which is good. Tom had you dealing with way too much."

"Where is he?"

"Spending the holiday in San Francisco."

"He's actually taking a vacation?"

"Hardly. A group of Indians has occupied the old prison island, Alcatraz, in San Francisco Bay. It seems that Indian treaties say they're entitled to any abandoned federal land. The feds abandoned Alcatraz years ago, so last week the Indians claimed it. Tom went out to help set up a support center on the mainland." Deanna tugged on Brady's arm and moved toward the kitchen. "I saw Mark's name on the volunteer list. Did you come together?"

"He was going to meet us. He's not here?"

"Haven't seen him. Who's us?"

"My brothers and a friend. We ran into Jerry outside and they're helping him haul extra chairs from the basement." A parade of church ladies entered the dining hall, each of them carrying a huge covered dish. "How many people are you expecting to feed?"

"At least three hundred. We're cooking for four. Only we're not cooking standing here. I hope you brought an apron."

Mark never showed up. For the first hour Brady looked up every time another volunteer arrived. After that she was too busy. She didn't sit down for four hours.

She was setting out fresh paper place mats on a table when Cullen came up behind her. "This is pretty cool," he said. "I can kind of see why you liked this place. These people are really happy to be here. I'm surprised, it's not like they're all poor or anything. I thought it would be mostly bums."

"Well, there are plenty of them. But lots of the others just come because they think this is where they belong."

"Where's Sam? He hasn't bugged me in a while."

"Paul ran him back to the house an hour ago. He was getting tired. See that old guy having trouble with the milk machine? Why don't you go help him."

Cullen nodded and walked over.

A girlfriend, she thought as she watched him help the older volunteer fill a pitcher of milk. That's impossible.

Life, stand still, she wished for the hundredth time that fall. But then Cullen laughed, a deep, rumbling, older-boy laugh. He gently took the pitcher from the old man and walked with him back to a table, listening politely as the man jabbered away.

I take it back, she thought as she watched him walk around the table, greeting and chatting with people one by one. I take it back and I'll never wish it again.

It was dark when Paul parked the car in the driveway. Lights were on all over the house, and Brady could see her mother and Mark through the living room windows.

As Paul and Mark greeted each other, Brady hung up her coat and then slipped into the kitchen, touching Mark softly on the back as she passed behind him. Her mother followed.

"What did you have Sam doing?" she said. "He was exhausted when Paul brought him back. He went right to his room to nap."

"I'm not surprised. The guys worked hard setting things up, and he was trying to do whatever Cullen and Paul did. How long has Mark been here?"

"Half hour or so." Mary stood in front of the oven with her hands on her hips. "I am not hopeful about this turkey. I have dismal luck cooking these things. At least we have Sylvia's cake."

Brady started to say something. She froze when she noticed that her mother's eyes were brimming. "What's wrong, Mom?"

Mary shook her head and wiped the spilled tears with the backs of her hands. "Not much that's new. Just kind of a tough missing-Will day."

Brady wrapped her arms around her mother and held tight. "I can't believe we all ran out on you."

"Actually, it was nice to have some quiet. You're a raucous bunch and I was glad to be alone for a while." She pushed back and held Brady by the arms as she looked at her. She glanced toward the living room and lowered her voice. "It was nice to talk with Mark. He feels awful about your conversation the other day. He's dealing with a lot, Brady."

"I think he's holding too much in. He probably really needs to talk to a counselor—or a very good psych nurse."

Mary pressed the back of her hand against her daughter's cheek. "Oh, honey, he doesn't need a shrink nearly as bad as he needs a mother."

Sam shuffled in, yawning. "Everyone's so noisy. Is the turkey done?"

"Beyond done," Mary said. "If people want to eat in the dining room, you'd all better clear your junk off the table. Otherwise we're in here."

Sam went to the kitchen door and shouted, "Mom says it's time to eat!"

"Not quite," Brady said when the guys appeared. "Sam was a little eager."

"I should get home," Paul said. "My grandmother is scheduled to descend about seven. I need to be there to block things for my parents. They haven't been face-to-face with her since Sally left, and Gran Cooper is a wicked shot."

Brady felt Mark sidle up to her. He slipped his hand into hers. "Sorry I didn't show up," he whispered. "And for the other night."

Before she could answer, Paul groaned loudly. "Don't be so shy, pal. You'd better give her a nice sweet kiss, otherwise I will."

Mary butted the oven door with her hip. She hoisted the turkey roaster onto the stove top. Without turning, she said, "Cullen and Sam, set the table. Brady, please mash the potatoes. Mark, I think he means what he says. Paul, dear, it's time for you to go home and cheer up your mother."

16

Grace dropped a stack of yellow typing paper on Mark's desk. "If you don't like it here, then why do you hang out in the newsroom?" she asked Brady.

Brady said, "I didn't say I don't like it, I said I don't want to work here. And aren't journalists supposed to be observant and accurate? I'm not hanging out; I'm here about once a week. That's it."

Grace nodded. "I am observant: always Wednesdays. Why is that?"

Brady shrugged. "We have this concrete date sort of thing. We meet here because you always have him working late, even now during winter break when everyone else is gone."

"Like I said, you could work here too, Brady. You're a natural editor. We don't pay a lot, but it can't be much worse than that cafeteria job you took."

"Took and quit. I only stuck it out long enough to buy Christmas presents. Grace, I absolutely do not want a job where I'm fixing things, okay? Especially where I'd be correcting my boyfriend's work."

"I didn't think of it that way. That's no problem, really. We could assign you—"

Brady held up her hand and shook her head.

Grace smiled. "Okay. I'll drop it. I need him for a few minutes more, all right? He's bringing some typewriters down from one of the classrooms. Then he's free for date night." She walked away, her clunky boots making a loud sound in the empty newsroom

Brady pulled her new art history text out of the bookstore bag and set it on Mark's desk. After flipping though a few pages she closed it and put it away. She had a week before the new quarter began. Why rush things?

She picked up the mug Sam had given Mark for Christmas, decided it was clean enough, and walked across the newsroom to the coffeepot. On the way back she spotted a stack of news photos on a desk near Mark's. As she sipped, she glanced at the top photo on the stack.

Alcatraz occupation continues read the caption. She picked it up, thinking about Father Tom. She set it down when the one underneath caught her eye. *Occupation supporters gather at supply depot.* This one showed twenty or thirty people milling around. Many held American flags and hand-lettered banners. She scanned it, half expecting to see Tom.

She set down the coffee mug with a thud. Coffee sloshed onto the desk.

She heard Mark and Grace laughing outside the door. Holding the photo in front of her so they couldn't see, she walked to her bag as they entered. She slipped the photo between pages of a book and then covered the bag with her coat.

Like a rare bird, she thought. A Sally sighting.

When Brady got off the bus at her corner, she saw the Coopers' Jaguar parked in her driveway. It was nearly ten o'clock—why was Sylvia visiting so late?

Brady walked slowly toward home. I can't go in, she thought. Not with this in my bag. I can't go in and not tell them about it. My luck.

Bad luck got worse. Before she could retreat, she saw Sylvia run out of the house to the car. She paused to kick snow chunks from around a tire. As she did, she looked down the street, saw Brady, and waved. Brady hugged the bag with one arm and limply waved back with the other. Sylvia put her hands on her hips, cocked her head. Then she motioned.

Brady obeyed, heart pumping faster with every slow step. "Hi, Sylvia."

"She called. She called the office and talked to Rob. She thought it less likely those phones were tapped."

"What did she say? Is she all right?"

"Yes, except for the obvious fact of having lost her senses. I thought maybe she'd call here too, so I came in to see you. I know you don't trust us anymore and won't tell us if you hear from her, but I didn't think you could lie to my face."

Brady glanced down at the bag in her arms. "I've been gone all day. I haven't talked to her in over two months."

"Two months," Sylvia echoed softly. Her eyes blazed. "Goddam her, why didn't she call me at home? I want to talk to her, Brady. I want to hear her voice."

"What did she say to Rob? I mean, if you want to tell me."

"She said she was fine. She called to wish us a happy new year, can you believe that? She said she was moving around a lot. She swears she hasn't been back to Minneapolis. Rob told her you found her messages in the library and got the postcard. She knew she'd been spotted in Ann Arbor. He warned her about the hunt for the money, Brady. He told her how they were tracking the money. She didn't know. He said she got very angry. She didn't talk much after that." Sylvia reached into her pocket. As she pulled out her car keys a white cloud of tissue fell into the dirty snow that had come off the tire. The tissue rapidly turned gray as it soaked up slush. "That settles it," she said. "No more Kleenex, so no more crying."

"Bloody hell," Brady muttered. "I may as well."

Sylvia looked startled.

Brady unzipped her bag. "I just made a copy of this to send to Paul. I was going to let him decide whether to tell you about it. I guess it doesn't make any difference who sees it. It's an old picture." She pulled out the Alcatraz photo.

Sylvia walked a few steps until she was under a streetlamp. "How long have you had this?"

"I found it today. It's a wire service picture and I think it's been sitting around the *Daily* for a couple of weeks."

"Rob and I have been discussing hiring a private investigator. He thinks we should have done that long ago, but we were so damn compliant with the FBI. Now maybe we should. We could send him to San Francisco."

"Sylvia, it wouldn't do any good. Look at her. She's staring straight at the camera. She knows her picture's been taken. I bet she was gone from there within a minute. We know the FBI takes photos of groups like this. They probably have their own shot of her. It might be interesting to show it to Agent Blake and see what he says. I bet they knew she was there and didn't tell you. I bet you trust the FBI agents more than they trust you."

That didn't make Sylvia any happier. Brady put a hand on her elbow. "I'm freezing. Why don't we go inside?"

Sylvia shook her head. "Rob's still at the office. I have to get him." Brady watched her open the car door and toss the photo on the front seat, glad she had another copy for herself.

Brady kissed Sylvia on the cheek. "I won't hide anything from you. I promise."

17

Another date night, and once again Mark wasn't ready to go. How many weeks had they been doing this, and was he ever ready to go on time?

As usual, noisy mayhem reigned at the *Daily*. Ringing phones, clacking typewriters, shouting, swearing, laughter. Brady casually sauntered by the noisy machines that spit out the wire service stories and photos. A stack of pictures waiting to be filed lay in a wire basket. She looked around, picked them up, then went back to Mark's desk. She looked around again, then dropped the pictures into her bag.

"Brady!"

Grace walked over. "You have a phone call. Well, really it's for Mark. But when I told the guy I couldn't see him in the room but I knew he had to be around because his girlfriend was still waiting for him, he said he'd talk to you. Name's Paul Cooper."

Brady didn't move. Grace pointed at the phone on Mark's desk. "Line two."

She waited for Grace to walk away, then she picked up the phone. "This is Brady."

"It's Paul. God, how incredibly lucky you're there. Well, not really. I guessed you might be there because Mark told me about your regular date thing. Have I told you I'm sort of seeing someone? Maybe I should do the same deal with her. Of course, she goes to Wesleyan, which is a ways from here, so it's sort of hard to see her too often. Shit, listen to me run on. If I'd known for sure I'd end up talking to you, I wouldn't have had those beers. She called."

Brady saw Grace watching her. She turned and dropped into a chair.

"She called straight to my room, like she didn't care if someone was listening. She didn't talk long because she was about to leave whatever town she was in. She was also pretty upset when she realized I was nursing a major hangover by having a beer. But it works, what can I say? I think she's lost her sense of humor."

"Where is she?"

"She wouldn't say. I told her you'd spotted her in the Alcatraz picture you lifted from the paper. She laughed then; I guess she still laughs at some things. She said she wouldn't be showing up in any more group pictures, so we could stop looking. She said she's going deep underground. She said if there's a bomb or gun battle with the FBI, not to worry. She's not there; she'll be out of reach of anyone's guns."

"Deep underground?" Brady whispered. "What can that mean? How can it be deeper?"

"God only knows. She gave me a couple of messages for you."

"Why doesn't she just call me?"

"She said why: She assumes your phones are tapped and she wants the FBI off your back as soon as possible. So she sent a message. I'm supposed to tell you that every day, no matter where she is, she half expects you'll knock on the door with the cops or at least Mom and Dad in tow, and if and when it happens, she'll still love you. Sweet, huh? She also said, and I assume you know what this means, 'Tell her I'm feeling something.' I suppose that means a guy's in the picture. Some dickhead radical, probably."

"Maybe, but maybe it has nothing to do with romance." Brady twisted the cord. "Anything else?"

"Just one thing, which I think was the real reason she called. Mom and Dad's anniversary is next week. She knows I always forget it. She called to remind me. Hey, tell Mark-man I'm sending him a couple of really wild albums to review. He'll love them. And don't stop checking the pictures, okay? I don't trust what Sally says. She can't stay hiding, not forever."

"I won't stop. I have a pile of them in my bag I'm taking home."

She sat still for a moment after saying good-bye, replaying the conversation.

Deep underground. Maybe Father Tom would have an idea what that involved, what kind of life it might mean. She'd go to the center tomorrow and ask him.

"Who were you talking to? You look as if you saw a ghost."

She stared at Mark. "That was Paul. He called for you, and Grace told me to pick it up. Sally had just called him. He talked to her. She's okay."

"Hey, that's great. Doesn't surprise me that she's staying on her feet, but I know you're glad to hear it. He say anything else?"

Lots. He's seeing someone, he's drinking in the afternoon, he wants me to keep stealing pictures from your newspaper. "He's sending you a couple of albums to review. That's all."

Mark brightened. "God, I like that guy. Shall we go eat? My treat tonight, anyplace you want."

Brady nodded, then bent over to pick up her bag from the floor. She glimpsed the top edges of the photos, and quickly covered them with her scarf. When she stood erect, she glanced across the newsroom. Grace was sitting on a desk, still watching.

18

Brady sat cross-legged on her bed, studying photos with a magnifying glass. Amsterdam, London, Berkeley, Boston, Paris. Trouble everywhere. Problems and protest in every corner of the planet. She picked up another picture. "This is ridiculous," she said. "She's not in Manila."

Someone knocked on the door and she looked up sharply. "Sam," she shouted. "I am not making popcorn. Get Cullen to do it."

The door opened and her mother looked in. "Just me. Don't yell."

Brady spread papers over the photos. "Come on in. How was dinner with Jed? I didn't expect to see you so early."

"We were both tired. It's almost the end of the week. I didn't expect to see your light on. Weren't you and Mark going to a movie?"

"We had dinner, that's all. Which is fine because I'm feeling lousy. Don't look so worried. I'm just cramped and bitchy. Had to register for spring quarter today too. Midterms aren't even finished, and already they want us to figure out next term."

"What are you taking?"

"More art history, anthropology, advanced comp, and, ta da, another quarter of Irish. That will be the toughest class."

"Still no science or math."

"I hope you're still okay with that. I think I'm doing the right thing."

"Then I do too." Mary leaned over and kissed Brady. "Hang in there, honey; you'll find something you love. You're only nineteen. It takes time and work to make dreams come true."

Brady recoiled. "Is that what you tell your patients?"

"Depends on the patient. It did sound awful, didn't it? Well, sometimes the truth is trite." She glanced down on the bed. Brady followed her gaze. A corner of a photo peeked out from under a sheet of class notes.

"What's this?" Mary said.

Brady sighed. "Go ahead, look." She pushed aside the papers.

Her mother only needed a quick glance to understand. "You're looking for Sally. Do you do this a lot? Good Lord, Brady. By some freak luck you found her in one photo and now you're obsessed with finding another."

Brady sat back against pillows. "She's been in two pictures, really. There was also the one the FBI took in Ann Arbor. Mom, I talked to Paul today. He had talked to Sally this afternoon. She told him she's going even deeper out of sight."

"Have you called Sylvia?"

"No."

"Then I'm going to do it. You cannot keep something like that from her."

Brady said, "I'm not. I'm sure Paul will tell them. He said the real reason she called was to remind him about their parents' anniversary."

They laughed together. When they finished, Brady dropped her head on her mother's shoulder. "I miss laughing with Sally."

"Let her go, Brady. She doesn't want to be found."

Brady looked up and saw a picture of Will that had been taken the summer after he got out of high school. She'd framed and hung it on the wall. He was perched on the hood of the car, tan and smiling, holding a bottle of Coke. "It's like I keep wishing for and chasing after impossible things. I wish I could be laughing with Sally. I wish Will weren't dead. I wish Sam had memories of Dad. I wish I could see into the future with Mark—but I don't really want to talk about that one, so don't look so excited. Maybe you should call Sylvia. There's the slight possibility Paul got . . ." Wasted, drunk, plastered, loaded—how many words could she come up with? " . . . sidetracked and forgot to call her. And if you're going downstairs, would you do something for me?"

"Of course."

"Please make Sam some popcorn. Maybe then he'll leave me alone."

19

When she walked into the newsroom, her heart sank. There was a large group around Mark's desk. No way she could sneak the photos back. She took a breath and walked forward. She'd wait them out. Grace spotted her and said something to Mark. When he turned to look at Brady, he wore a grim expression. She looked at the others. Theirs matched. What the hell was going on?

He bolted up and walked toward her.

"I knew this would be a surprise, but I didn't think it would be a bad one. Just wanted to see if you felt like an early supper. How did your poli sci exam go?"

He tipped his head and grabbed her elbow. "Let's talk in the hall." As he guided her out, she glanced back. Everyone was watching.

He led her down to the end of the hall. "What's going on? People were looking at me like I was a leper or something."

He didn't answer. He stood staring at the floor with his hands slipped into his pockets.

"Mark, would you tell me what the hell is going on?"

"I don't know how to say it. I thought I'd have more time to figure it out."

"How about one word at a time?"

"You're not welcome in the newsroom anymore. Management rule, not mine."

"Why?" But she knew—someone must have seen her taking photos.

"Because of Sally. Because you're a friend of Sally Cooper's who has been linked to the FBI. People have been working on a couple of stories that were connected to the bombing. Sally's name came up. After Paul called here yesterday, Grace put some things together. She did some checking around. Apparently at least two people in campus administration have described you as an FBI informant."

"That is pure bullshit, Mark. Did you tell her that? I've answered questions about Sally, sure, and for a while I cooperated with the agents because I thought it was the best thing to do. Her parents asked me to."

"Of course I told her it was BS. But you're on file somewhere as the girl who led the FBI and U security into Walter library. People seem to know you've cooperated with them. Grace and the other editors are really mad about this. They don't want anyone to be able to suggest that the FBI is linked to the *Daily* staff. A newspaper has to be absolutely untainted."

"I'm not even talking to them anymore, Mark, you know that."

"Which, according to Grace, is even worse. You chatted with Sally's brother on our phone. Grace says all the FBI needs to get a wiretap warrant for our phones is the possibility that you or I might be trading tips with Paul about Sally."

He was so still, so glum. "Oh, no, Mark. Don't tell me that they're kicking you out too."

"They talked about it, but, no. I guess I'm not on anyone's list as an informant."

"Mark, I'm walking away from here now. I won't come back, I won't bother you again in this place. I do not want to get you in trouble. Tell them that."

He leaned against the wall, arms crossed, brow furrowed. "I loved seeing you come into the newsroom every week. I loved watching you stroll around and take it all in. You'd have really fit in here too, Brady."

She kissed the right side of his chin. "Not my scene. I quit playing social worker because I couldn't handle chaos and stress. This place is even worse. No way I'd suffer the insanity just to fix stories about basketball games and tuition hikes."

He stretched his arms over his head as he laughed. Then he straightened and snapped his fingers. "One of the stories they were working on that got Grace started on all this? It's about Father Tom. He's been transferred from St. Bernard's."

"Transferred?"

"I don't know what's going on, but he's gone."

20

Dee was sitting behind the desk in Father Tom's office.

No, clearly it was her office now. The overflow of clothing and books was gone, the walls had been cleared of posters and clippings, there was a vase of flowers on the coffee table. Dee hung up the phone. She waved Brady in.

"What happened to Tom?"

"The archdiocese got him reassigned to a church in South Dakota. It's good to see you."

"You're in charge?"

Dee pushed back in the chair. She nodded as she tapped a pencil against the desk. "Don't hate me for that."

"Of course not. You're perfect, Dee. You know I loved him, but I wasn't blind. You'll be way more organized than he was. Still, why did they do it? Has he been banished, or did he ask to go?"

"He was sent. He heard from the archbishop on Monday and he was gone by the weekend. Nothing formal was announced until two days ago, after he was gone."

Another departure, another missed good-bye. Brady's chest tightened. "Why?"

"The archdiocese of St. Paul and Minneapolis does not like supporting a hotbed of radicalism. It's been going on for years, of course. But ever since Tom gave those deserters sanctuary, there have been a lot of complaints from church members." She seemed to weigh her words. "The pressure to remove him really got strong after the bombing, when it got out that people involved in that were regulars of Bernie's After Dark. There are even some pretty loud rumblings about closing the center."

"They can't do that. It's ridiculous."

"It's reality."

"This place is so much more than a political center. Tom never did enough to publicize all the things that got done. He could have had so much more support from the church members if he'd worked at that. Dee, what you need—"

Dee raised a hand to hush her, then waved someone in from the hall. Mrs. Woitz entered. She was carrying a plate of cookies and a clipboard. "Deanna, here are the receipts from the bake sale, and some gingersnaps. Connie Brisco made them and—oh, honey, here you are again, looking so pretty. We sure miss you, Brady. Isn't that some news about Father Tom?"

Brady nodded. She suspected Mrs. Woitz considered it good news.

"My arthritis is not too bad these days. I've got some new medication."

"That's good."

"Birthday Brigade's in the library. Don't you leave without saying hi to everyone."

When Mrs. Woitz was out of sight, Dee grinned and said, "Do you miss it, or what? Now tell me what you were going to say."

Before Brady could speak, Jerry poked his head in. "Hey, I heard you were lurking around. Welcome back."

"I'm not back. Just getting the scoop on Tom."

Jerry shook his head. "Love the guy with all my heart, but man, he pushed it too far and now we've got to pick up the pieces."

Brady sat back. "The world needs people who push, Jerry."

"And it needs ten times as many to clean up later. I know what kind we are. Dee, okay if I go ahead and order that Xerox machine?"

Dee nodded. Jerry blew Brady a kiss and disappeared. Dee got up and closed the door. "I miss Tom like crazy," she said, her voice near breaking. "Make no mistake, I'm mad as hell at him for jeopardizing the day-to-day work we do here, but oh, I miss him."

Brady said, "I wish I could have said good-bye."

Dee sat next to her on the sofa. "You were going to tell me what I should do."

"It's just a dumb idea."

"I doubt that. Go on."

"I know St. Bernard's has a church bulletin, but you should publish one for the center. Somehow you should get the word out about all the things that go on here. And you could have interviews with people who use the center, and maybe the volunteers, and maybe, oh, I don't know. Stories about the neighborhood, even. You could almost make it a neighborhood newsletter."

"I've thought of something like that. We could send it to donors and foundations. Businesses in the area. Media outlets. People with money and clout."

"And normal people, but yes. Exactly."

Dee stretched out her legs and chewed on her lip. After a moment she said, "I have a little money for this kind of project. I think it's a good idea, if I can find the right person to take it on. Someone who's familiar with the center. Someone people like and would talk to. Someone I could count on to get it done."

Brady said nothing.

Dee said, "Welcome back."

Brady lifted the poker and prodded the bottom log of the pile. Everything shifted, and sparks flared and swirled around.

The front door opened and closed. She heard a book bag hit the floor. "That smells really good outside," Cullen said. "But it's kind of smoky in here. Should I open a window?"

"I already did."

"Didn't you open the flue?"

"Yes, but the chimney's so cold, it didn't draw up the smoke right away."

"Do we have any hot dogs?"

"I don't know, but that sounds kind of good, doesn't it?"

"I'll check. What are you burning? Love letters? Don't tell me you broke up with Mark. No, you'll never break up with him. Nineteen and you're locked in for life."

"Probably so." She sighed, then laughed with Cullen.

He sat down beside her and lifted the poker from her lap. He prodded the logs. "I won't tell him about the sigh. Where's Mom?"

"Took Sam to the dentist."

"Where are these pictures from and why are you burning them?"

"I took them from the *Daily*. Please don't tell Mark. They were being filed or thrown out or whatever they do with old stuff and I wanted to look them over." She tossed one of the photos into the flames. It curled up and darkened before catching on fire.

"So I shouldn't tell Mark, huh? You realize, of course, that you've handed me excellent blackmail material. Weird, how the photo paper curls like that. You seem a little moody."

"I'm pretty happy, actually. I went back to the center today. I'm going to start working there again."

He groaned. "I do not want to be in the room when you tell Mom."

Brady ripped a photo in two. She held one piece above the fire until a tongue of flame leaped up and caught it. "She shouldn't go too nuts, because I'll be doing different stuff. I get to write a newsletter. It'll go out in the neighborhood."

"That could be cool. They paying you?"

"Hardly anything."

"You can't afford that, Brady. Remember, you owe me twenty bucks."

"I've figured that out too. I'm going to call Sylvia, suck up my pride, and ask for a favor. I'm going to ask her to twist arms and get me a part-time job at the art institute. She knows everybody there. Any job will do. I'd be happy to wear an ugly uniform and guard pictures."

"She'd do a lot more, I bet."

"I'm not asking for more. I'd like being a guard, anyway. I'd like to memorize every painting and get familiar with all the galleries."

"How can you handle school with two jobs?"

"Lots of people do it. I'll tell you what: Double that twenty I owe you if I don't get straight A's this quarter."

"You're on. You're going nuts, aren't you?"

"Maybe I am, because I've also decided to ask Mom to loan me money so I can go to Europe this summer. I'm going to make Mark go too."

"You're asking her for money so you can take a trip with your boy-friend?"

"Yep." She tossed two more pictures into the fire.

Cullen whistled. "Definitely nuts." He laid the poker on the hearth. "So what's this all about, besides indulging in a little moody pyromania?"

Brady tossed the rest of the pictures into the flames. "What this is all about, little brother, is knowing the difference between letting things happen and making them happen."

PART FIVE

1

Brady dumped her bookstore bag on the kitchen table and picked up the notes that had been scrawled in red crayon on typing paper.

Mom and Brady: Rob kidnapped Sam and me for the weekend. Going up to the lake with him and Mark to cut firewood and get the boats out. Don't panic, Brady—Rob says he'll get us back in time so I can help you move into the dorm on Sunday. C.

Brady: Dinner and orchestra with Jed. Might be late. Sylvia wants us out there for dinner tomorrow since the guys are all at the lake. She's anxious to hear about your trip. Call her tonight to say yes or no. Mom.

Brady let loose a happy howl. It was the last weekend before the new school year started, she had the house to herself for the night, and the boys were gone for two whole days. She flipped on the radio, switched it from her mother's favorite classical station, and found some good music. She cranked up the volume and started making a sandwich as she sang along with Janis.

She was reaching into the fridge for a Coke when she realized that the pounding she heard wasn't a thumping bass, but someone knocking on the front door.

An exasperated mailman waited impatiently on the front step.

"Sorry," Brady said.

He handed her a package. "For Brady Callahan. I need a signature."

She signed. "Thanks a million," she called as he sprinted down the steps. She scratched the back of one leg with a foot and read the return address label on the parcel.

Moira Duffy, Libraries and Archives, University of Ulster.

She said, "What the hell?"

Grabbing her sandwich and soda from the kitchen, the package under her arm, she went up to her room. She sat on her bed and stared at the package. "This is stupid," she said. "I'm not psychic. I could stare for hours and not guess."

She ripped off the paper and slid her nail across the tape that secured the box. "University of Ulster. Well, if this is an IRA bomb, it goes off now," she said as she lifted the lid. "Ka boom."

Inside the box, on top of gray cardboard wrapping, was a letter.

> *Dear Miss Callahan:*
> *It was so very nice to speak with you last March.*

Huh?

> *As I mentioned in our conversation, I joined the library staff in 1965 and, therefore, did not have the pleasure of knowing your father. Several members of the faculty do remember him with affection and wish for me to convey their regards to you, especially Dr. Dennis Boylan, who was of great assistance to me with this project. I regret I could not attend to your request sooner, as I was on medical leave for several months.*
>
> *My original skepticism and pessimism about fulfilling your request has been proven wrong! Dr. Boylan was very helpful. He recalled an event in 1946 that was broadcast over the radio in the Six Counties. The event marked the retirement of one of the eminent scholars at the university. Your father was one of several participants who read that day. With the cooperation of the archivist at BBC Ireland, I was able to track down a recording of the event.*

Brady set down the letter and dug into the cardboard wrapping. Inside lay a black vinyl LP wrapped in plastic.

> *Program notes list him as having read several poems. Unfortunately, the quality of the recording was so poor that only three could be transferred to an LP, which is enclosed.*
>
> *The funds you sent to cover the project were more than sufficient. Wonderfully generous, in fact!*

Brady closed her eyes and said, "Sally. Oh my God, Sally." She smoothed the letter under her hand.

> *As you suggested, the remainder of the money will be used for university scholarships.*
>
> *Dr. Boylan refused to translate the poems. He said it was your father's strong wish to be read only in Irish. He consented, however, to translate the titles. They are recorded in the following order: "The Hero's Sleep," "Sister of Mercy," and "A Blessing on Thee."*
>
> *It was my pleasure to work on this project. I hope it brings you and your family great joy.*
>
> > *Cordially,*
> > *Moira Duffy*

Brady picked up the record and wept.

Why am I scared to do this? she wondered. What am I afraid I'll hear? What am I waiting for?

Brady unwrapped the plastic and took out the record. She dropped it on the turntable, turned on the power, and set down the needle.

The third time through, she could listen without crying.

Fourth time—she thought she recognized a few words.

Fifth time, she said, "Poor Jed. He doesn't have a voice like this. But then, no one on the planet has a voice like this. Oh, God, I don't remember this voice at all."

Seventh time: "Yes, that's Dad."

She heard a car door slam and ran to her window. Only a neighbor.

Brady got paper and pencil from the desk and her Irish dictionary from the bookshelf. She sat down by the speakers. She started the record again, grabbing words out of the air and writing them down. She gave up after scribbling a few and just listened.

The first poem ended. She said aloud, "If you want to feel something, Sally, you should be here. Why the hell aren't you here?" On the record, her father cleared his throat, said, "Sorry. Bit of a cold," and then began reading the second poem. His smooth baritone rolled out the words.

Siur was sister, she knew that. *Trocaire,* mercy.

Then the next one. *"Bennacht Fort."* "A Blessing on Thee."

She listened to them all again. The next time, halfway through "Sister of Mercy," Brady turned off the stereo. Her fingers tapped out a rhythm as she stared at the window and the dark September sky.

She went to her desk and dug through papers in the deep bottom drawer until she found the copy of the Alcatraz photo. She opened the top drawer and pushed things around until she found the magnifying glass. She looked at Sally. She looked at the people around Sally.

Indians. Students. Grandmothers. Priests.

Nuns.

She closed her eyes and thought about the Ann Arbor picture Sylvia had shown her. Yes, that one too. In both pictures, Sally was standing by a nun wearing a habit.

Tell her I'm feeling something, Sally had said.

Brady sat back. That was it, that's what Sally had done, where she'd gone.

All those books she'd been reading. Reclaiming your spiritual roots, Brady had teased her.

I can't live in this world, Sally had said.

Going deep underground, she'd told Paul. Away from shoot-outs and bombings. Out of reach of anyone's guns.

Not even the FBI would blast down the doors of a convent.

But was she out of reach of her father's friends and connections? Not likely, not once he had an idea where to look. Rob knew generals, ambassadors, senators. Surely he knew an archbishop or two who could crack open cloistered doors.

Would the Coopers believe her, Brady wondered. How, exactly, do you convince people that their daughter is hiding with nuns? Should she even try? She dropped her head on her arms. If Sally was happy, if she was feeling something, if she was done running and was building a life out of sight, did Brady dare turn her in so she could be sent to prison? Prison.

It's not a betrayal.

Brady listened to the recording again. When she reached the spot where her father cleared his throat and spoke in English, she whispered, *"Bennacht fort."*

A blessing on thee, Sally.

Forgive me.

2

"You're not writing, Brady. You're daydreaming."

"Dammit, Sam. You're supposed to knock when you come into my room."

"This isn't your room anymore, Brady. It's been mine for three years, so why should I knock?"

"Well, when I'm in here using my old typewriter, you knock."

Sam banged on the door. "I'm knocking, okay? They want to start the party."

Sylvia's laugh floated up and in through the window. "Sounds like it's already started."

"Everyone's here and I'm supposed to get you. Well, not everyone. Ms. Bitch hasn't showed up."

"Sam, you know her name."

"Carol's not here. I heard Mom tell Sylvia that she might not come."

"That's Carol's problem, not ours. She might not love our mother, but we love her father, so don't make a big deal out of it if she doesn't show up, and don't call her names. I'll be down in a minute. I want to finish this letter so Sylvia and Rob can take it to Sally this weekend."

"I heard a new joke. Why don't I tell it to you and you can put it in the letter?"

"Good idea. What is it?"

A minute later he was running away as she threw an eraser. "That's so obscene," she shouted after him. "I can't believe you know a joke like that."

He called from the stairs, "I bet she'd like it."

I bet she would too, Brady thought as she resumed typing.

At this point, Sally, I know you're rolling your eyes and thinking, Bloody hell, not another leave-nothing-out, obsessive-compulsive, rolling-in-details letter from Brady. Well, pal, it's not as if you don't have the time to read my overly-long letters. Five more years of time, as it happens.

I don't want you to miss a thing. That's mostly selfish. When you're out, I'll want to talk with you about everything, and I expect you to hold up your end of the conversation. Okay, I'm letting you miss one thing. Sam just told me a very obscene joke to pass along, which I won't do. I bet the prison censors would black it out. You'd like it, though.

You probably remember him as a sweet skinny little boy. He's changed this summer.

Back to the news. Mark and Paul started a beard-growing contest this week. I guess that's what a year of law school does to the brain---you start thinking that stunts like that are a great idea. I don't think it will last long, because Cullen joined in, and after about two days it was obvious he would have the best beard by far.

What real-world news are you getting these days? Are the others still fighting over which soap operas to watch? It's probably just as well that you can't watch the Watergate hearings; you'd go nuts. Nixon has refused to turn over any tapes or papers to the investigators. How much longer can he hold out and keep lying? Your dad says that Nixon just doesn't understand why people don't love him, fall at his feet, and let this all slide now that the troops are out of Vietnam.

I'm going to Colorado next week. Deanna is taking some of the teen volunteers from the center to Aspen, to a youth conference on solving world hunger. She asked me to help chaperone. Kind of surreal to hold a conference on hunger at a posh resort. I guess summer rates are pretty cheap. Dee has a great group of kids going, they're really committed and active. The center got some nice publicity earlier this month when Congress finally raised the minimum wage to $2 an hour. Dee was interviewed by _Time_ about the impact it would have on working-class families. Oh, she really liked your idea of starting a program for kids whose moms are in prison. She said she'll write you to get more details of what you think might be important to do. I told her to contact your lawyer so she could be approved as one of your correspondents.

What magazines do you get in the library there now? Make a list if there are any others you want. It's disgusting and outrageous that they won't allow _Rolling Stone_ anymore. Speaking of magazines: I'll have a very short article in a Milwaukee magazine next month. It's about some of the paintings that went out on loan from the art institute to their museum while we're closed for remodeling. The piece is short, but it's a start.

My period was late. I'm okay, it was a false alarm, but talk about panic. When I told Mark I was late, he was happy. His exact words: "Jeez, Brady, now can we get married?"

Like I said, law school is messing with his mind. Obviously, his is totally fried. Not surprising, after pushing through college in three years and then going straight to grad school. At least Paul took some time off before he jumped in.

I don't know why I'm so scared about marrying him. Well, yes I do. I don't care how close we are, 22 is too young. Besides, sometimes I feel like it's not me he wants to marry--- it's my family.

Big item in today's paper: The defense secretary finally admits that we bombed the hell out of Cambodia for two years back in '69-70 while claiming to respect its neutrality. Nixon and his men acted so bloody pious when they lied. Still do.

Okay, now you're thinking, Stop with the bitching and just cheer me up. How about this: I haven't seen Paul drink or smoke dope all summer. Okay, it's only the middle of July, but let's be optimistic. What has he told you about Marti? They've been together for three months, which has to be some kind of record for him. She's very nice. Still, I wonder if she's maybe, possibly, just perhaps, a little bit intimidated by your mother???

I bought the books you mentioned. I love the Woolf letters, but I'm having trouble with the Thomas Merton. As you know, I have an argument with the contemplative life. There's so much that needs to be done in the world.

Will I have to quit swearing around you when you go back to the abbey in five years? If you go. They'll forgive you and welcome you back, won't they? I mean, that's their business, after all. Compared to all the sins going down in the world, you showing up at the door using a fake name hardly ranks.

But I hate to think of you not being out here with me once you're free.

They're all standing below the window and yelling. Time to toast the couple, it appears. What's the rush, I'd like to know. After all, they've dated for almost four years. Jed may have finally persuaded her to wear a diamond, but it wouldn't surprise me if it's another four years before there's an actual wedding.

She's so incredibly happy.

Forget them and celebrate me, I say. I went to the advising office yesterday and---Hurrah!---talked them into giving me credit for the museum studies class I took in London last spring. Now it's almost certain I'll graduate---finally---in March. Unless I drop out of summer school and go back to Europe. Three IRA letter bombs went off in London this week, though. If I go, I'll head to France, especially if Mark can get some time off and go with me. That's doubtful, though. Summer law clerks are such slaves. Whether I go or not, I will definitely come to see you this summer. Maybe the end of August? I think my car can handle one more trip to

West Virginia. As I've complained before, what a bizarre place to put a federal prison.

Okay, I'll stop. You know, letters are the perfect way to communicate with a friend---the writer gets to pick the topics and the other person can't argue or interrupt. Not to suggest you would <u>ever</u> do either. Obviously, I like rambling on about everything under the sun, so you're stuck with it.

Sally, I so want to have a record of these days, that's why I go on and on when I write. We have to keep talking about things and people---otherwise they fade away. Last night Sam and I were talking about Will. He can hardly remember him. That makes me so sad.

Write and tell me about everything---what you think, what you hear, what you read, what the latest oppressive rules are, who's breaking them, who's new, why she's in there, who's causing trouble. I want to hear about everything that goes on in Alderson prison.

I think it's important to know and remember what we can. These are the things that happened---some of it by chance, some by choice. This is the way life is. Let's not forget anything. You never know---some of it might make sense someday. Hell, we might even find something to laugh about. I'll count on you to help me with that.

This has gone on too long.

Love,

Brady

MARSHA QUALEY is the acclaimed author of seven previous novels: *One Night, Close to a Killer, Thin Ice, Hometown, Come in from the Cold, Revolutions of the Heart,* and *Everybody's Daughter.* Her books have appeared on numerous best-of-the-year lists, including ALA Quick Picks, ALA Best Books for Young Adults, IRA Young Adults' Choices, and *School Library Journal* Best Books of the Year. She lives near Minneapolis, Minnesota.